GW

The Border Bandit

G·K
Hall
&Co.

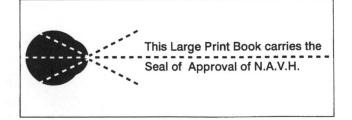

The Border Bandit

Max Brand

G.K. Hall & Co.
Thorndike, Maine

Published in 1997 by arrangement with Golden West Literary Agency.

G.K. Hall Large Print Western Collection.

The text of this Large Print edition is unabridged.
Other aspects of the book may vary from the original edition.

Set in 16 pt. Plantin by Minnie B. Raven.

Printed in the United States on permanent paper.

Library of Congress Cataloging in Publication Data

Brand, Max, 1892–1944.
    The border bandit / Max Brand writing as Evan Evans.
        p. (large print) cm.
    ISBN 0-7838-1876-9 (lg. print : hc)
    1. Large type books. I. Title.
[PS3511.A87B596   1997]
813'.52—dc20   96-20711

The Border Bandit

PART I

THE ORDEAL

CHAPTER I
Oliver Goes West

To understand all of the circumstances of this history, you must go back a long time to the days when a repeating rifle was a thing to be dreamed of, but never known. You must go back so far that a revolving pistol was something to be stared at and wondered over, while the wiser and older heads were inclined to disapprove and declare that a bit of machinery so complicated must go wrong in a pinch.

In those days a cattleman hated a sheepman with a mortal hatred because the sheep sheared off the grass to the roots, so that it required whole seasons to recover its best growth. And those were the days when the sheepmen walked with guns in their hands, scanning every horizon for fear a group of cowpunchers might come into view. Those were times when an unbranded cow belonged to the first comer. And so did an unbranded calf, for that matter, if you happened to be able to get away with it without the knowledge of the owner.

Those were the days when the railroad branched feebly here and there west of the Mississippi; but the great, strong trunk lines which afterward penetrated far and wide through the land, bringing rivers of profit and rivers of law and order, also, were not so much as imagined.

Indians were then a force worth thinking about, especially if you lived in the Southwest, where you had to consider those wild Romans of the plains, the Comanches, who looked upon Mexico as their natural plunder ground.

In those times, the United States threw out little groups of soldiers here and there through the western wilderness and dreamed that they were actually controlling a region so vast that most of it was a white blur on the geographies which the tobacco-eating politicians in Washington had studied in their boyhood. The soldiers did their best, which was not much. Usually, they arrived after the mischief was hopelessly ended. And when the Indians had raised the devil, the troopers came down and rode frantically, bravely along the departing trail — but they often rode in vain.

It was then, too, that ladies cinched themselves in at the waist to imitate a wasp as well as they could, poor, tortured souls. Skirts brushed the ground and raised a little cloud of dust, and to show an ankle was considered most highly indecent. The gentlemen, too, of that epoch, were fellows who walked about in tightly fitted trousers that were strapped under the instep, and they had long-tailed coats fitted in close around the hips.

No débutante in these degenerate times ever

studied so assiduously how to rise, to sit, to walk, as did the gentleman then. If you can tell a lady or an actress today by her walk, you could tell a gentleman in the same way, in that time. For in that epoch there were such things as social un-equals. You could tell a man from a gentleman. Yes, there were different ways of rearing, differ-ent ways of approaching life, different ways of education.

Men prided themselves upon their "sensibili-ties." And not to have a tear in the eye when a stirring passage in poetry was read was to be considered a clod. And what poetry there was, and what prose! What proselike poetry, and what poetrylike prose!

Men made speeches on the street, when you stopped and asked after the health of their fami-lies. There were set phrases for everything. A mask of formalism was thrown abroad to cover the reality of a man and a woman. You could talk with a man for half a year without scratching through the surface crust of mannerism which overlaid his soul of souls.

And you must know that on the day that Oliver Tay approached Siddon Flat, he was just such a product of just such upper classes except that he was, if anything, far more so. A most romantic product to be sure! He was a handsome youth, but his dress and mannerisms were such that an intelligent observer might have guessed — and quite correctly — that some influence in early life had combined with his environment to give his

11

outward appearance an effect which was rather too handsome — one might almost say too beautiful. Oliver was a joy and delight to his mother who had done everything in her power to bring her boy up as a proper gentleman. The young man was quite conscious of his own good looks and was even well pleased to wear his blonde hair unusually long so that it had a way of curling on the ends. There was nothing unconscious about our Oliver. If there had been, his good mother would instantly have dispelled any illusions and brought up before his eyes the full picture of his perfections.

She was a rarely discerning woman. She had been much in the world, and she knew a great deal about men and women and their affairs; but one thing she knew better than all else — and this was that her son was perfect. Having such an honest conviction, she would have felt that it was treasonable to her to allow him to grow up without the proper amount of self-respect. She taught him that he must be sacred to himself, and you may be sure that she did not teach in vain because there is nothing in this world that men under thirty take so seriously as they do themselves. And Oliver was only twenty-one!

He had been soberly equipped for this expedition into the wild West. One would have thought from his mother's white face and her many tears that she was sending her darling into the heart of Africa. And, as a matter of fact, considering exactly what Oliver was, it is very doubtful if

12

deserts and jungles and lions would have been any more dangerous to Oliver than this same American West.

But first you must know what it was that brought Oliver so far from civilization.

The reason was that an uncle of his had been so void of taste and a sense of propriety as to go into the wilderness and become a trader with the Indians. There he had worked for many years; and the rest of the family, as fast as they could, had tried to forget that there had ever been such a relative. He was buried. He was long dead, certainly, so far as Oliver's mother was concerned, when she heard from a lawyer in New York that Crossman Tay had died in Siddon Flat and that he had left his estate to his nephew, Oliver.

"I regret," said Mrs. Tay, "that poor Crossman has closed his eyes upon this world; but I presume that the best disposition of his estate, as you call it, would be to turn it over to charity."

The lawyer was a hard-jawed fellow with no sense of the finer side of things. He said brutally, "Ma'am, Crossman Tay has just sent a second ship from New Orleans to New York. The profits of the first voyage were over fifty thousand dollars!"

But I must interrupt, here, so that you may understand. Fifty thousand is nothing, now — a mere gesture, you say. But in those times it was different. The man who had the mansion on the hill, and drove with two fine trotters to his car-

13

riage, and who owned the mill, besides invested capital in banks — why, that man was worth only his forty or his fifty thousand dollars.

Mrs. Tay closed her eyes and did some swift mental arithmetic. She was always good at figures. "Twenty-five hundred dollars a year!" she breathed, opening her eyes. "Crossman was, in my opinion, a very wonderful man."

Said the lawyer, "I'm very glad to know that you have that good opinion of him, ma'am. I am merely mentioning his profits of one shipload. And he has done other things besides send his purchases by ship. And he has sent more than one ship. In a word, this estate is a matter of something like a quarter of a million dollars. However, if you wish to hand it over to charity, I shall make the necessary arrangement."

Mrs. Tay turned white, "Sir," said she, "it is not a jesting matter."

"That was what I thought in the first place," said the brutal lawyer.

And that was why Oliver Tay was embarked for the great West.

They had consulted the biggest map that they could find. They had located the border readily enough. But as for Siddon Flat, why there was not even a dot the size of a pinprick to indicate that Siddon Flat was anywhere in the Southwest.

"What an ignorant and stupid map maker!" said Mrs. Tay.

"Why, Mother, it may be only a village," said her son.

"Stuff!" said Mrs. Tay. "My dearest child, consider that Siddon Flat is the name of the city in which your dear Uncle Crossman lived! Do millionaires live in villages which cannot even be located on the map?"

From this background, then, Oliver was launched upon the sea of life, with the tide carrying him West.

CHAPTER II

In the Stage

Oliver was quite oblivious of all the others in the stagecoach, with the exception of one person. The rest were simply rough, rude fellows — clods. To Oliver, they simply had no existence, for he had been taught by his mother that this world has sundry needs of common flesh and bone; but that is no reason why people of culture should be aware of their existence.

However, it has been said that there was an exception. It was only a partial exception. It was a girl who was sweet eighteen — and extraordinarily sweet at that. So much so that Oliver Tay occasionally allowed his eyes to rest upon her in spite of the fact that her clothes were very, very ordinary.

Oliver's mother always said, "The clothes do not make the man, my dear; but they always make the woman."

Oliver's mother had no poor friends on her calling list. And when she thought of what the vast fortune of Crossman Tay would mean — of how it would of course revise her calling list upward — why, Mrs. Tay almost fainted with delight.

Now when Oliver first looked on this young girl he was fairly and frankly dazzled. His wits spun about in his head. And he had to take hold of himself with a firm grip and say, "Are you some common fellow, or are you Oliver Tay?"

After having thus consulted his better nature, he found it possible to look steadily at her — though with just a little effort — as when the sun is behind thin clouds, you might say. However, at the second glance he discovered that the material of which her coat was made would certainly never do; and, as for her bonnet, it was simply impossible. He decided this rather sadly, to be sure, but also firmly. He was always firm with himself, was Oliver. His mother insisted on it.

And thereafter he only allowed himself to be aware of her out of the corner of his eye. He forced himself to consider her as one considers a lovely painting on a wall. But nevertheless a little ache would creep into his heart with a most irritating persistence. To speak just a dozen pleasant words to her would have been a joy to Oliver, but then Oliver never flirted.

So Oliver kept his head turned to the wide, hot, glimmering desert of the North, or to the ridiculously big mountains in the South. Oliver was accustomed to Connecticut mountains; and he felt that these monstrosities were out of all proportion — they were absurd. What could one expect of people who lived in surroundings which were in themselves cartoons of Mother Nature?

Oliver decided that this was good enough to write to his mother.

Also, he would write to her about the girl. He would have nothing to report, because this afternoon the hoydenish creature had actually climbed up to sit beside the driver; and she sat braced back and held the reins of the wheelers while the weather-browned old stager grinned down at her and loved her with all his heart. And all the time laughter kept bubbling from the lips of this girl, and odd little musical, ridiculous cries which made tickles and wriggles run right up the spine of Oliver Tay and settle in the smiling-nerves of his cheeks.

But he controlled himself. You may be sure that he was his mother's son in a crisis of this nature. And, when she returned to her place and attempted, for the tenth time, to address something to him, Oliver crushed her by failing to hear; and he turned his head to the north and looked magnificently forth across the desert.

He was showing her his three-quarters view, which he felt to be his finest angle. He had tried them all before the mirror. Because Mrs. Oliver Tay always said, "Every girl makes the most of herself. Pray, why should not every man?"

So Oliver Tay made the most of himself. He knew, for instance, exactly how the blond hair that escaped beneath the brim of his hat framed his ivory face. And he knew just how his big chin was supported by his graceful, tapering fingers. Oliver's chin was the one fly in the perfect ointment of his mother's life. For it was entirely too large, too broad, too heavily and bluntly provided with bone. His mother one day lost her temper completely.

"Your father's grandfather was a sailor," sobbed Mrs. Tay, "but why should that be visited upon me?"

However, between them they evolved a way of arranging the stocks of Oliver to make them appear a little more broad and a little lower and fuller, so that the chin did not appear, after a time, to be so dreadfully massive. For his mother's sake he had studied for weary hours to learn how to make the best of it, and how to hold his head tilted back a little, so that the angle of the perspective might cover the only fault in his face. The only fault. Yes, surely there was no other. Mrs. Tay could not find one. And Oliver himself agreed that his features were perfect.

So, as I have been saying, he looked across the northern desert and allowed the perfection of his beauty to sink in upon this hoyden of the West.

Then the stage rolled into Siddon Flat.

Oliver Tay was accustomed to making a sensation. But he had never seen men who, at the sight of him, threw up their arms and screamed and whooped. He was amazed, and puzzled. These poor, rough savages! He smiled a little to himself. Mrs. Tay would be amused, also!

The stage halted. He stepped daintily down; and just then it seemed to Oliver that he heard the voice of the girl, behind him, saying, "What will he do? Cry, I suppose, when they —"

That is to say, this was what his ears told him the girl was uttering, and uttering about him. But he knew that his ears were deceiving him. No person in this world could possibly take him lightly, least of all a woman.

Just across the street, as the letter had said, there was a long, low-fronted building with the sign CROSSMAN TAY painted in great, uneven letters of red. It was a shock to Oliver. It was a rude shock. He was prepared to find his estate vested in the low marts of trade. But he really was not prepared for red paint.

He crossed the street slowly. It was ankle-deep in the foulest dust, and at the very first stride the careful polish on Oliver's boots disappeared, covered by an alkali white. He advanced, however, toward the main entrance of the store and he found it easy to go forward, for the dozen or more men who were in his path turned around, and gaped at him, and instinctively opened a path before him through which Oliver stepped with that little, cold smile which Mrs. Tay had taught him to wear for the public.

But, just as Oliver reached the wide doorway, a weaving figure came toward him from the interior. It was wrapped in a brightly painted buffalo robe, and it staggered from foot to foot, rolling wild, reddened eyes. Oliver knew at once that it was an Indian. He had seen an Indian once before, in Boston — or a white man dressed up and painted like an Indian on the stage, which was just the same thing.

So he was only mildly interested. He only hoped that the creature would not jostle dustily against him. Alas, that was the very thing that happened. They wavered opposite one another, drawn by the singular magnet which catches passers-by; and, before Oliver Tay could dodge again, just as he was slipping past, the shoulder of the redman lodged heavily against his chest.

Instinct told Oliver what to do. A trip with his heel and a shove with his shoulder deposited the red man with a heavy thump and grunt upon the floor, and Oliver went on. He went on toward a tall, thin man with weary eyes, who was watching all of this.

"I am asking for Henry Luger," said Oliver.

"I'm Henry Luger," said the tall, thin man.

"My name," said Oliver, "is Oliver Tay!"

"Is it?" said Luger dryly. "The important thing just now is: What's the name of the Indian you just knocked down? Have you got any idea of that, young man?"

"Certainly not," said Oliver, much offended.

"Well," said Mr. Luger, "that's White Hawk, the great Comanche."

"Really?" said Oliver, and he covered the slightest of yawns.

Mr. Luger regarded him with a dubious frown; then he led the new owner into his private office, but only to cry out, as he glanced through the window, "By the good old Lord Harry, there's Marian Barge!"

"Ah," said Oliver, "is that her name?"

"Why, Tay, didn't you ride in with her, four days on that stage? Lovely, eh?"

"I really didn't notice," said Oliver.

CHAPTER III

Scalp Locks

The conduct of Mr. Luger was strange but remarkably sympathetic. He seemed to realize at once that it was almost like death to Oliver Tay to have to breathe the foul air of this trading town. He declared that everything could be rushed through so that Oliver might be free within three days. There was a prospective purchaser for the business — a good, reputable business man who would pay a third down and give excellent references for the rest. Oliver was delighted.

"And by the way," said Mr. Luger, "how tall are you?"

"Just two inches above six feet," said Oliver.

"Ah?" said Luger. "If I were you, Mr. Tay, I would wear no weapons while in this part of the country. If I were you, I would remain exactly as you are — exactly. You will find that it will save you a great deal of trouble, I am sure."

Oliver hardly knew what could be the meaning of this advice; but, since he felt that it was given in good part, he accepted it with a smile and departed. And all day long, as he wandered about the streets of the town, he admired the strange sights and the queer people: Mexicans, Negroes, Castilian Spanish, desert rats, pushing Yankee business men, all blending in the queerest of hodgepodges.

But though these creatures appeared rude, they seemed harmless. Not an offensive move was made toward him all of that day, so that he began to feel that the legends about the rough, man-killing cowpunchers was the merest myth. To be sure, they turned and stared at him, without the slightest sense of taste. But Oliver was used to being looked at. He rather liked it, in fact. So he walked until evening, returned to Mr. Luger's to have dinner, expressed his opinion of the place and wondered that Mr. Luger could exist in it, and then walked back to the hotel.

It was only a short distance. Not more than fifty steps, all told. But the alley was dark and narrow, for half the distance; and Oliver did not see the half-dozen swarthy shadows stealing softly behind him. The first warning of danger was a noose that flipped accurately over his head and was drawn tight around his neck, with a jerk that cut off all chance of making noise, and Oliver was tied in a neat bundle and removed softly.

Half an hour later the stifling blanket was removed from his head and he found himself lying beside a fire looking up into the face of White Hawk. White Hawk was very pleased. And though Oliver had read much about the immobile hauteur of the natives of the desert, he found that White Hawk was just like a child with a toy, so much did his features light up as he drew forth his scalping knife and sank his broad fingers in Oliver's flowing golden locks.

Oliver had never looked upon his hair in that light. But now he could see that, from a certain viewpoint, all of his care and the care of Mrs. Oliver Tay had been wasted for the construction simply of a perfect scalp lock. He did not shudder. It was too dreadful for shuddering. He lay stiff as a stone and wondered how heaven could permit such things to happen.

A woman's voice sounded and stayed the hand of White Hawk. A thrilling thought of another Pocahontas darted through the soul of Oliver. In that flash, he saw himself translated into a school text and a rather miserable drawing. But, when he looked up, he discovered that it was an antique and dreadful mask of a hag, the most hideous creature that he had ever beheld. However, what she had to say influenced White Hawk. He presently relinquished his purpose with a sigh.

Alas, if Oliver could have known!

For the oldest squaw and the wisest of White Hawk's domestic circle had just finished persuading him that if he would sell this strapping big fellow south of the Rio Grande to the silver mines, he would receive the price of two drunks and a roll of lead for bullets.

That sage counsel was taken, and two days later Oliver was striding across the desert in a line of sweating, down-headed wretches like himself, save that all of the others were Negroes, or

25

Indians, or half-breeds of one sort or another. Oliver staggered along in this line, more than half naked. For the very first thing that had been done was to take possession of the incredibly wonderful clothes of the white man.

So Oliver was walking across the stones and the cacti and the fiery sands on burned and weary feet; but, when he winced and dragged back, a brute of an Indian rushed up on a tireless devil of a horse and with a bull whip slashed the sun-scorched back of the son of Mrs. Oliver Tay. And in this torture, Oliver wondered that he did not scream and weep and wring his hands.

But there was something dreadfully insensitive in Oliver, it seemed. There was something which would have displeased his mother almost as much as his big blunt chin. For, as a matter of fact, when the agony stabbed him to the heart, sometimes a wave of weakness rushed upward to his throat; but there it was always locked back behind his set teeth. And if the tears swept into his eyes, they were burned out again by a strange electric fire that shot through him.

They crossed a river. They were examined by firelight. A Mexican in a tall-crowned, wide-brimmed straw hat, smoking a cigarette, walked up and down the line of captives, which had been stripped of clothes for this inspection. And when he came to Oliver, would he not start and cry out: "Good heavens! A white man — an aristocrat, among these scoundrels, this riffraff?"

No, the Mexican did nothing of the kind. But

he kicked the shins of Oliver to make him lift up his feet, and then he grunted and pointed out to the slave-selling Comanche the poor condition of those feet.

The Comanche was a fair businessman for one of his kind. He argued with much heat, it seemed to Oliver, that this was the prize of the whole procession, in poundage, and in beauty.

But the Mexican merely snarled. He took a bony forefinger and sank it into the plump ribs of Oliver Tay and rubbed his sharp nail up and down across the rib bones. And though Oliver did not understand Spanish, it was plain to him that the other was saying, "Do you call this pudding a man?"

However, the deal was ended, and Oliver advanced to another stage of trouble. For three days he was forced to march across the desert. He really could not do it. When he looked down and saw the condition of his feet, he knew that the next step would be his last. But somehow there was always something in him which supplied the endurance for still a little more pain.

Then the caravan halted, and Oliver was allowed to tend to his feet. They waited for a whole week for another herd of wretches, and then they struggled on again. For fifteen more days they marched across the desert. And Oliver's white skin became a brown-black hide, and his lovely golden hair became a stiff thatch of sun-faded hemp. And his feet were covered from heel to toes with deepening calluses. Two hundred and twenty pounds of Oliver had rolled into Siddon Flat on the stage coach. But only a hundred and seventy pounds of him reached the silver mine.

Then he went to work at the most hideous treadmill that was ever conceived by the mind of man. All day long he was forced to climb up sagging rotten ladders from the depths of the mine, carrying baskets of silver on his back, supported with a strap that passed around his forehead.

Even the Indians and Negroes, inured to such labor, presently wasted and died under this dreadful strain; and Oliver brought to the task a body which was hardly more than bones and sinews. What place had muscle in the world for which Mrs. Tay lived? However, Oliver did not die. He wasted, certainly, another ten pounds or so. But just as his vitality wavered between burning low and burning out, there was an accident in the mine — a drift was closed by a fall of rock — and there was an enforced vacation for half a week.

At the end of that time, Oliver could go on. And he did go on. It would be pleasant to write that his nimble wits soon contrived a means of escape; but, as a matter of fact, Oliver was much too weary to even attempt to think, most of the time. He ate food. He labored like a devil. And he slept. His life was divided into those three parts, and not even the image of Mrs. Oliver Tay entered his mind more than once a week; and, as for himself — why, he well-nigh forgot that there was such a person as Oliver Tay.

He did not hope. He simply existed. And this thing went on for six months, which is an eternity, when a man is twenty-one. Three months of that time were spent in a trance of labor. Then he began to recover. Legs, back, and arms began to be equipped with such a luxurious robing of muscles and sinews that, although the overseers piled a double load upon him, still he could carry it with ease up and down the ladder. He grew stronger every day. He grew so strong that, before the end of the six months, he had spare energy; and he could begin to think again.

And as his lethargy fell away he began to really suffer. Before that, only his body had been in torment. But now his soul could endure the pangs, also.

CHAPTER IV
In the Silver Mine

Half of the time in the steaming heat of the deeps of the mine, and half in the broiling sun at the mouth of the pit. Oliver Tay was like one who passes from boiling water to frying pan, a process which was rapidly killing off the others who had entered this servitude when he had. He saw them wither, weaken, fade, and die, one after the other, without paying any particular attention to them, because the woes and the good of others were never much in his mind. His good mother had taught him otherwise.

But now that his frame resisted the torment — in spite of the double burdens which were laid upon him, in spite of the fact that he was sometimes worked both by day and by night shift — now that his whole big body was turned to iron, Oliver Tay one day heard a sigh before him, as he was climbing up the ladder from the deeps of the mine. The fellow in advance of him staggered and wabbled to and fro. Oliver deftly swung to one side so that the man, in falling, might miss him, and happily strike two or three of those in the rear and dash them from their foot and hand holds, and so crunch them to bits on the hard rocks at the bottom of the shaft.

Such was the cunning of Oliver Tay; but, on this occasion, though the man above him was plainly nearly gone, yet he did not fall. And presently a faint, feeble voice sounded from him in broken Spanish, "Courage, *amigos,* for I shall not fall on you!" And with that, he bent to his labor again and went up the ladder with sagging knees.

Big Oliver looking upward with knit brows, noted the leanness of those knees and thighs, and then glanced down at his own Herculean legs. And he stared at the bent back of the man above him, with the spinal column thrusting out all its length, with every notch to be counted in it. And it seemed to Oliver that he was beholding a miracle of the very first water, for this man above him seemed to be struggling so hard not for the sake of himself as much as to spare the poor, wretched slaves beneath him.

A tremor of emotion swept over Oliver Tay. It reached the pit of his throat. It passed through and dissolved the inward might which had enabled Oliver to endure his own miseries; and he shuddered through all his huge body, so that a man next behind him snarled in Spanish, "Are you going to tumble, you great lump, and sweep us all to the bottom?"

But Oliver paid no heed. He merely shook his head to clear his eyes of the tears. Then he hurried on. He reached out a great, brown, corded arm and lifted the ponderous weight of the ore basket from the shoulders of the slave before him.

And he heard a stifled and groaning voice exclaim, "In the name of heaven, is there an angel with me in this torment?"

But the chief miracle, to Oliver, was that the weight of the two baskets bothered him no more than had the weight of one. He carried them lightly up to the surface, for this act of grace had poured an incredible strength through all of his limbs. He was hardly breathing fast as he returned the burden to the other at the top of the ladder. He found himself looking down at a man of middle height, with a broad, strong frame from which suffering in the mine had stripped away the flesh. He was a gaunt scarecrow, and his eyes looked forth at Oliver Tay out of two deep, dark holes.

"You are the Englishman!" said he in an English as broken as his Spanish. And his voice was filled with the greatest possible surprise. It was as though he had said, "And the devil has done this much for me!"

"I am not English," said Oliver.

And merely in speaking to this man, he felt more kindness flow through his soul than had ever possessed it before that moment from the instant of his birth. He could not help smiling with gentleness, and his mercy and pity overflowed and enveloped the smaller man.

"Ah, ah!" murmured the other, "I have been a blind fool! I have never seen you before! Now, friend, I shall not live two days; but, from this moment until my death, I shall no longer pray for my own soul but for your deliverance."

And Oliver knew that it was true. And as for himself, while he strode along in the line of the slaves, he pondered upon this event. It seemed to him that all was better in this world than it had been before. He was filled with a strange kindness for the miserable, stumbling, cursing slaves before and behind him. Yes, those who cursed were the most valuable; those who were silent were sure to die before long. And yet he himself had been one of the silent for these months and months.

The stranger whom he had saved staggered, turning back toward the mine; and the long whip of the driver reached out like a dragon's tongue and flicked across his shoulders. Oliver could hear the horrible hiss of the bull's hide. Then, as Oliver Tay passed the driver, he turned his head a little and smiled straight into the man's face. It had an odd effect, that smile of his; for the driver stood like one turned to stone, as though he had been confronted by the Medusa's face. Afterward, the fellow hurried back, trembling, to the shack where the guards lived.

"Fernando has the chills and fever," they said when they caught sight of him.

"It is the big gringo," he told them, panting. "He is turning mad, at last. His eyes are as green as the eyes of a cat; and he will be doing mischief around here, one of these days. Heaven keep me out of the grip of his big hands!"

"Double his loads again," said the others.

"No man could carry double the load that he lifts ordinarily. It could not be done."

"Nevertheless, try. Will you break the heart of the dog, or will you have him break ours some black night?"

So Fernando, the driver, went back, and at the next round he did as he was told. He gave Oliver Tay a great basket with an order to bring it up filled. And coming up the ladder under that vast weight, every muscle in Oliver's body stretched and crackled like breaking strings.

"Comrade," said the white man he had helped, and who was now just behind him, "you bear that for my sake."

"Ha!" said Oliver Tay. "I tell you, it is nothing."

But still there was much left to this day; and all through it he was forced to carry that new vast basket. At length, after dark, he was allowed to leave his place in the line, and he walked to the fire where his shift of slaves had their meal. Behold, the great pot in which the corn was cooked, seasoned with goat's fat and a few shreds of goat's flesh, was empty and polished. He had been purposely detained until the meal was over.

However, he had missed other meals before this. What stung him was the fierce, prying, hateful, envious eyes of the other slaves, as they lay on the ground and stared up at him. They detested him because of the strength that was in him, the strength that enabled him to endure a labor under which they were crushed. And he, looking about for the first time with cleared vision, saw that they were human, indeed, but something less than of human worth. They had been ground under the heel until there was less soul in the pack of them than in one mongrel cur that begs its food in the street.

"My friend!" said a voice gently.

He turned, and he saw that it was his worn companion of the ladder holding out a double handful of pottage. They were not clean hands. And dust and ashes and cinders had blown from the smoldering fire upon the food. But six months before this, Oliver Tay had ceased thinking about such little things as cleanliness. He devoured that food with a dreadful eagerness, and then lay down at the side of his new companion and stretched his mighty arms above his head and felt new strength rush back into his body with the touch of the damp, cool earth.

"Now tell me what you are and how you came here?" said his friend.

Oliver liked up through the dusk to the coming of the stars. The ghostly face of Mrs. Tay formed before his eyes. Then that image vanished, and there was nothing.

"I shall tell you," he replied at length. "I am nothing. I have lived like a man asleep. Nothing real has ever happened to me, until I was sold to this gang of devils. But what are you?"

"I have a longer story than yours," said the other. "My name is Roderigo Venales. I came from Florence to Mexico City, lost my money at dice, took to the hills, lived a gay year or two taking purses. Finally I was caught; and they hesitated as to whether I should be hung at once, or thrown into a dungeon to rot, or given to this living death. They chose the worst of the three for me, and so here I am."

"Do you hear that baying of dogs through the hills?" said Oliver.

"Yes, they are hunting that poor fool who ran off last night."

Oliver raised himself on his elbow, and he looked about him. They lay in the pit of a great funnel of black mountains that sent their naked sides dizzily up against the sky. And here and there across these slopes there were always watchers, waiting for a smoke signal by day or a fire signal by night, announcing the escape of a maddened slave. And besides, there were always strong bloodhounds in the camp to follow trails.

But Oliver whispered, "Now close your eyes and sleep, Roderigo Venales. For, a little later, you and I will leave this camp!"

CHAPTER V
Out of the Frying Pan

It will be seen what this undertaking meant, when it is known that although Venales had been tortured close to death in the mine, still he shrank from attempting to escape.

When a slave tried to escape and a party went in pursuit, two or three of the workers in the mine were always taken along so that they could see what the dogs did to the fugitives when they were pulled down. On one of these occasions, Venales was a witness. He had never forgotten, and he tried to tell Oliver Tay what it was like. But Oliver sat in the darkness with his thick-muscled forearms wrapped around his knees, and he tilted his head back and back to that angle at which he had learned from the mirror his chin appeared less brutally heavy.

He was not thinking of mirrors, now, and he was not thinking of looks; but he was smiling a little at the stars and wondering at himself. For he found, when he looked into his heart, that he had not the slightest fear of death. Indeed, he was seeing himself for the very first time; and, just as his eye could wander through unfathomed leagues of the stars which were strewn across the universe of night, so he could turn his glance inward and probe a vastness of new-found self. All new!

He was quite sure that though his mother could recognize his face, she would never be able to know the heart of her son. He had seen other worlds, and there was still an unknown continent to explore in himself.

Then he said to Venales, "When the time comes, you'll go along with me. I know a way."

He did not know a way. He had not the slightest idea of a way; but still he felt that one might as well die at once as to drag on a wretched existence here, half underground and half out of it, with the whip to season the labor.

The wind, falling away a little, allowed the sound of the booming voices of the hounds to float more clearly to him. He felt no hatred of them, but neither did he feel any fear. It would soon be a grand race. He could remember, as a boy, shouting and clapping his hands when the greyhounds turned the flying rabbit, and caught it, and broke its back. Why, this was the same thing, with men for rabbits!

Those voices from the mountains were echoed suddenly by a clamor from the kennels, where half a dozen of the great brutes were always lodged. And they got each day, as Oliver Tay knew, more solid food than any toiler in the mines — save himself — because he had the strength to elbow the other slaves aside, and stand for a double turn at the pot.

Then a guitar twanged and a Spanish song floated softly forth. Something about love, and spring, and the moon, of course. He had learned Spanish while he was at the mine — learned it little by little, each word usually driven into his mind with the lash of a whip. One rarely forgets such lessons.

And after that, a horse neighed from the stables. Horses!

He stood up and looked across to the low-lying barns and drew in a breath of the cool night air.

"You gringo, lie down!"

That was the guard, gun at shoulder. Those guard muskets were loaded with small shot — ragged pieces which would blow a man to bits. Juan had tried to rush the guard two weeks before; and, after the gun went off, Juan was a headless man.

So Oliver lay down and closed his eyes, but he was only waiting; and, after a little time — was it an hour, or two hours? — he raised his head again. The whole mass of the slaves slept, and as they slept they groaned with weariness.

He touched the arm of Venales. "Now creep behind me, Roderigo."

For the guard sat with his back to a tree, his rifle across his knees; and, by the way his head had fallen to one side, Oliver knew that the man slept. He went first, and Venales behind him. He could feel the fear of Venales like a cold wind, following. It filled Oliver with pity.

When he had crawled to the feet of the guard,

he saw that it was Fernando; and he was glad because there was no other man whom he would be so happy to kill. But now this matter of killing.

There was the gun. He could lift it from the knees of the sleeper and fire the charge into his breast, but that would be to rouse the whole camp. Or he could take the throat of Fernando in both his hands. But a choking man will kick and make a flurry like a hen with its head off.

However, there was something else — for at the hip of Fernando there was a broad-hafted knife with a blade a foot long — almost a sword. He drew that knife from its sheath and considered the proper place. If the point ground against a rib, Fernando would have time to utter one screech — his death cry and death knell of the fugitives, also. However, one must take some chances.

He poised the knife and thrust it home. It went very easily, Fernando slipped softly to the side, and Oliver lowered him to the ground lest there be a noise. Then he picked up the fallen musket and gave it to Venales; and they went on side by side, their bare feet making no sound.

At the door of the stable a man stepped suddenly out before them. He seemed to realize the truth in a flash of intuition and thrust his hands over his head.

"Mercy! Mercy!" he whispered. "I see nothing."

"Strike!" breathed Venales through his teeth.

But Oliver shook his head. "Bring us to the

best two horses in the stable," he said.

And the fellow instantly led them on. He selected a bay and a gray. Then Oliver bound him with rope and gagged him.

"The knife is better," said Venales. "Through the back, *amigo!*"

And even in the dimness of the barn, Oliver could see the flash of his teeth as he grinned with a hungry thirst for blood. "Let him be," said Oliver.

They saddled the horses and led them out into the night. There was not a sound. Only, presently, one of the dogs wakened, snarling, or perhaps it had merely had a bad dream. Venales was busy thrusting into the saddle holsters the two pistols which he had taken from the stable guard.

"Are you ready?"

"I have a horse, a musket, and two pistols," said Venales; "and my brother is at my side. Why, I am ready for everything, beginning with fighting and ending with death. You will see that I can be a man."

But Oliver needed no further proofs of that. You would have said that Venales had gained not a horse and guns only but also twenty pounds of flesh and inches of stature. His head was raised for the first time. When they sent the hounds after Venales, they would be trailing a man, not a slave.

Oliver's foot was in the stirrup when a gasp and then a thrilling scream broke from the stable.

"I told you the knife was safer!" called Venales.

And instantly he conjured himself into the saddle, by a sort of magic, and was showing Oliver the way out of the camp.

"You ride the wrong way!" gasped Oliver.

"No," said the calm voice of Venales. "The river is best for horses."

How calm he was, now that he was in the saddle — not spurring his horse wildly, in spite of the clamor that was breaking out in the camp, but sending it along at a gentle gallop. Now that they drew clear of the building, Oliver could see that his companion was right. There were other trails, but they were rough and deep with soft, loose sand, and the river road was evenly graded, winding up the valley.

Some one rose out of the ground before them — so it seemed — and stood on the bridge across the little river.

"Who goes?"

"Friends!" shouted Venales, galloping his horse a little faster; and he fired the musket at the sentinel.

Oliver, riding across the bridge, saw the dead man roll over the edge and disappear toward the swift, black waters. But it was no more to Oliver than the fall of a stone.

And, as they turned up the river road, he was laughing softly for joy in the strength of his horse — laughing for joy, too, at the easy way in which Venales was sitting the saddle before him. A hooded hawk is a worthless thing; but give her eyes and freedom, and then see! So it was with Venales!

The dogs were already raging behind them. Horses were squealing and snorting as the riders mounted. And beneath these sounds there was a deep, groaning murmur that came, as Oliver knew, from the wakened slaves in their pen. From the camp behind him, two fires were lifting red heads. And now, far ahead of them from the hills, another fire flashed in answer.

Still Oliver laughed; for he was free, and as long as this knife remained to him, he would stay free. They could take his body, but what was that? His soul would slip through their reaching fingers like water through a sieve, or like a pigeon for its home in the sky.

The black earth rushed beneath them. The stars slid back overhead.

"They are all gathered on this side of the river," said Venales, reining back. "They have blocked us here. But we'll swim the current. Eh?"

Oliver looked at the white water and felt that it was death, but yonder was Venales sending the gray horse like a silver streak from the bank. They went with a churning of high-flung foam, and without waiting to see whether they rose or no, Oliver flung his bay in pursuit. The water leaped up with a roar into his face. The serpent coils of the currents tore at him. The bay held its way but was swept downstream, though pointing its nose valiantly up and toward the shore.

Oliver, with his head clear of the water and the

stars in his eyes once more, threw himself out of the saddle and swam with one hand gripping the pommel. Thus lightened, the horse made swifter progress. His feet found bottom; his shoulders heaved suddenly high out of water, and Oliver scrambled back into the saddle as they heaved up the bank.

The laughter of Venales was there before them. Who would believe that this wild man had been a staggering, cringing, dying slave only a few short hours before?

"Will they follow?" asked Oliver, pointing back to the flying shadows which swept up the river road.

"Are they riding for their lives?" answered Venales. "No, they will never follow. There are only the men and the dogs of the outer guard."

Only those men and those dogs! However, nothing was terrible until it was found and faced. Like two happy children they galloped their horses across the sands toward the black, bold mountains which walked up into the upper sky, where freedom was.

CHAPTER VI

The Baying of the Hounds

They were in the hills when they heard the baying of the hounds. They were in the throat of the valley with walls as steep as the walls of a room when the music of the dogs came baying in soft, distant thunder around them. They were on the crest of a divide when the noise of the pack crashed about them, just at their heels.

Venales whipped out of the saddle. His horse did not lift its head. Its strength was spent.

"They are no good to us, now," said Venales, "and," he added, "there was only one charge for the musket. How many hounds are there?"

Oliver was already on the ground, listening. "I think that there are six," said he.

"And there is one bullet in each pistol. That will leave four. Tell me, Oliver, will you take this gun and swear to kill one brute with it?"

"Keep the pistol," said Oliver. "I have never known how to shoot. This little tooth will do me." He waved the knife against the stars and laughed again.

"Patience, heart," called Venales. "Let me try the pistols, first. They may turn the crew. Who can tell?"

That instant, the pack burst up the ravine and topped the rise, running hard and low; and, at the view, every voice slid up the scale and hung on a wild, terrible note of triumph.

Oliver looked at Venales, but still the other held his fire. He stood with his head thrown back, smiling, the starlight glimmering on his starved, naked shoulders. Both the pistols were poised. You would say that he was about to fire at a target for some cheerful little wager — a glass of wine, perhaps. The wine would be their own hearts' blood, this night, if he missed.

How fast those brutes came. There was no accounting for such speed and such wind. Far, far behind them their masters could hardly be heard, cheering them on. A pistol cracked, and the brindled leader threw himself into the air, snapped at his own flying ghost, and dropped dead upon the rocks. And the dog beside him received the next slug. He dived along the ground, rattling the stones, and lay without a quiver so close to Oliver that he could have touched the sweating flank.

The others in that pack turned right and left. They had seen enough to give them pause, all of them except a black monster who now shook himself clear of the shadows in the cañon and came stalwartly on. He was a vast beast, like a boarhound; but he was glistening black as the face of a pool when there is no moon. He drove straight onward, howling like a demon, and bounded at the nearest goal. That goal was Oliver.

There was no way of meeting that charge without being gashed by the yawning teeth, so Oliver slipped to one knee and let the danger fly past across his shoulder while he stabbed upward.

The black monster screeched, and rolled off the narrow trail and thumped heavily down the first stages of the precipice that opened on their side. Then, with its death cry ringing up behind it, it fell into the great gorge below.

That was a stalwart pack. There were still three dogs ready to fight if there was a chance in fighting, but there seemed no chance here. They had seen their fellows go down. So they backed away, howling, to tell their masters that the prey was at bay.

"Now we have two winded horses," said Venales calmly. "And yet those nags that are working up the cañon cannot be much fresher than we are. So let's walk our mounts along, for a little, and keep the dogs back, if we can. In five minutes there will be enough wind in our mounts to carry us downhill."

He was the master, for horses were as new to Oliver as guns. They jogged the down-headed nags along the slope with the dogs following eagerly, edging nearer. Then the noise of the other riders came at them openly, as the posse cleared the mouth of the gulch. It was only a question now, of which horses were the freshest. And though, when they mounted, it seemed as if they could get no more out of their nags —

still the pursuit did not gain. It fell back, little by little, and little by little, until there were only the dogs, and then the far winding of a horn, sounding the retreat.

The pack turned back; and Oliver and Venales knew that they were safe for this night, at least. They had broken through the ring of the guards. They had the free stretch of the open mountains before them.

They entered that space with a determination to follow no frequented trails and to ride near no habitation. For seven days they pushed steadily ahead, living on birds which they could trap with simple little snares, and rabbits caught in their runways. It was work which made Oliver lean, but Venales seemed to grow fat on it. Every day his eyes were brighter and his cheeks ruddier, until it was plain to Oliver that it had not been labor that crushed his companion in the mine but the bitterness of slavery.

And, all that time, no sign or sound of a pursuit approached them. There are mountain wildernesses to this day in Mexico where an army could be hidden safely. And there was three times as much wasteland in those times. Two hundred miles of rough country lay between them and the silver mine when, at last, from an upper slope of a mountain, they looked down upon twinkling lights in a little valley; and Venales, trembling with the cold that blew through his rags, decided that it was time for them to change their ways.

It was a widespread rancheria to which they descended in the middle of the night, and all went for them as by magic. In the gun room of the old house they armed themselves to the teeth with long heavy rifles, pistols, and ample stock of lead and powder. They invaded the kitchen for dried meat and parched corn and salt and flour, and in the corrals they selected two stout mustangs to continue their journey.

When they set forth again, they knew that there would be a fresh pursuit behind them. But they were warmly dressed; they had found food; and their hearts were consoled for their privations. So, in a safe camp the next night, they consulted as to what their plans should be.

To Oliver Tay it seemed that the safe way was to point their course steadily to the north until they came to his own land. But Venales had other ideas on the subject. He pointed out to Oliver that this was the land which he knew. In the same country he had lived the wild life before, and he knew how the law could be dodged. But north of the Rio Grande —

"North of the Rio Grande," said Oliver. "I am a rich man. There will be no need of wearing masks and holding guns at the heads of people, Roderigo."

"Not for you, then," said the other. "But am I to live on your charity, *amigo?*"

"Consider, Roderigo," said Oliver simply, "that you are one with me. You are my brother. What you have is mine, and what I have is yours.

There is no question of charity."

The Italian smiled faintly. "This is kind talk; and it is talk which is true while we are here in the mountains," he said. "But when we leave them, and when we come back to your own people —"

"They will think as I do," said Oliver stoutly.

"Have you a father and a mother?" asked Roderigo.

"I have a mother," said Oliver with a sigh.

"Will she wish to have me as one of her family?" said Roderigo. "An outlaw, a bandit, a man-killer, my dear Oliver!"

And, watching the gloomy face of Oliver, he laughed aloud. "I understand it all," he said. "If you go north, you must go alone. If you stay in the south, I shall teach you how the eagles live, *amigo*. I shall teach you how to be happy and owe no man for your happiness and have no obligations in this wide world except to your gun, your knife, and the horse you ride. Is that something to you?"

CHAPTER VII
Fanning a Revolver

Oliver Tay had no intention of becoming a border bandit.

By a sure messenger he dispatched a letter to the coast where it would take a ship to the States and find his mother and assure her that he was well, and that he was following on the heels of that letter as fast as he could go. In the meantime, so long as he did not become a robber himself, was there any harm in associating with the little band which Venales was collecting? None in the world, surely, and Mexico owed him a little entertainment, as anyone would agree.

Besides, they were as jolly a lot as you would find in a day's ride by train. Venales had known them all before, here and there. It was astonishing how much he knew of people and things. A glance at man or beast was sure to store away in his mind every interesting fact concerning it. So he knew exactly enough about each one of his followers to wish to enroll him in his band. For ten days they drifted here and there through valley and lowland; and wherever they went, they added a few followers.

"I am leaving in a day or two," Oliver Tay would say gravely to Venales.

"Yes, yes," Roderigo would agree. "Do you think that I would have you turn bandit for the sake of friendship? Tush, dear lad, never in the world!"

He meant what he said, and never once did he strive to draw Oliver into his schemes. But life was so wonderfully pleasant that Oliver found it hard, very hard, to drag himself away from the band.

Perhaps the majority of them were very black villains to other people and in other places, but they showed him nothing save what was good in them. They had heard concerning him the one thing which opens all hearts — charity from one sufferer to another. And Roderigo Venales was never tired of talking on that theme behind the back of Oliver Tay, and of telling how the giant had taken the ore basket from his breaking back, and of how Oliver had opened the way to liberty.

"Now, upon my solemn soul," Venales would say, "he got freedom for us both, not so much because he would have dared it for himself, but because he pitied and wished it for me. And, when we stood in the pass, *amigos*, and the great dogs came leaping toward us, what did he do? He gave me both the pistols, and in his own hand he kept only a knife — that same knife, I tell you, which is now at his belt!"

As a matter of fact, Roderigo had discovered

that it was not altogether a matter of bad policy to praise Oliver so much. For, the more he magnified Oliver, the greater he himself became. Here was a god among men, and yet that god had suffered all dreadful dangers and perils for the sake of his friend, Venales. The men of the band loved to hear these tales, and they loved to sit about the campfire and learn of the dreadful life in the mines; because more than one of them, sooner or later, would be sure to enter them.

So Oliver found himself made once more into a demigod, with this difference. Before, he had been worshiped by a mother. Now he was admired by men who, he knew, were nearly wholehearted scoundrels; and yet praise, even from them, was wonderfully sweet. He would never let them admire him to his face. But they showed their affection in a thousand ways. No matter what he wished to do, the best talents of the crew were at his command. If he wished to explore the powers of that same famous knife which he had used upon the black dog, there was sure to be the cunning little thief and slippery snake of an information-getter — Capiño.

Capiño had commited nearly every sin of which mankind is capable, and, what was more, he carried the tokens of them written most visibly in his face. But it was his delight to do all he could for Oliver, and for hours at a time he would show him how to manage a knife in hand-to-hand fighting. There is a science in such battles, almost like the science of the rapier, filled with rules rich with stratagems — more interesting than any rapier, however. For a small sword only pricks the flesh daintily and discreetly, whereas a knife opens a great wound.

And, when they were finished with their hot work of lunging, and thrusting, and half lunging, and sweeping for the legs, and overhanding cuts at the head and face, and little whiplash strokes that curled toward the wrist, then Capiño would have his big friend stand up and try throwing the blade. Oliver learned how to hold it in the palm and dart it forth with the full sweep of the arm, smoothly, easily. And, though Oliver would never equal the venomous precision of Capiño, still he made such progress in this art that many a time the little thief would leap into the air and strike his heels and his hands together.

"Let any of you stand up to Don Olivero!" he would snarl at the others. "Stand up to him, any of you, if you have any doubts as to what he can do!"

They had no doubts. For they could see enough with their own eyes.

Perhaps Capiño was with Oliver more than any other man when they were about the camp; but, when Oliver went forth to hunt in the hills, he always had with him a dark and silent man. Like an Indian he was more inclined to use gestures than words, and he was more filled with the lore of the trail than any book. To go out with Antonio Morales for a single hour was to learn that the secrets of the world must be read in his way.

And Oliver rapidly picked up enchanting paragraphs of information. Not that he could for an instant rival the woodcraft and the mountain craft of Morales, who knew, it seemed, which way the mountain goat would run, and which way the antelope would dart, and when the eagle would turn in the air; but Oliver learned a vast deal of other things. No schoolmaster could have poured him so full.

For this was a time when the doors of his mind and his heart were open. He had just escaped from a dreadful peril; and he told himself that very soon he would be back in the traces once more, living the life of his mother's wishes, and being the sort of a man which she wished him to be. But, in the meantime, here was a little vacation interval in which he could rest at ease and enjoy himself without a thought for the morrow. Surely, he had earned a few days of this relaxation.

So he would be off up the trail with Morales, reading a new book of life and loving every word that it brought to him. Sometimes they were gone for forty-eight hours. And sometimes water and food did not pass their lips in that time among the sunburned mountains. But at last there was always a kill, and then a fire, and then a feast, but not too much — never so much food that one could not sleep lightly as a cat, when on the open trail. But how to tell the print of lobo, coyote, bobcat, mountain lion, black bear, grizzly, and a hundred other kinds that run the Mexican flesh trails, and how to tell all the deer, and how to know their ways and their coverts — Oliver read deep in such lore as this.

Then he would return to the camp; and there, when he was not with Capiño, he was sure to be found at the side of Carpio Vega — tall, noble-faced Carpio Vega, looking like some young Roman patrician, gentle, courteous, well-bred, kindly, considerate, soft-voiced but strong as a giant — almost as strong as those muscles of Oliver Tay's, fresh from the torture school of the mine.

Antonio Morales taught the trail, but Carpio Vega taught the revolver only. He was almost the only man in the band fortunate enough to possess a revolver, and he was most skilled in the use of it.

"A gun is a very good thing for hunting deer," said Venales to Oliver; "but pistols are best for close work, and nearly all our work is that! Do we ride down on danger like a cavalry charge? No, we slip along like snakes and bide our time."

"Come, Venales, do you think that I shall ever do such things?"

"You? No, of course not. But nevertheless, you watch Carpio Vega and see if you can learn his art."

"Do you call it an art?" said Oliver, smiling. "Capiño with a knife — yes, that is a clever, devilish art. And Morales on the trail is wonderful, too. But a revolver — why, what is there to that?"

"I will wager a hundred golden pesos," said Venales gravely, "that you cannot learn to shoot as he does, fanning it at his hip!"

"I don't know what you mean."

"Wait, and you will learn! Or you will try to learn. But the wager?"

"Why, I shall take the wager for the sake of the fun."

That was only at the beginning, but afterward he discovered what "fanning" a revolver meant. It was the newest of all the arts of guncraft, just as the revolver was the newest gun; and it was displayed by Carpio Vega most unexpectedly when a curious grizzly invaded their camp in the night. Someone fired and wounded the bear in the head; and the creature, crazed and blinded, charged straight for Carpio Vega. He did not flee for safety, though he had no rifle. Instead, he jerked forth a revolver, and that weapon began to chatter with a wonderful speed. Half a dozen tongues of flame darted from the hip of Vega. The bear halted, half wheeled, and fell dead.

Every one of the six bullets from that death pistol had found the head of the monster.

When Oliver went to ask a question, Carpio showed everything to him. The trigger of the revolver was filed away. To fire it, he held the gun solidly at his right hip. Then with his left hand he cuffed back the hammer as rapidly as he chose, and so he did away with the necessity of cocking and pulling the trigger. But, jerking the weapon each time he struck it with the palm of his left hand, how could he ever strike a target?

"Ah, that is a secret," smiled Carpio Vega. "I have tried to teach others. Do you wish to learn?"

And when Oliver said that he did, still Carpio smiled.

CHAPTER VIII
The Gift of Death

Afterward, Oliver learned the reason for that smile. Not a man in the camp could master the secret of "fanning" a revolver. Not a one of them all but had failed.

But Oliver had one vast advantage from the first, and that was a Herculean power of wrist which enabled him to hold the weapon steady as a rock while he was stroking the hammer. He tried twenty shots twenty paces from a big stump of a tree. Two of the bullets struck, and Carpio declared that he was highly impressed.

He took Oliver with pounds and pounds of ammunition to a spot where they stood in front of a flat-faced cliff. And there he bade him blaze away, not a shot and then a look at the target but a revolverful at a time. Bullets were no object, then. And the whole problem, with each loading of the gun, was to learn to group the shots as closely together as possible. At thirty paces he put up a bright silver peso for a target, and Oliver splashed the half dozen shots at it as rapidly and accurately as he could. When he had finished, the peso was moved; there were remarks from Carpio Vega; and the lesson was resumed in the same fashion.

How many quintals of powder and lead Oliver blew away in this fashion he could not guess. But though he saw little progress in his work, Carpio Vega was contented. And in fact, the groupings were growing smaller and smaller. And now, where the peso was put up, the slugs flew in such a small group that they spotted the rock all around the silver bit of brightness — spotted it like a stone under the hammer — and not a very inaccurate hammer, at that.

Until, at the last, Oliver learned that there was a sort of explosive rhythm about this matter — to bring the gun forth, to sweep the palm of the left hand back with just sufficient force to knock back the hammer without jarring the gun too much, to press down with the strength of the forefinger inside the trigger guard where everything including the palm of the left hand tended to jerk the muzzle of the weapon up, and all the time to keep one's eyes wide open and looking earnestly at the target.

"What is the secret that makes Carpio Vega so wonderful?" asked Oliver of Venales.

"I will tell you," said the leader. "He never squints. That is all."

Neither at a target, nor at a man, nor at a fact in life! Carpio Vega truly never squinted but looked wide-eyed and frankly at the full truth.

And suddenly, one day, he stood behind Oliver and watched him empty three guns at a target, in rapid succession. And, as Oliver threw down the weapon, groaning, "I never can master the infernal thing!" — the voice of Vega came most unexpectedly:

"Don Olivero, do you think that I could manage it any better?"

Oliver turned and stared at him in bewilderment, a little flushed.

"I am not jesting," said Carpio. "I have worked at this thing for more months than you have practiced days. But it is an art. Unless one is born with a gift for it, it can never be mastered. I, it is true, have the gift. And therefore I can manage it. But you have a greater gift, my friend. I have had you firing at pesos. Do you think that any man in the world could strike a peso at that distance? No. Except by a little luck. But you would put a bullet inside a rabbit, Don Olivero; and you would be able to fire all of those shots while another man was counting one!

"Now, you must remember, the head of a man is as large as a sitting rabbit!"

There was so much grim point to the last part of this remark that Oliver cried out, "Why, Carpio, I am tremendously interested in all of this. But it is only a game with me, you know. Nothing but a game, Carpio. Why, man, you don't doubt that, do you?"

Carpio Vega dropped his head a little; and, after he had considered the face of the ground, as though to draw wisdom from it, he said quietly, "This is all very true. But did you never hear an old story, Don Olivero, of a man who asked for a gift from a god, and wished for a touch of gold?"

"Yes," said Oliver, smiling in turn. "And what has that to do with this?"

"You remember," said Carpio, more gravely, "that the trouble was that whatever he touched turned to gold."

"Yes," nodded Oliver, "so that he could not eat food. It was gold. Water was yellow metal. He would have starved."

"But he was mercifully given the power to wash away the golden gift in the waters of a river?"

"Yes, that was the story."

"Now, Don Olivero, suppose that a man is given the gift of death and there is no river in which he can wash the gift away!"

Oliver, listening, was startled. And he frowned at his companion. "That is a gloomy thing to say," he remarked. "You don't mean that, however, Carpio?"

"If I had been a very good friend to you," said Carpio sadly, "I should never have taught you this thing. But do you know that I started because you asked, and because I did not think that you could learn? I thought that you were too slow and too — good-natured, Don Olivero. I forgot that you, too, had been in torment."

He laid a hand on the shoulder of Oliver. So much sympathy and generous understanding shone from his handsome face that the heart of Oliver was deeply touched. There was some mystery about this man which he could not understand. There seemed to be all the virtues in him that could be wished in any man, and yet he lived apart among the rough fellows who had been gathered by Venales. Even Roderigo himself seemed uneasy if he were left for a moment alone at the side of Carpio Vega. For his own part it had always seemed to him that Vega was as superior to the rest of the crew as the light of the sun to that of the moon.

He said suddenly, "Tell me, Carpio, what brings you up here to lead this life? These fellows arc not your kind. This is no life for you. Why are you here? Can you tell me?"

"I can tell you in one word," said Vega quietly. "I have just been speaking to you about a gift which is not a gift of gold?"

"Yes."

"I have just said that it is plain you have been given this gift of death, Don Olivero. Why, then, to be plain with you, I have been given the same gift. And that is why I am here!"

And Oliver, looking at him in pity and alarm, understood. And he wondered how many men this calm, handsome Carpio Vega had killed, and who they were, and under what circumstances? There was no use asking, for he would get no answer; but he knew, now, why the others in the camp shunned the company of Carpio. They, too, feared the "gift" which was his. Even Venales was not beyond its reach.

And for a whole day after that, Oliver kept his hand free from the revolvers. But after that, the fascination of what was only a game to him drew him back to the work. For to make that gun turn into fire and leaden death, gave him a wonderful satisfaction. Not that he would ever use it — no, to be sure! But still, it was a great thing. It was a toy from which he could not keep his hands.

In all this time, for weeks had passed since Venales collected his crew about him, until they now amounted to more than a dozen men, it must not be thought that there was no occupation for them except to lie about in a mountain camp and idle their hours hunting a little, and fishing a little, and playing a game of cards, or throwing knives at a mark, or practicing at odd targets with rifle or pistol. No, they drifted here and there, from spot to spot, and now and again some among them would disappear in company with Venales. Sometimes they were gone for a day, sometimes for five. And when they returned, perhaps they rode newer and finer horses, and drove cattle before them. And always, when they returned, they had their pockets filled with money.

It was all divided according to a strict rule. It was placed in the center of a circle, with the men sitting cross-legged around it. And Venales called off the names of his band one by one, and asked if there were any reason why this man should not receive his portion. And sometimes there were objections raised, as that such and such a fellow had skulked in the moment of danger. But all of those questions were instantly voted on by every voice except that of Oliver. And, after that, Venales would ask if there were any reason why the next man should be punished, or should have an extra reward for daring and cunning. And sometimes two, and even three shares were voted to a man who had distinguished himself. But always Venales got for his own purse two full shares and no more, unless the band actually voted him more, as it usually did. It was a sort of democracy, with a passive tyrant at the head of it.

Sometimes Oliver, standing by and watching, wondered if Oliver Tay, the son of Mrs. Oliver Tay, could really be standing there among those mountains, and among those men. Sometimes, too, when a knotty point arose, they would bring their differences to him, as to an impartial judge. And then he strove to banish every prejudice from his heart. With a gathered brow and a serious mind and a fast-beating pulse, he considered the matter and gave his judgment; and in every case it was the final word.

So that Venales was fond of saying, "How many throat cuttings have we been saved by our judge?"

Oh, it was a wonderfully cheerful and busy and yet careless life. And with new learning flooding in upon his mind every day, Oliver wondered if any other man was so happy as he.

It was a shock to him when Venales came to him one day, as he stood beside little venomous Capiño, practicing with the knife, and said, "Oliver, *amigo mio*, I think that the time has come for us to part, unless you care to stay here alone for a fortnight. For the whole band is riding with me tomorrow. Yes, and I wish that I could have three times as many of them. We have a thing to do that needs an army. And perhaps we shall be gone for a month, so, dear friend, if your heart is aching to be gone to your own country, this is the proper time to start."

CHAPTER IX
"To Rob, Roderigo?"

It brought Oliver Tay to a standstill.

He had never realized before that the careless freedom of this life was so dear to him; but now that the opportunity of leaving was thrust upon him, so to speak, he shrank from the departure.

And Roderigo Venales went on gently, "Or, perhaps, you would come with us?"

"I?" exclaimed Oliver. "To rob, Roderigo?"

"Tush!" said the bandit. "Rob, man? No, no, but simply to ride with us and see from a distance how the thing is done. You sit at a play, Don Oliver, and see robbery on the stage. You think nothing of that. Now this will be a different matter. You will see it on a real road, in the real mountains. And besides, it will be a grand affair. We wait for a caravan, my friend, loaded with silver that has been dug out of the ground by tortured men. And you know what that torture is. Tell me, then, is it not even a good thing to tear the money out of the hands of the tyrants?"

So said Roderigo Venales, growing red and puffed with passion as he spoke; and Oliver, remembering the manner in which he had slaved through many months of agony, could not help but smile at the thought of seeing such treasure fall into the bandits' hands.

"I shall go, Roderigo," said he. "Mind, though, that I shall take no part."

Venales seemed wonderfully pleased. He could not keep from laughing with joy and pressing the hand of his friend; and, when he had gone and Oliver turned back to the art of knife throwing, he thought that there was a glitter of delight even in the eyes of Capiño, himself. And he wondered why.

He had a clue to the reason furnished him not much later that same day. Carpio Vega came to him, as usual, with a pair of revolvers. They went down to a place apart from the camp, which was not half a mile beneath the timber line. Far beneath them a river called with a melancholy voice up the steep walls of its cañon. Where the dim print of an old trail curled over the lip of the ravine, Carpio Vega halted with his pupil. They were out of gunshot hearing from the rest of the crew, unless some stragglers had slipped after them to witness the trial — because there was an immense deal of interest in the progress of Oliver in this work. Here Carpio stooped and picked up a section fallen from the side of a rotted tree stump. He tossed it into the air; and it hung for an instant above the cañon, staggering in the wind as it fell.

"Shoot, Don Oliver!"

The back of Oliver had been turned, at that moment. But he wheeled about, with gun coming with practiced smoothness into his hand. He saw the spinning slab of wood, and the gun spoke. A single word of five quick syllables, and as the muzzle of the gun bucked and jumped with every recoil, the falling section of the tree rind reeled before the shock — 44-caliber slugs of lead were tearing through it.

All five went home, as the wood dropped out of sight past the verge of the cañon; and Oliver nodded with a sigh of satisfaction. "However," said he, "it was a large target, Carpio, and at close range."

"It was smaller than the body of a small man," said Carpio Vega, whose eyes never made mistakes; "and it was at about thirty or thirty-five paces. Oliver, do not ride with us, today!"

"Ah?" said Oliver.

"It is too dangerous," said Carpio.

"I am only a spectator," said Oliver.

"Let me ask you," said Carpio gravely, "if a race horse loves to use his speed?"

"Of course."

"And when a greyhound sees a rabbit, does it start a chase?"

"Well, but what of that?"

"And when a hungry puma sees a young, helpless colt in the pasture — ?"

"It dines on horseflesh that day. Very well. But what does all of this aim at?"

"Let me tell you, Oliver, that there will be fighting in this work which we have ahead of us. And when the fighting is hottest, can *you* keep out of it? Or will you, too, become a border bandit like the rest of us?" And he pointed to the gun in the hand of his friend.

"You only fired five times," he said, apparently changing the subject on purpose. "Why did you keep the sixth shot?"

"For someone who might come at me from the other side," said Oliver.

Carpio Vega shook his head with a smile of mingled admiration and sadness. "Yes," said he, "you should keep far away from fighting. Because, Oliver, when you start to fight you may start to kill. And that would be the end of you, I think!"

Such good advice, so pointedly brought home, should have carried the day. And, of course, it did not. For though Oliver thought the matter over and knew that if he saw these companions of his in danger he would be shrewdly tempted to come to their assistance, still he decided that he would have the moral strength to resist giving a helping hand to thieves in the midst of an act of thievery.

And, when the band rode out, with all their packs made, and their camp left desolate behind them, with the fire turning into ashes, Oliver was one of the train, riding at the head of the procession with Roderigo Venales.

It was like the march of a little army. There were twenty-two men in this assembly now. Of these not more than fifteen or sixteen kept in a close body. The remaining half dozen were thrown out ahead and on either side, riding from one commanding point of view to another to make sure that no ambush had been posted for them. As for the rear, the speed of their marching was considered to protect them enough at that point. And what marches they were!

For they traveled Indian style, with two or three horses for every man. Each one of the animals was a chosen mustang, ugly as Satan and just as tough. Each man had his gun thrust into a holster which passed under his right knee, muzzle down and the butt ready to his hand for any emergency. And each carried at least one pair of pistols in the saddle holsters; while most had another and lighter pair at the hip; and several carried even a third set, to say nothing of a knife or two to polish off the equipment.

Besides, there were some four or five of the new-fashioned revolving pistols in the lot, but outside of Carpio Vega and Oliver himself, the men of the party had not yet mastered the intricacies of the new weapon enough to feel at home with it. They were surer with their heavy, long-barreled, single-shot pistols; though some had double-barreled pistols of a wristbreaking weight.

They traveled solely in the morning and the late afternoon; and all through the blazing middle of the day they lay by in a camp, and rested, and let the horses graze, with no serious employment except for a short target practice which Venales insisted upon every day. And which was the secret, as Vega confided to Oliver, of the success of the bandit leader. In the first place, he saw that every one of his followers had plenty of the best weapons; in the second place he made sure that those weapons were kept in perfect order; in the third place he insisted that they keep in good practice with them.

For eleven days they pushed through the mountains at a terrific pace, with the horses growing leaner every march until they were nothing but muscle, bone, and fire. After that, the march was conducted with more slowness.

"Because," said Venales to Oliver, "whether we win or lose, we'll have to march faster coming back than we did going out."

Twice they caught sight of the dangers which were adrift for them in this mountain wilderness. Once a scout rushed back to them on a foaming horse with word that soldiers were straight ahead, coming up the gulch. And the bandits straightway melted up the side of the mountain like so many mountain sheep. From the top of the crest they watched two score of weary cavalry troop pass beneath them. They saw the soldiers discover traces of their trail. They saw them mill about and send out a few scouts, who strove for a futile moment to solve the trail problem up the mountainside. And then the soldiery marched on up the gulch, and Venales went his way.

"But why did they give up the hunt?" asked Oliver of little Capiño, who was often at his side.

"I shall tell you," said Capiño. "They have

72

never been robbed by us, and they don't think that they ever will be. Besides, they saw enough evidence to promise them a good deal more blood than glory if they *did* catch up with us — which they could never have done."

However, there was enough in the sight of those soldiers to make Oliver very sober; and the very next day as they rounded the shoulder of a hill, they were warned back into covert by the scouts. Looking down through three miles of crystal-clear mountain air, they saw six score riders in good formation trooping up a broad, sandy valley.

These, too, went by. But how many other parties were out policing these wilds, and how quickly would they gather on the trail as soon as the alarm went out? However, Venales seemed to have no doubts and no worries. They pushed straight ahead on their course as soon as the danger cloud was below the horizon, and four days later they were at the spot.

Here they made themselves ready for their surprise attack and their gambling throw for a great fortune.

CHAPTER X

The Silver Train

It was a perfectly chosen spot.

A deep-worn trail, ground into the rock by many centuries of mule hoofs, turned here from the windings of an upper valley and twisted around the neck of a mountain for a distance of a quarter of a mile, or so, before it dipped out again onto a lower, broader tableland. Now, upon the lower side of the narrow trail, where it turned the face of the summit, there was a five-hundred-foot fall of almost sheer precipice down to a water that foamed brown and white through the heart of the gorge and kept deep voices rolling from wall to wall. To stand there one moment was to feel oneself washed far away into a world of illusion, as the roaring of the ocean makes the seashore a place more enchanted than real.

On the other hand, the face of the upper peak shot up above the trail at an angle almost equally dizzy. One could not possibly ride a horse or even a mule up it or even across it. To climb it was a slow, wretched process of digging toes and grasping hands and would have been quite impossible, had it not been for clusters of tough-rooted shrubs which grew along the mountain, inserting their roots with wonderful cunning in rock crevices where no opening appeared.

Down this trail the treasure caravan was to pass. The plan of Venales was simply to leave his horses on the farther side of the mountain and post his men among these same bushes; and, when the treasure was passing rush out at a signal and attack the party. Oliver, as one with some eye for battle, could not help being delighted with the scheme. But what was the treasure?

Venales could tell him about that in the utmost detail, and particularly about the owner of the treasure, who was sure to ride in this train — Diego Venustiano, the proudest, sternest, fiercest spirit in the whole of Mexico.

The story of Venustiano was an epic, a thing to be dreamed rather than to be believed, a gigantic and terrible fiction which fitted this wild mountainside and the thick-throated voices that were forever bellowing from the deeps of the ravine.

For Venustiano came from a little mountain town in Aragon, of a good old stock which had sent out its scions some centuries before to fight the Moors in Granada, and to sail into the western seas for the conquest of a new world, and to fight the stubborn Dutchmen among their flooded fields and fortress cities. They had had both glory and wealth as a result of their exploits, had the Venustianos. But the wealth departed, as it has a habit of doing in Spain; and, as for the glory, it was as precious as ever but a little obscured by time and a trifle moldy.

So Diego, when he was a young man of twenty, decided that he would leave the little town and go where many of his ancestors had made both fame and fortune many generations before — to Mexico. To Mexico he went, as soon as he landed fell into the bad graces of a politician in Vera Cruz, and presently found himself snatched away in the night and sent exactly where Oliver himself had been dispatched — to the living torture of the mines.

There was a grim justice in it, perhaps. Because those earlier Venustianos had wrung their money from the land by means of the slave labor of the poor Indians, and now their descendant was put to the same labor that had killed off millions and millions in another day.

However, Diego Venustiano was not the stuff which died easily. He survived. He grew hardened to the labor just as Oliver had done. But instead of being in the mines for six or seven months, he was in that inferno for as many years. He grew inured to the pain and the effort. And then he began to learn. Literally, he was studying mining from the ground up. The time came when he knew as much or more about silver mining than any man in Mexico.

At the end of this time his opportunity came. Rumor said that a fire in the mine — a fire which wiped out a score of poor miners like so many smothered rats — was started by Diego. While all was in a turmoil, he chose the proper moment and slipped away. Pursuit could not catch up with him.

And from that moment he began to wander through the land with a mule, on the trail of silver. His trail carried him over more thousands of miles of country than would carry a man half way around the world — a trail, also, which led deep through the legends of Indians and peons. Wherever a clue offered itself Venustiano was willing to take the thread of rumor, hearsay, or the least plausible evidence, and follow it as far as keen wits, leathery endurance, and a heart of steel would carry him.

For half a dozen years he toiled and moiled. And then he made his strike. It was not much, but it was a possible introduction to something. He struggled away at it by dint of the labor of his single pair of hands and opened a drift into a mountainside, only to find the vein pinching out the farther he went. For two years, single-handed, he struggled with his problem. And in the meantime, the silver which he took out, he laid by as a prize. At the end of two years, the vein disappeared.

But Venustiano did not give up. He felt that that vein *must* reappear. For three more years he labored in the depths of the earth, probing here and there, until at last a shaft which he had sunk recovered the lead. Recovered it, too, in such a fashion that a single year of the working of it made Venustiano a rich man.

Those riches were lost to him by the keenness

of the robbers who swept down and carried away his treasure train as the mules carried the loads of silver down the mountain trails. The second year of the working of the mine the same thing happened.

Then Venustiano took new measures. He gathered an active little army of forty or fifty men, and for an entire year he went on the trails of the bandits who haunted the vicinity. That year he made rich bags. For the robbers were only accustomed to being hunted by the stiff and stodgy military. Now, however, it was a case of hawk hunt hawk; and Venustiano hounded them through the mountains, wore them down, surprised their camps by dreadful forced marches through the midst of a bitter winter.

He gave no quarter. All the suspected he killed without mercy. How many of the innocent went down before his wrath, no man could guess. The government sent out to investigate; but the investigator took away more silver than information, and Venustiano was allowed to finish his campaign. By the time that it had ended, quiet had been brought back to the mountains. That section of them was wiped clear of trouble.

For eighteen or nineteen years, then, Diego Venustiano had been working to learn how to mine silver, to locate a claim, to open its rich veins deep within the rocks, and then to make his transportation road safe for his deliveries of the bullion to the lowlands. After that, for six years he reaped each harvest undisturbed. And every harvest exceeded the others that had gone before as Diego spread the drifts of the mine here and there, sinking rises or shafts until the heart of the mountain was honey-combed. But no man could say that he was not the wisest miner in Mexico.

How much money he had made, none could tell. It was said that the silver he took from the ground had been invested here and there, in agricultural lands in the rich plateaus where there was both rich sand and plenty of water; and again it was believed that he had sent thousands across the seas, to buy up extensive lands in old Spain, to which he intended to retire when the time came. But the time had surely not yet come.

He was not more than forty-five years old. He had built up a magnificent machine which tore the metal for him out of the ground, and he remained with a stern might to see that the machine operated to its fullest capacities. Each year he in person escorted the silver train down from the mines along this trail.

When Oliver had listened to this tale he could not help exclaiming, "But how many men, Venales, will come down with that train?"

"Why, perhaps a hundred."

"A hundred?" exclaimed Oliver. "A whole hundred, with such a leader as this Venustiano? The man seems to be a very devil."

"There will be fifty or sixty mules loaded; and there will be probably a man to every mule," explained Venales. "They carry some sort of arms

— a pistol to this man, a gun to that, an old musket to the other. But those fifty or sixty men may not count. I think that they will run for cover the instant that a hot attack begins."

"But if they do not?"

"Why, if they do not — if they stand their ground and fight like men, there's no doubt, Oliver, what will happen. They will eat me up and my party like nothing whatever. There is no doubt about that."

"So!" said Oliver. "You have undertaken this march against that chance?"

"Exactly," said Venales with perfectly good cheer. "But besides the muleteers there will be perhaps thirty, perhaps fifty men as well armed, as straight shooting, as brave, and as well led as my own crew."

"However, you expect to beat them?"

"I think that the chances are about even. The surprise should turn the trick for us. For seven years, now, there has not been a whisper of trouble in these mountains. The robbers have avoided them like a plague-ridden marsh. And even a wise man like Venustiano will begin to think that the world is afraid of touching him. As for myself and my men, you know that we have secretly ridden five hundred miles. No one can suspect that we are here. And so, friend Oliver, we sit down and take our chances at two hundred thousand pesos in good money. Is it worth while?"

CHAPTER XI

The Fight with Don Diego

That was a question which Oliver could not help turning over in his head for a moment, before he made his reply. "There is one thing sure," he said at last. "If they beat you, you cannot run away uphill or downhill. It will simply have to be along the trail, either ahead or behind, and they shooting at you all the time that you are running."

"True," said the bandit. "In case we are beaten we are, as you say, completely wiped out."

"Tell me," said Oliver, "do all the men in your party know this and are they still hot for the fight?"

The other smiled. "What is your own opinion?"

"For my part," said Oliver, "if it came to such a thing as this I should think that Carpio Vega and Antonio Morales might very well be up to risking their lives for a good fortune. And perhaps that little devil, Capiño. But as for the rest — I should think that it was entirely above them."

"You are right," nodded Venales. "But they are the sheep, *amigo*. And we four are the goats who lead them. We tell them that it will be an easy matter, that the muleteers will take to their heels at once. So we get them up to the place where they begin the fight. And, having once begun it, they will either battle it out or else they will die. And men with their backs against the wall are sure to fight. You have seen my fellows in action. You know that they have teeth. And, if we fail, our failure will cost Don Diego more blood than even he has ever seen before in one day, the cruel devil!"

"Is he a devil?"

"I tell you this," said the other. "There is no man in the mountains who will not swear that Diego Venustiano is the wickedest and coldest hearted in the world!"

He spoke with a good deal of honest emotion, and Oliver could not help believing him. But they had no chance for further talk because, in the midst of this, word was brought in suddenly that the leading men of Venustiano's party had been sighted up the trail; and there was an instant scurrying to cover. Long before this, every man had had a place appointed to him; and now they scrambled to their covert behind rocks and shrubs, a wild-eyed lot, who yet melted instantly into a silence and a stillness as complete as the ground on which they lay. Or, if there were any murmur of noise from one of them, the sullen booming of the waters in the gorge covered it.

Oliver saw them disappear, and then he in turn took up his chosen site. It was higher up the slope behind a nest of broadleaved cactus, a place to which he had to work by a bit of painful climbing. He would not be able to see what went on without standing up and exposing himself in his place of retreat, but once the shooting began, he felt that he could take it for granted that all eyes would be busy on the trail — too busy to pay much heed to the figures up the slope.

But, after he was in his place, a long wait followed. For a half hour the sun burned steadily, mercilessly down upon him. And what a sun! When one moved about, it was endurable with a stir of air; but sitting motionless it seemed that the brightness and the heat were gathered by a burning mass. The band of Oliver's hat became a gripping band of hot iron, and the shoulders of his coat seemed to smoke as at the touch of fire.

But at the end of the half hour, all thought of physical discomfort left him; for three riders came into view along the upper trail, three men on the finest of horses, three fellows with keen eyes and heads that turned constantly from side to side, so that it was plain that they were the chosen advance guard of the main body of the escort. Oliver, peeking out toward them, in as much guilty excitement as though he, too, were about to become one of the robbing party, felt his heart sink so far as any hope for the success of Venales was concerned. For if Venustiano was able to collect such fellows as these around him, it was fairly sure he would crush the bandits at the first attack.

After these men in advance, there was a considerable interval; and the sound of the hoofs of their horses had almost died out around the bend when another group approached — a dozen men mounted on mustangs, all armed to the teeth much after the fashion of the bandits.

And, indeed, it seemed to Oliver that the bandits were a group of respectable citizens, compared with these picked watchdogs of Diego Venustiano. He had seen rough fellows and wicked crews before; but the Indians of White Hawk, and that copper-faced scoundrel himself, were as nothing compared with these villains. Behind them came the string of the mules down the trail, with little packs settled on their backs — little but ponderous enough to make the poor beasts grunt.

Silver bullion was in those packs, and the heart of Oliver leaped at the though of it! Raw silver, fresh from the mine! He set his teeth again. To the mind of any thinking man, knowing what Oliver did of mining methods in Mexico, there was a broad stain of red upon that bright metal.

But it seemed that the nodding river of mules would never end — a peon for every two of the animals — a down-headed, sleepy fellow, carrying, as Venales had predicted, almost anything in the way of a weapon.

Oliver counted the packs roughly. There were more than four score of them, and his brain reeled a little when he thought what this meant. Truly, Don Diego had learned how to tear treasure from the rocky ribs of the earth!

Then, at the rear of the procession, came a compact body of twenty-two or more riders; and Don Diego was among them. Oliver felt that he could have picked him out at a distance of half a mile by something lofty and stern in the carriage of his head and in the set of his broad shoulders. He took off his hat to wipe his brow. There was not a touch of gray in his black hair. There was not a touch of gray in his narrow, pointed beard. And these fellows who rode around him were so many human tigers, trained to fierceness.

Alas, Venales! What would become of him and his men? Surely, he would see that the thing was impossible — now that the difficulties were directly beneath his eyes.

The rear guard itself was halfway along the face of the mountain, and Oliver was telling himself with every step that the horse of Venustiano made that the attempt was now given up, when he saw Venales stand up from behind a shrub near the road and call out in a clear, gay voice:

"Now, *amigos!* They are ours! Go at them, my lions!"

Such a voice, like light through the darkest night — like pleasant spring after the hard winter of their suspense and their waiting — made Oliver understand instantly why Venales was a famous leader.

Don Diego did not need to have the danger explained to him. He shouted, "Steady, my children! Steady!" And snatching out a pistol with a long barrel, almost like a carbine, he fired it point-blank at Venales.

That bullet might have ended the fray before it had begun, had Don Diego been as great with pistols as he was in mining. But as it was, he missed Venales, as the leader slipped down toward the trail, still shouting.

For a dreadful moment it seemed to Oliver that the hearts of all of Venales' men had failed them, and that they were afraid to follow their leader. Pistols and guns flashed along the line of the rear guard. And Venales dropped into covert behind a rock as a crashing discharge rattled about him, splashing lead across the stone that sheltered him. They counted the marks after the fight was over, and then it was found that no fewer than eleven pistol and rifle shots had clipped the face of the stone behind which Venales crouched. And the instant that that discharge was over, drawing steady aim, at point-blank range, the men of Venales poured their answering volley.

The shock reminded Oliver of what he had heard of the effect of first broadsides at sea, when the weight of lead seemed to make the enemy heel over in the water. So, now, the rear guard of the treasure train staggered and fell into confusion; and, maddened with two or three bad wounds, one of the mustangs leaped over the edge of the precipice and fell into the void with a scream of agony and fear.

How many saddles were emptied by that first

discharge, Oliver could not tell. He was far too excited. He stood up, though wildly delivered bullets now and again whizzed uncomfortably near to him. For now the bandits, with a yell of exultation as they saw the effect of their first fire, left their places of ambush and stormed down at the riders of Venustiano.

The latter blanched from the shock. And, as they wavered back and forth, it seemed to Oliver that they would certainly have fled at once had it not been for the voice of Venustiano, ringing sharp and high above the fight, calling them his children, bidding them be of good cheer and remember that they were fighting under his eye. And when had he failed to reward the smallest deed of valor on his behalf?

Oliver admired the rich man with all his heart — as much, in fact, as he detested all that he had heard of him. This was a slave master, to be sure, but what a leader! And Oliver saw two of the opposing party, and watched Venustiano beat them down and back with a consummate ease. And as Don Diego fought, still more than half of his attention seemed to be given to the rest of the battle. He appeared to be far more concerned with what was happening to his men than to himself.

But it seemed a lost cause which Venustiano represented. His men were dropping all about him. The heart was gone from them so far as that fight was concerned, when an unexpected succor poured back into them.

CHAPTER XII
The Rally

Looking across that little battlefield, it seemed to Oliver that the cause had been won for Venales — and a fair enough cause, at that. Because the cruelty of a pirate seemed to him preferable to the cruelty of a slave driver.

The advance scouts of Señor Venustiano were far ahead, almost too far away to come to the help of their master in any but a long fight. And even the advance guard of a dozen villainous warriors was back at a distance of the entire length of the column of pack mules.

And now, as they strove desperately to get back to the scene of the fighting, they were blocked and worried in their progress by the mules themselves, which were bunched in confused knots, filling the trail here and there so that the men had to climb over them or work a bit up the difficult slope to get past.

Between that advance guard and the rear were the muleteers. There were some two score of these fellows; and, at the first glance, they had seemed to Oliver like negligible fighting stuff — mere lumpish creatures hardly above the dignity of the mules which they conducted. But it

they somewhat belied their
...ive mustangs do. There was
...uality in this herd.

...t, they stood wavering, undetermi...
...do, and it always seemed to Oliver th...
...les had thought of detailing merely fou...
...e men to charge this motley, ragged line,
...y would have scattered at once. However, they
were given time to herd together. And then some
fighting instinct wakened in them. Suddenly the
nearest group surged backward, shouting: "Venustiano!" which was the battle cry of the guard,
just as "Venales!" was the rallying signal of the
bandits.

These peons came with old muskets, with pistols, with knives, with clubs; but they came in
earnest, blind with fighting madness; and their
spirit was what counted. And behind the leading
group, the rest of the peons gathered rapidly,
until all were pouring back, screeching: "Venustiano!" at the top of their lungs, until the crackling of the guns was fairly drowned.

Their impact had an instant effect. The raging
men of Venales, in the very act of sweeping the
last of Don Diego's escort aside, were struck on
the flank and hurled back. Don Diego himself
urged his nearest followers back to the fight. And
taken in flank and in front, the men of Venales
gave ground, and wavered.

Oliver saw Venales himself standing with a
crimson stream trickling down one side of his
face, swinging a broken rifle like a club, with the

all form of Carpio Vega be
…io Morales like a raging pan…
…hile little Capiño held back for
…seemed wondering whether the tim…
…me to fly.

For a moment these four kept up the…
…out, once they were down, all was over.
fought against them, too, for the advance gu…
was working back rapidly toward the scene of the
encounter. And when they arrived, nothing but
a miracle could save the bandits.

All of this Oliver saw, and he knew the meaning of it with an eye and a brain as calm as his
heart was excited. But then a strange thing happened in him.

The cause of law and order was forgotten. He
remembered, merely, that yonder were his
friends, men with whom he had eaten and drunk
beside the campfire; and now their backs were
against the wall, while he stood by and merely
watched.

From either hip he whipped out a revolver.
From his lips came a cry that tore his throat,
"Venales! Venales!" And he rushed down the
hillside.

That shout from the great throat of Oliver
overwhelmed the deep booming of the river beneath, the explosions of the guns, the roar of the
fighters. It came flooding down from the hillside
like the thunder of a lion; and the peons, who
were nearest, looked up and saw a picture which
they were never to forget.

They saw a giant whom the advantage of the ground made more enormous still, and who was set off in flashing finery. For all the early training of Oliver had not been forgotten; and if he had no polite clothes to show among polite people, he had taken instead from the loot of the bandits which was freely offered to him a Mexican jacket which luckily fitted his bulky shoulders and clasped his torso with flaring gold lace and bright buttons. About his hips was tied a brilliant, flowing scarf of scarlet silk; and down the seams of his trousers ran rows of burnished silver buttons, so that he dazzled the eye as he came sweeping down with the hat gone from his head, his hair, which had grown almost down to his shoulders, blowing wildly behind his head, a revolver spitting fire and death from either hand, and the continual thunder of "Venales! Venales!" on his lips.

Who could blame the peons — centered as they were on the battle in front — if when they saw this charging monster they did not perceive, also, that he came alone, a single man whom a single bullet could stop, no matter what his size? As a matter of fact, he seemed to them, surely, the leader of a strong reserve of bandits who would sweep them over the precipice at the first impact.

The dozen who were nearest did not give themselves a chance to recover from the first thought, the first shock. They turned; they dropped their weapons; and they fled stumbling, and screaming, *"Todo es perdo!"* That cry ended the battle.

"All is lost! All is lost!" yelled the rest of the peon rout; and, turning after their companions, blind with fear, wild with excitement, they fled. Some ran up the trail and some down, scrambling past the mules with the hysterical strength of fear to buoy them.

Those who rushed up the trail had an easy enough flight. Those who went down it met the returning advance guard; and, though there were enough of these to turn the current of the fight again, they were instantly involved in the flight. All flocked together along the trail, and a dozen times it seemed to Oliver that those on the outer edge of the precipice would be thrust off to destruction.

He himself, after his single charge, remained where he was and saw the bandits scatter up and down the way, pursuing the fugitives; but the most important fugitive of all needed no pursuing. For, as Venustiano strove furiously to rally the flight, two men as strong as lions burst upon him, one big and strong, one swift as a cat. Now he struggled no longer, but lay in the hands of Antonio Morales and big Carpio Vega.

As for Venales, he was going briskly up and down directing the management of affairs. With a stained handkerchief he wiped his wounded face; and his cheerful voice had already brought assurance and good cheer to a dozen of the peons, who vowed that they would remain with this peerless leader and help him to conduct the train of mules to their destination, whatever that might be.

So, without pausing to glorify himself or his men, he went up and down the trail, putting all things in order, and arranging for the disposal of the mules in their line. Some packs had to be shifted, also; for three of the mules had been struck down by random bullets and their cargoes had been added to the other packs.

And by the time that the others had returned from the pursuit, and the wounds of the injured had been tied up and cleansed with the water in the canteens, Venales had the entire procession in readiness for instant marching. Then he returned and joined the happy throng of his followers.

They were sadly thinned in numbers by that brief and murderous battle. Seven men were dead. Three more were so badly wounded that they would be unable to help themselves. And there remained a scant dozen in the fighting force. Unless Oliver Tay were added.

And Oliver, seated on a rock, watching the turmoil which had followed the fight, wondered why it was that his heart leaped, and his very soul was warm with gladness, when the thing that he had done had been to help a gang of cutthroats to the enjoyment of a royal prize. However, the happiness was there in his heart. Border bandit though he had become, it would not go down. And pride was there, also. And it seemed to Oliver Tay that for the first time in his life he had lived utterly and completely, and used to the full the powers that were in him. To be a giant for one instant — why, what does it matter if afterward one must be a dwarf and a slave to life?

But if he was a little elevated in his own thoughts, it was nothing compared to the adulation which was around him. They had looked up to him before as to a just man, a brave man, and one with an open heart — most certainly proved by the manner in which he had carried Venales with him to liberty. But now it was a different matter. He was a demigod. Yes, he was surely more than mortal.

These were men who believed in miracles. And here was the first that any of them had actually seen performed. So they felt that in Oliver Tay there had been visible the actual presence of the power of heaven. They did not flock about him, grasping his hand, thanking him, clapping him upon the shoulder. The thing that he had done was too great for vulgar congratulation. Even Venales, to whom nothing on earth was sacred, paused for a moment as he approached Oliver and looked up into his face with something like fear.

CHAPTER XIII

The Division of the Spoils

They weighed two or three representative packs from the train and thereby estimated the weight of the entire treasure. Then, in a semicircle, like so many starved wolves, they waited to divide these spoils.

The speech of Venales was curt and brisk. To himself he reserved three shares. To Morales and Carpio Vega who had taken the great Venustiano, he suggested two shares apiece. And then he made a little pause as a grim-faced bandit yelled, "And Don Olivero? We would be dividing death and not silver among us, if it were not for him!"

"There are seven from among us gone to the devil on this glorious day," said Venales; "and therefore we can afford to be generous. Besides, as you say, if Don Olivero had not charged them singlehanded like a troop of cavalry, there would be no silver for us. Therefore I say: Five shares to him. Is that too much?"

They answered with a cheer that it was not. They would gladly have given more. For to each of them went a fortune. Had they not all ridden forth more than once and risked their lives for the sake of a total booty not a third as great as that which was now to go to each individual among them?

"Now, then," said Venales, "we have only to find a tree tall enough to be worthy of the hanging of the fiend, Venustiano. Then we march on!"

Oliver Tay looked across at the prisoner. And to his bewilderment he saw that the stern man was on his knees, his hands clasped together, his eyes fixed upon his hat, which was set on a rock before him. And there he prayed. Not with a white face of terror, but rather as one at his devotions in a church.

Oliver, stepping nearer, looked curiously at the hat and saw that in front of it there was supported the little golden image of St. Christopher, the patron saint of travelers. Well might Don Diego pray now to the saint who had guided him on far voyages and dusty trips after fortune — now that he was about to take the last and greatest journey of all. And yet there was something childish and touching in this devotion that melted the heart of Oliver.

The tree had been selected. It thrust out from the edge of the cliff; and, from an outer limb, they proposed to leave Venustiano dangling over the abyss.

"Stand up," said the dark Morales. "Your time has come, you dog!" And he dragged the prisoner to his feet.

A savage, scar-faced fellow shook his fist in the face of Don Diego. "Do you think that praying now will keep you from torment?"

"I have no hope," said the doomed man calmly, "except in blessed St. Christopher and the mercy which he may win for me."

"Cover his eyes," said Venales mercifully.

"I thank you," said Venustiano; "but I prefer to look death in the face. It is my way, if you please!"

They brought him swiftly to the edge of the cliff; and Oliver, remembering his own days in the mines, and seeing the set, cruel face of this slave driver, could not doubt that the man deserved death. And yet something was melting in him. He thrust himself suddenly among them. "My friend!" he called.

"Hush! Stop! Be quiet there! Stand fast! Don Olivero has something to say to us!"

They stood instantly still, with eyes of affectionate awe fixed upon him; and Oliver Tay could not help half loving them, for the very sake of the power which he had over them. "Now," said Oliver, "you have offered me many thousand pesos in hard cash —"

"It is not enough!" shouted someone. "You shall have half of the entire treasure, Don Olivero! All is owing to you!"

He raised his hand; and there was a drawn breath, and then silence again. His eye wandered for an instant from them and down through the dizzy void of the cañon to the mumbling waters far beneath. To die was like that — entering an unplumbed abyss. Then he looked back at Don

Diego. The face of the man was as hard and unrelenting as the granite cliffs themselves.

"I am about to offer back the money. I will not have the treasure, not if you were to offer me all of it," said Oliver. "I have another request. Will you grant it to me, all of you?"

They heard him, breathless. Each man saw great treasure added to his own share by this act of renunciation. It seemed madness on the part of the big man, but they yelled instantly that whatever else he asked for should be his.

Only one voice was raised in protest, and that was from Carpio Vega, who called, "I have guessed at the thing which he will ask. Do not grant it, friends. It will be the ruin of him and of all of us!"

They turned on Carpio Vega with a universal snarl, and a volley of shouts tore at him, "Not grant it to him? Even if he asks for our lives, are they not his? Has he not saved them? Was I not down with a knife at my throat when his shout came thundering down the slope and saved me? The weight of his voice was enough. The very sight of him made them run. I tell you he killed a man with every bullet from his guns. I saw it with my own eyes. And now shall we refuse him whatever he asks of us?"

In the midst of a storm of such protest as this, what could Carpio Vega do? As a matter of fact, he lighted a cigarette, shrugged his wide, capable shoulders, and half turned his back upon them and their proceedings.

"Very well, then," said Oliver. "If you will give me what I want, take back the silver. Let me have Don Diego for my own share!"

They were breathless.

Then Venales said: "I understand. Don Olivero was through hell in the mines, *amigos*. He was through it with me. And now he wishes to pay back some of the pain to Venustiano. Can you blame him?"

Could they blame him? No, there was enough Indian in their blood to make them sympathize entirely with this suggestion. They raised a brief, fierce shout, "Give him Venustiano! Let him tear the devil to pieces, bit by bit!"

So they gave Don Diego into his hands.

What Oliver did was to take the horse of Don Diego by the bridle. He led the prisoner to it and waved him into the saddle; and, for an instant, Venustiano sat there, staring down at Oliver with a face convulsed with many emotions. It had been easy enough for him to die; but it was far from easy for him to accept life again in a single word and a gesture.

"Señor, señor," said he in a shaken voice, "I have owed a great loss to you alone, today. The battle was already over when you came. Am I to owe you a greater gift, also? It is the will of St. Christopher. His name is sacred!"

There had been an instant wave of shouting from the crowd, when they heard and saw what Oliver intended to do. Little Capiño clasped his hand.

99

"Do you hear me, Don Olivero? You have wits, and you have enough strength for a herd of oxen. But this man is not a man. He is sold to the devil. There is no good in him, no kindness, no gratitude. Do you think that he would be grateful? No, I swear by my true soul that he would only laugh at you when he was once safe. And when he is free, he will hunt us down as he has hunted others. Will you believe that?"

Antonio Morales, Venales, and others flocked close, arguing, begging.

But Oliver waved them back. "You have made a gift to me," he said sternly. "Are you taking it back again?"

They gave ground to him, at that; and he led the horse of Don Diego up the trail, until he and his prisoner turned the first elbow curve. Then he said briefly, "You have heard what they say of you. Now, Don Diego, I have been in a mine. As they said, it was torment. And if you have run such a one as I worked in, you deserve to be burned to death, an inch of you at a time. However, I could not stand by and see a brave man die. I have given you your life, and I shall not bargain with you about it. Only I have to make one request of you."

There was a glint of light in the eyes of the other. "I understand at last," he said, sighing, and nodding, and then with a stern smile, "You could have had silver, but not safe money. That silver has not yet been taken to a bank, is not that true? And one cannot eat raw silver. And so,

Don Olivero, you set me free now on condition that I pay you a little later, a good ransom of money — coined money?" His eyes were like the eyes of a hawk, as he stared at Oliver.

But the latter smiled. "I shall swear this oath to you," said he, "that if money could have bought me, one peso from those robbers, yonder, would mean more to me than a million from you. But what I have come to ask of you is that in return for your life, you forget what has happened today — and the men who have done it!"

A blankness of astonishment fell like a curtain across the face of Don Diego. And then a shadow of gloom followed. It was not hard to make out that he had promised himself already all the sweets of a most exacting revenge upon those renegades of the mountains — Morales and Carpio Vega first of all.

CHAPTER XIV

The Other Side of the Rio

He let his eyes wander a little anxiously down the trail. He glanced at his horse. It was a choice one, of course. For should Diego Venustiano trust himself to the back of anything but a blooded beast? They were alone, he and this one man. "It is a hard condition," he said coldly.

"Harder than dying?" asked Oliver.

"That is already a thing of the past," said Don Diego. "I have almost forgotten it!"

"Good!" said Oliver. "I see that they have described you to a hair. When you reach your home, you will not sleep day or night till you have gathered a little army; and then you will come flying through the mountains on the trail of Venales. Is not that true?"

"Hunting is the sport of kings," said Venustiano. "And why not, Don Olivero?"

"You are very cool," said Oliver. "However, there is one thing that would make me trust you; take off your hat and swear by the image of St. Christopher in the brim of it never to remember this day, never to send out hunters on the trail of Venales and the rest of us, never to give information or word of what has happened except

102

what your men give for you! Why, Don Diego, you are vastly rich. What is the loss of one year to you? You will only take a hundred poor devils and grind them to death in your mines to tear out the silver faster, and so you will make it up. Will you be reasonable?"

"There is a pistol in this holster, still loaded," said Don Diego, clutching the butt of it.

"Good!" said Oliver. "Draw it, man; and make an end of this argument! We will fight fairly and squarely. I stand here and wait for you to make the first motion!" And he smiled at the thought, keeping his own hands free from his holstered guns.

Don Diego, looking down at that wind-blown golden hair, and the terrible, joyous smile of the giant, knew that there were simply two ways of dying. One way was with a rope around his neck. And another was to take a bullet through the heart from the gun of a man who never missed his target. There was no cowardice in the soul of Venustiano, but he was preeminently a man of reason. And he saw now that it would be folly to uphold a lost cause against such an enemy.

He said quietly, "Will you tell me why you do this? I have offered you a free fortune!"

"Today," answered Oliver freely, "I go back to my own people. And I wish to go with clean hands. Do you understand?"

The eyes of the Spaniard opened a little. "Señor," he said gravely, "I understand you at last and ask your pardon. I am ready to take that oath of which you spoke."

"No," added Oliver. "Now that we understand one another, I think that your bare word will be enough."

The hand of Venustiano was extended, and Oliver took it instantly.

"To whom do I give my promise?"

"To Oliver Tay."

"Señor," said Don Diego, "I think that today you have given back to me something more than life. You have given me my word of honor."

"*Adios,*" said Oliver and turned his back on Don Diego, and Don Diego's gun, and walked freely, without fear, back to rejoin the company.

"There need be no fear of Venustiano," he told Venales and the rest. "He will not hound you because of what has happened today."

And something in his manner of saying it, made them believe him.

That night, when the camp slept, Oliver started. He had taken from the common treasury — they would have given it all to him, if he would have accepted — five hundred dollars in gold coin and a handful of silver. He took from the stock a strong bay, able to carry his weight through the mountains to the north. His pack was small, but he had a rifle of the finest make in the holster beneath his right leg; and, after the schooling which Antonio Morales had given him, he would never lack for meat on his journey. Two fine new revolvers completed his equipment when he said farewell to Venales, Morales, Vega, and little Capiño. The others were as grave as stone; but tears were in the eyes of Capiño, and he could not speak.

"Brother," said Roderigo Venales, "tell me this thing: Have we offended you?"

"You have loaded me with nothing but kindness," said Oliver gently. "But I have another life waiting for me north of the Rio Grande, and I find that I have come to like this mountain freedom so well that it is hard and harder for me to go. Who could tell, Roderigo? In another week or so I might come to you and beg for a place with the next raiders! And after that — no, I have become a border bandit once for the sake of my companions at arms, but —"

They did not argue, but let him go; and he left behind him a message of farewell for all the rest.

"Because," said Oliver Tay, "if I say good-by to them all, they will start persuading; and only a little persuading would make me stay, perhaps!"

So he rode off under the stars, and three of the four remained starkly standing and looking after him; but little Capiño sat down and buried his ugly face in his hands.

"Morales and Vega," said Venales suddenly, "we have lost the biggest part of our strength with that gringo!"

They did not answer. Their silence was their strongest assent.

And one of the wounded, waking a little from his sleep, cried out, and then slept again.

"When he goes back to that life which is waiting for him north of the Rio Grande," said Venales, "who can tell what he'll find? Perhaps everything will not be as sweet for him as he thinks. He may be ready to regret us and the things which he has left behind him, just as we are already regretting him. Because we have lost our judge, *amigos!* In all the weeks he has been with us, has there been a single argument settled with guns or knives? No, the word of Don Olivero was beyond reproach; and we trusted him enough to give all our disputes freely into his hands. But after this, there will be another story. There are fifteen of us, now. Trust me when I say that there will be fewer than that before this silver is turned into coin! Vega, you loved him more than the rest. What do you say?"

"He was a brother to me," said Carpio Vega, "and I say: Let my brother leave the robbers and the cutthroats behind him."

"That is one manner of speaking," nodded Venales. "You, Morales, know him nearly as well as Vega, though neither of you worked in a mine with him and saw him in the middle of Hades. What do you say?"

There was a saying among the brigands that the devil was no wiser or more secret than a snake, and that Morales was a veritable serpent for wisdom and silence. He looked down at the ground for a moment, and then he raised his dark eyes to them. "I say that Carpio Vega and I should follow him, trailing him to his own country. Then, if everything is not well with that life which he left behind him, north of the Rio Grande, and if he yearns to come back to us, Carpio and I will be there. When he sees us, he may know that he needs us as much as we need him."

"You speak the very thing that I have had in my mind," said Vega. "And your shares?"

"Give us all the coin that you have left. We trust the rest of our money to you," said Morales. "Vega, will you ride with me?"

"Why not?" said Carpio Vega, gloomily bowing his handsome head. "Morales, you are a tempter inspired by —"

"Hush!" said Venales. "Take your choice of the horses. Mount and ride. When we have disposed of the loot, I shall send away all except Capiño and a few of the best. We have done enough, and it will be time for us to disappear. I shall drift slowly north with those whom I keep with me. Before long, we shall be in Juarez. Look for us there when you need us. And good fortune go with you, my friends!"

Even Carpio Vega, wise as he was, could never have trailed Oliver Tay north without either losing the way, or coming so close as to be seen; but Morales traveled with a flawless instinct. And Oliver was never aware of the two shadows which followed him.

He came out of the mountains. He descended to the valley of the Rio. He crossed the river and turned onto the old trail toward Siddon Flat, traveling in haste, now. For his horse was lean; and he himself was dried and starved by the long march, the many fasts for food, and the torments for the lack of water. But it was not that he rode to regain mere ease of life and comfort. He was hurrying in a sort of terror, lest his new life just to the south might roll up behind him and over-whelm him like a bright cloud, filled with danger but filled with splendor, also. He rode in the haste of one striving to recover his old self.

So he wound through the mountains again, and at last saw beneath him the jumble of adobe hovels and frame shacks which made up the Flat. Down to it he sped, rousing his tired horse to a swift gallop, driving it along with merciless spurs. And so he swept down the main street to the spot where he had lost all touch with his old self, and drew rein.

A cloud of his own dust blew around him; and, staring through the mist, he saw in great rough red letters, painted across the front of the store which had once been "Crossman Tay," the legend:

HENRY LUGER & COMPANY.

CHAPTER XV
The Fortune of War

It seemed more than odd to Oliver — that new sign; and it gave him his first forebodings of trouble. But it was only the first of a series of little shocks which were to come to him during the next few seconds of his life. For, as he dismounted and stepped through the doorway of the store, the first person that he encountered was pretty Marian Barge, looking a bit browner and a bit rosier and altogether more lovely than he had thought a girl could possibly be.

She looked at him once and started. She looked at him again and then cried, "It's Oliver Tay!"

"It's I," said Oliver, smiling down at her with his broad-brimmed Mexican sombrero in his hand. "Is there something wrong with me outside of my queer getup?"

But she only looked at him in a frightened way, and then past him at a little group in the distance — a woman and a man talking with tall, lean Henry Luger.

And Oliver, looking in that direction, suddenly shouted, "Mother!" and lurched forward.

To his bewilderment, Mrs. Tay put her dainty hand before her eyes and fell back into the arms of the tall gentleman with her. She fell back with a scream of terror. "It's Oliver's ghost!" cried she. "Help me, Peter!"

That was Cousin Peter Sydham, who had always come to dinner once a week — Peter Sydham, long an authority on horses and etiquette and clothes, and therefore almost a god in the eyes of little Mrs. Tay. He was the example according to which Oliver had been framed from infancy. And now Peter Sydham supported Mrs. Tay with one arm and with the other fended off the rushing "ghost."

As well try to fend off the charge of a long-horned steer. Oliver, now two hundred and twenty pounds of sinew and iron, brushed through that defending arm and caught up his mother. One part of the mystery he saw through at once. "You have not had a letter from me?" he cried. "The letter didn't get through to you, Mother?"

"Letter? Oh, no! Oh, heavens!" cried Mrs. Tay. She uncovered her eyes for an instant; but what she saw seemed to overcome her again, and she sank limply against the breast of Oliver.

"This way!" called Henry Luger, as cool as ever.

And they were in a little private office, where Oliver could put his mother in a chair and kneel in front of her, holding her hands.

"Are you better now?" he asked her tenderly. "What a scoundrel I was not to hurry back sooner than I did!"

"Oh, Oliver!" moaned his mother, and then her eyes went miserably past him. "Oh, dear Peter — what shall we do, Peter? What will Oliver think?"

"Think? Of what?" asked Oliver. "I don't want to think. Only to be happy and — Gad, Cousin Peter, with all respect to you, what the deuce has Cousin Peter to do with me?"

"Oh, Oliver!" moaned the little woman. "You mustn't say it. Peter — Cousin Peter — I mean, I am his wife now, Oliver."

It brought Oliver to his feet smartly enough. He stood back against the wall and turned his eyes straight at Cousin Peter.

He had always thought of this man, in the old days, as a sort of a hero, an old Roman of a rather smart fashion, as sort of a latter-day Spartan, and a pattern for rising youth. But during the larger part of a year his eyes had been practiced on men of different patterns. He had known the sad nobility of Carpio Vega, and the panther grace of Antonio, and the craft and wisdom of Venales, and the light-fingered and dangerous deftness of Capiño. Last and not least of all, he had before the eyes of his mind one figure like a thing of rock — Diego Venustiano.

Contrasted with such a background as that which was still drifting through the mind of Oliver, Cousin Peter Sydham shrank from hero to plain man, rather soft in body and pink in the jowls. His careful clothes looked not a little absurd to Oliver, used as he was to the tatters or

111

the barbaric splendor of the costume of Mexico. And, besides, as Cousin Peter stood now, expanding his chest a little, and striving to be imposing, and to bear down Oliver with his glance, as he had always done so easily in the past, Oliver could not help smiling a little, in sadness and in contempt.

Before that smile, Cousin Peter's eyes shifted. His face flushed. And a dreadful little moment of silence filled the room.

Mrs. Tay-Sydham sat with her hands clasped, glancing from one of these big men to the other. And then she cried out with a touch of irritation, "You mustn't look at your father like that, Oliver!"

"Father?" said Oliver through his teeth. "Father? This?"

Of course, it was very wrong of him. He should never have expressed himself in this fashion. But he had been very long in a wild land of liberty, and now the striking muscles along his arms were twisting like snakes that coiled, and flexed, and uncoiled again.

Cousin Peter felt that something must be done to uphold his dignity. "Oliver!" his mother cried, when Cousin Peter said firmly, "You had better leave me alone with this young man, my dear. He needs taking in hand, it seems." And he made a step toward Oliver.

"Listen to me," said Oliver Tay. "I don't want to call you a sneaking rascal, Cousin Peter; but I'm confoundedly tempted to do so. Now, what does all this mean?"

Cousin Peter hastily retraced his steps.

"A nasty thought comes into my head," said Oliver. "There was no wooing from Cousin Peter before. Could it be that after a quarter of a million dollars came into our hands it made any difference to him?"

"Oliver! Oliver!" wept Mrs. Tay-Sydham.

But Oliver had no pity. She had used a very wrong word only a little time before. For now he was thinking of that dead father of his, and the thought made him as hard as steel.

"As for the money," said Cousin Peter, "and I should have known that it was the cause of this scene, every penny shall be accounted for. Every penny of your money —"

"My money?" snapped Oliver, growing a bit blacker. "Do you mean to say, Mother, that my inheritance from Uncle Crossman has been in the hands of Cousin Peter?"

"Oh, Oliver," said his mother, "after your death, when I was so bewildered — and no one to look after that great fortune —"

"After my death," said Oliver dryly, looking at his new stepfather. "Very well!"

"I tell you," said Cousin Peter, his face blotched with white and purple, "I tell you, Oliver, dear boy, that you mustn't misunderstand. Everything will be accounted for. If there were unlucky investments, goodness knows that they were no fault of mine!"

"Unlucky investments!" said Oliver grimly.

"One cannot help a few mistakes in money matters!" said Cousin Peter.

Mrs. Tay-Sydham suddenly looked at her returned boy and found, indeed, that there was not a vestige of boyhood left to him. He had utterly changed. The curve of softness was gone from his cheek. His soft neck was now a mass of stiff sinews. And the chin, the unfortunate chin, the vulgarly big chin, stood out in dreadful prominence. One could call him a markedly handsome fellow; but never, never again could he be called beautiful. Her heart ached for him. But it ached still more for Cousin Peter. For, to her astonishment, she saw that her husband was unmistakably and terribly afraid of this young lion. He shrank back. His glance wavered toward the windows and then toward the door. And so his wife ran to him, and took his arm, and helped him face her son.

"I followed him in everything, in every step that he made, and everything was for the best. If the wretched investments seemed to turn out badly after the store was sold to Mr. Luger —"

"Who empowered you to sell this store of mine, Sydham?"

That grim, impersonal name shocked the last vestige of color from the face of poor Peter. "I meant to say," he gasped, "that the unlucky results of the investments made in your behalf —"

"The investments made in my behalf were unlucky, eh? But those made in your own behalf were excellent?"

"The fortunes of war," began Sydham.

"Confound the fortunes of war!" said Oliver. "What's left to me?"

"Oliver!" wailed his mother; and yet she shrank more protectively close to Cousin Peter. For her huge son seemed to be growing bigger and bigger with the passage of each moment. And dreadful features cropped out in terrible relief — such as a gun at either hip well holstered in worn leather, and a workmanly looking handle of a big knife in the front of his gun belt.

"You will be taken care of," gasped Peter Sydham; "remember that — on my honor — always taken care of! All any young man could want I will promise to see that you have and —"

"I'm stripped, then," said Oliver slowly. "You've done a thorough job of it, for fear the ghost might turn up, eh? And you've married my mother to keep me from asking too many questions. Why, Cousin Peter, I knew that you were a clever fellow in lots of ways; but I never before guessed that you were such a good business man."

He stepped forward, and Cousin Peter winced back with something like a groan of fear. But Oliver went straight past them and out of the office, where he was aware of Marian Barge, a little frightened, and tall Henry Luger, with cold, curious eyes. So he knew that the voices which had been raised within the office had sounded farther than he guessed.

He saw, furthermore, another figure which interested him more than all the rest, and that was a form muffled in a painted buffalo robe. Oliver was after it in a trice. It whirled; a knife flashed; but knife and man went to the floor before the fist of Oliver.

He stood over the fallen man with a gun in his fingers. "Get up, White Hawk," he said. "We need a little friendly chat, you and I!"

CHAPTER XVI

Companions in Arms

There was a hurly-burly of running forms and many voices, in the midst of which White Hawk rose slowly to his feet with a trickle of crimson running down his face and his composure utterly unruffled. He seemed far more interested in the gun in the hands of Oliver than in the rest of what was happening, until a gruff fellow with a flashing steel badge on his vest said crisply to Oliver, "This looks like assault and battery, young feller. You'll have to do a bit of explaining!"

"Keep that copper-faced hound in sight," said Oliver, "while I explain how, nearly a year ago, I bumped into White Hawk one day in this same store; and, more because he was drunk than because I was careless, he was knocked down. On account of that, he kidnaped me and sold me south of the river to the silver mines. Now, Sheriff, how will it turn out?"

The sheriff considered gravely and spat. "Witnesses?" said he.

"Not a one," said Oliver.

"Then not a chance to get him," said the sheriff. "You let it drop, young man; and, if I was you, after what I'd done to White Hawk, I'd get out of this part of the country by the next stage. There is more Comanches than luck in this neck of the woods, and you believe me!"

No matter what right might be on the side of Oliver, he could not help seeing that logic was overwhelmingly in favor of what the sheriff had said.

And therefore it was that, as the light of the day mellowed and turned rosy in the evening, Oliver sat alone on a fallen rock fragment at the edge of the town and turned his affairs slowly over in his mind.

All was totally changed for him. There remained of his old future only the chance of living at the cost of a stepfather who, because he had wronged Oliver most shamefully, detested and feared him. And those whom we have most wronged are those whom we will most loathe. And if Oliver loved his mother still, that very love taught him that the kindest thing he could do would be to remain out of her life, for a time at least; so all that road to the future was blocked to him. And he remained in a land of danger — much danger since this second encounter with the Comanche chief. It had all happened so suddenly that it seemed to Oliver almost like a scene from a play, crowded as it was with ridiculous coincidence.

To convince himself that this last year had been real, however, he had the sight of the big sombrero which hung on his knee, and the weight of two revolvers at his belt.

A horse pattered down the road, slowed, went by at a walk, stopped. He looked up into the face of Marian Barge.

"Mr. Tay —"

He stood up.

"Do you know that White Hawk has ridden out of town in a towering rage?"

"I could guess at that, thank you."

"And do you also guess that he has two hundred braves waiting for him back yonder in the hills?"

"I could even suspect that."

"Then you don't know," said she, "that the next stage leaves in twenty minutes, or you wouldn't be sitting here!"

He stood at the head of her horse, rubbing its soft muzzle with the back of his knuckles. "I am trying to make up my mind," said Oliver, "about the happiest thing to do."

"The safest thing —" began the girl.

"The happiest thing," said Oliver. "May I walk with you a little way?"

She looked down at him gravely, but with a gleam of excitement in her eyes.

"Somehow," said she, "I knew perfectly that you wouldn't run away, even from White Hawk. And, if you are staying overnight, dad would be glad to have you, I know. If you wish —"

"Don't I — just!" said Oliver, most ungrammatically.

And he walked up the road beside her.

Mr. Barge had wise counsel to give. He had

fought too many Indians to hold them lightly. "But," said he, "when the other chap is an Indian, never turn your back. So maybe the best thing is for you to stay right on here and see the thing through."

"Thank you," said Oliver. "That's what I have in mind."

"Only," said Mr. Barge, "a good deal depends upon what you're gunna turn your hand to."

The bright head of the girl lifted, and Oliver felt her eyes glowing at him.

"What would you aim to be doing?"

"I don't know," said Oliver.

"Then, what have you got a liking for?"

"I don't know," said Oliver, "except that I want plenty of elbowroom, clear air, and exercise."

"That sounds like cattle," declared Mr. Barge. "Come out in the cool, and let's talk it over."

They sat on homemade rockingchairs on the little veranda; and, as they sat there, two shadowy forms of horsemen drifted through the starshine and paused just beyond the gate.

"Now what might they be?" asked Mr. Barge in a murmur.

"Not Comanches!" breathed Marian Barge. "Not Comanches, Oliver!"

She had caught at his arm in her fear — generous fear for him alone, he knew; and a great warmth went flooding through his body. Then, leaning forward, he eyed the outlines of those figures steadily. "I think," said Oliver slowly, as up, "that I know those men."

...nistled a soft-low note, and that note was
...ntly answered from the road, and the horses
...re twitched about, with their heads pointing
...oward the house. Oliver laughed a little, and
strode down from the veranda.

"You mustn't go!" cried Marian Barge, following hastily. "You mustn't go. It may be only a
trick."

"No, not a trick," said Oliver. "I thought that
I was riding away from my destiny, but it seems
that it was following me all the while. Just wait
for me a moment."

He went down the footworn path to the gate
and into the soft dust of the road, where the
mustangs stretched out their heads curiously to
snuff at him.

"I knew you, Morales," said he, "and you,
Carpio. Why have you come after me?"

Morales lighted a cigarette, and the flame of
the match showed the dark and sinister beauty
of his face. He said as he snapped the match
away, and the fragrance of the tobacco smoke
drifted through the air, "Don Olivero, we were
lonely in Mexico, and we thought that you might
be lonely here. So we came to ask."

"*Amigos!*" said Oliver, and gave them each a
hand.

If he had not strength enough to stand alone
in this country, here was power to help him, and
free hearts to pour it forth.

PART II

THE WARPATH

CHAPTER XVII
War Medicine

All through the night Yellow Wolf had traveled so long as the moon shone; but, when it passed behind thick clouds, he paused and made camp in a stubby group of willows. For one does not travel in the dark night, particularly when on the warpath, seeing that the weather in which one leaves this world is the weather which one will find far off on the shore of the happy hunting grounds. That other land is apt to be dull and misty enough, wherefore there is all the more reason that one should wish to take with one a good, bright, burning sun. One wishes to join the battle under the broad, white noonday; and then, if one's spirit departs, it journeys in a breath to the eternal hunting grounds and there enjoys fair weather unceasingly. Who, therefore, will care to risk death by night when no moon shows, and then, through eternity, stumble and grope through the dark fields of heaven with never enough light to see the shadowy buffalo that browse those phantom pastures?

Yellow Wolf, like a good Comanche, knew all of these things. He had sat at the knees of the elders of the tribe through the long winter evenings. And even on the warpath, as a boy, he had been willing to subdue himself and listen, and learn. Would you have proof that he had not listened in vain?

Behold him, then, as he starts for his journey in the pink of the morning. He strips off his clothes. He steps to the verge of the standing water; and his image lies before him and turns its head as he turns his, staring toward the far-off mountain, now turning from black to blue in the dawn light. He dives in, swims with swift effortless strokes beneath the surface until he is half way across the pool, and then turns, and floats on his back until he touches the shore again. And this is water which, not very long before, was ice and snow!

Standing once more on the shore, he whips the water from his body with the edges of his hands. Then he puts on the breech-clout. He steps into moccasins beautifully beaded; the work of a squaw's entire winter, perhaps, has gone to the decoration of those moccasins. He steps into tight-fitted deerskin trousers; and you must notice, now, the fringe that goes down the outer seam, fluttering in the breeze like hair. It is hair, human hair, at that. And, to make it really important, it was hair taken from the bodies of dead victims, slain by the hand of Mr. Yellow Wolf, himself.

He goes to his hobbled horse. It is a beautiful little pied animal with great prominent eyes, and those eyes fill with terror as it sees its master approach; for you may be sure that Yellow Wolf is not a gentle rider. To him the four legs of a pony serve in lieu of wings, and he scorns to fly across the earth less swiftly than the buzzard which sails on effortless pinions through the blue-white sky above.

Upon the back of the dainty piebald, Yellow Wolf throws a clumsy Indian saddle, with a harsh wooden frame, made to torture the horse without giving great comfort to the man. But the iron body of Yellow Wolf scorns petty comforts and rejoices in a little pain as much as any holy anchorite that ever laid the scourge on his own back for the sake of having the wounds of his soul healed in heaven. The horse is saddled. The rawhide thong which ordinarily trails from the neck of the mustang is coiled over the pommel of the saddle.

Then Yellow Wolf looks to his adornment. Before he stepped into the pool, he had removed some eagle feathers from his hair. Now he restores them to the proper place. Those feathers are a little timeworn; but they are honorable, you may be sure, because Yellow Wolf himself caught the bird who raised them. He caught that eagle when he himself was only a little boy, and he saved the feathers until he should become a warrior and of a reputation which allowed the wearing of such adornments. The first time a foe felt the full blade of his knife as he counted coup, Yellow Wolf took those feathers and dipped the tips of them in the heart's blood of the fallen enemy. That is why the broad ends of those feathers are so discolored, but Yellow Wolf regards them with infinite satisfaction.

His hair is now dressed and he turns to other matters. First, he draws from its case of antelope hide, running down the right side of the saddle, beneath his leg, a long, ponderous Kentucky rifle, such as, at one time, had been sure death in the hands of the frontiersmen who were raised to its use. But Yellow Wolf has never been able to afford enough powder and shot to enable him to practice with the weapon and become expert with it. Now and then he fires it. And he would not dream of coming out on the warpath without it because he regards with a sort of superstitious reverence this weapon of the white man. It is great medicine., And, being in his possession, it is his medicine. It is almost like a household god, to Yellow Wolf. He sees that it is well. At least outwardly it seems as handsome as ever. For every day he rubs and caresses it, and admires the shimmering beauty of its octagonal barrel.

Now he restores it to its handsome, beaded case. And he turns to the more effective part of his equipment. His knife he need only draw from the sheath and instantly restore it to its place. Because he always knows exactly the condition of that knife. It is as much a part of him as his hand. He is aware by instinct if the steel be tarnished or the edge blunted or nicked. Every day, and two or three times a day, it is almost subconsciously polished and whetted, often on the horny bottom of his naked foot, or finished on the palm of his strong hand. The knife, then, is always in order; but the bow and arrows are another matter. Arrows, for instance, are continually altering. The wood itself, unless it has been most carefully seasoned, is very apt to warp a little. And that will spoil the arrow for all except the most hand-to-hand fighting. And the continual chafing to which they are subjected during the jostling of each day's ride is apt to injure the feathers which must keep the arrow true in its flight, as a rudder steers a ship. He examines these arrows, one by one. Some are shorter and thicker of shaft and headed with a very small point. Those are the hunting arrows. The buffalo arrows, you may call them, since ten are used on that game for one used on any other. Other arrows have longer, slenderer shafts, with heavier heads. Those heads are not simple, like the hunting arrows; but they are curiously and cruelly barbed, so that, once having entered the flesh, they cannot be drawn out but must be cut away with the greatest of care.

Now Yellow Wolf sighs as he looks at those arrows, the pride of his heart. And straightway he sits down on his heels and replaces one of the rudder feathers on a war arrow. And he takes out another war arrow and scowls as he observes it; and his throat swells thick as he thinks of the words which he will address to Three Crows, the arrow maker, on his return to the Comanche village. Fool of a chattering magpie! He must be blind, not to tell green wood from old! Look, therefore, at this arrow, which might be the last in the sheaf, and upon its truth the life of the warrior might depend! However, the rest of Yellow Wolf's stock suited him well enough. Considering the journey, their condition was all that could very well be expected.

He looked at the rest of his accouterments. The big oval shield, made of the strongest back skin of a buffalo bull, and sun-hardened until it was almost as light as wood and as tough as steel — the big shield does not need much attention; but he looks it over with care. Yonder is the rent made when the war ax of an Apache hero clove even through the stout fabric of this shield. That strong-fingered squaw, Little Minnow, had sewed up the rent with strings of gut. And here toward the top of the shield were two small holes drilled through and through. Bullet holes, those, received while swinging in a flying charge around the covered wagon of a traveler across the plains. They served Yellow Wolf, now, for peepholes, often of use in the midst of a hard and close hand-to-hand battle.

That shield was blanched and white over all of its surface, except for the yellow figure of a buffalo wolf which was inscribed in the exact center. So skillfully was it painted that even a child could guess what it was. And, for this work of art, Yellow Wolf had paid no less than six buffalo robes, all well cured, and all softened and suppled. He took his name from that fine figure on his shield.

The shield examined, he gave a look to his lance, fourteen feet long, or perhaps a trifle more, longheaded, slender of haft, with a balance which he knew so well that its weight and its awkward length never confused him. Last of all, and most important of all, he gripped his bow with an affectionate might. It was four feet long, made of the best selected wood, and proved in the hands of Yellow Wolf time and again. All his arms, then, were in good order, and he had spent a full fifteen or twenty minutes handling them, after the old maxim which was always going the rounds in his tribe:

"When the enemy is seen, it is too late to begin to ask questions of the war bow!"

So Yellow Wolf asked his questions, always, well beforehand.

Now the arms were looked to, and there remained only one thing to take his attention, and that was a little skin of a field shrew, which hung from around his neck, suspended by a narrow lariat of horsehair. That was the medicine bag of Yellow Wolf, no less important to him and to his soul than his scalp and warlock.

He took the little medicine bag in both his hands and raised his face to the sky and stood for a moment in silent contemplation of the blueness of the heavens, and the sweep of the rosy clouds across it. Prayer passed from the soul of Yellow Wolf and blew away toward the heart of heaven. Then he stooped, picked up a handful of the ashes from his dead fire of the night before, and threw them into the air. The wind blew them swift and far, straight down the valley before him. Yellow Wolf took this as an excellent omen, and he hastened to spring into the saddle and start on his journey once more.

CHAPTER XVIII

The Coyote

He came to a triple forking of the valley, with a stream running brown and white through the heart of each. This was not as it had been in the map which had been drawn on the ground for him by White Hawk.

He dismounted; and, sitting on his heels, he sketched again upon the ground the whole set of instructions which he had received from his chief. Yonder stood the tall mountains; and here was the deep valley; and, as for the two smaller ravines, perhaps they had been considered too small to be worth notice. As for the streams which ran through them, when White Hawk was in this region there had been only one stream, instead of three; perhaps because it was not the season of melting snows.

Having assured himself upon this important point, he took his way again down the deeper of the valleys. But now he proceeded with the greatest caution, and every time he came to a sharpheaded hill, he dismounted and crawled snakelike to the top of it. There he would lie, scanning every feature of the valley before him with the attention and the intelligence with which a white man might scan a printed page.

He had come to the sixth or the seventh of these hills in this slow progress before he saw what he expected, and this was a little log cabin set down in the center of a broad-bottomed hollow, through which the river ran; and the noise of its talking rose sleepily and brimmed the valley from wall to wall.

It was a pleasant place. Here and there were ample growths of trees; though they never extended in a dense forest, but left the ground open and free to the cattle which dotted the valley with little dim bits of color. Now and again the sound of lowing rose in mellow notes above the chanting of the river. But all of these sounds were so faint and so far that when a blackbird whistled near by, it drowned out all else. Yellow Wolf, lying out flat and leaning on his elbows, scanned every detail with the utmost attention. He wrote all down in his memory. He would be prepared to speak of the minutest particles of all of this picture. He could say where the trees stood, and how far the log cabin was from the edge of the running water, and where it was that long strips of the soil had been turned up by the edge of the plow and now lay black beneath the sky — a blot upon the landscape, in the estimation of Yellow Wolf. He had heard the elders of his tribe say that wherever the white man came to graze cattle, there the Indians might still live, also; but that where the white man came to turn over the ground like a stupid mole, there the Indian must fight for his existence.

Just why this should be, Yellow Wolf did not know; and he did not ask. He did not pretend to be a philosopher. It was enough that the older heads should do the thinking, while he would content himself by doing whatever fighting came in his way. Scalps and buffalo robes were enough to fill the widest horizon of his imagination. He had no desire to grow into a medicine man.

However, since that item of the plowed land would be of importance, he considered its extent, also, and thought that it was only a tiny spot on the face of this fine valley. He admired, too, the solidity with which the log cabin had been erected. And he noted the stacks of hay, weather-blackened at the tops, and the outsheds, and the tangle of fencing which served to split the land into convenient portions of corral and pasture near the little house.

The wind had changed, now, and blowing up the valley it carried to his nostrils the scent of the wood smoke which floated from the chimney above the roof of the cabin. It carried to the nostrils of Yellow Wolf the fragrance of cooking food, far other than foods which he had known in his life. The smell of these delectable oddities made his nostrils quiver and widen and brought a sense of emptiness into his very soul.

However, he quelled those emotions, and be-gan to take note that he was not the only inter-ested watcher of that cabin. There was another not a hundred yards down the valley, crouched behind a rock — a spirit as secret and as fierce and well-nigh as subtle as his own — a little coyote with pricked ears studying the chances of gaining a meal for himself from all the tantalizing odors which tangled so joyfully in the air that blew from the house of the white man. Yellow Wolf, amused by the attention of the coyote, felt the minutes slipping by less slowly, while he waited in case chance might bring the white man out to his view.

Clouds gathered suddenly across the face of the sun. The wind turned sharp and rattled down a shower of rain that stung the tender skin between the shoulder blades of Yellow Wolf, but he did not stir limb or eye from the picture before him. White Hawk would have been proud of the steady nerve of his pupil. It was not a vain sign — the trimming of scalp locks which quivered down the outer seams of his trousers, or the two locks which dangled from the head of his spear. Yellow Wolf had killed before, and he was worthy to kill again. If only kind fortune would bring a white man's scalp to join the Apache prizes which he already carried!

The shower ended. The cloud scattered and ran for the edges of the sky like mischievous boys who have been throwing stones. The sun burned down with a kindly heat against the earth, once more. And at last the owner of the shack came forth. Yellow Wolf had been prepared for a great spectacle. White Hawk had given him a description in some detail. But still, he was shocked and moved with wonder.

Yellow Wolf was himself a big fellow; and, if his legs had not been bowed a little, after the true Comanche type, he would have stood a shade over six feet, with ample bulk to back him. But he knew that if he were at the side of this white man, he would be over-shadowed — not only by mere width of shoulders and by sheer inches in height but also by a certain air of magnificence and bigness which flowed forth from the stranger. One did not need to ask if he were as strong as his bulk promised. One needed only to see the wave of his hand to know that his arm was robed with immense might. One needed only to see him walk in order to make sure that he could run like an antelope.

But what stirred the heart of the Indian more than all else, perhaps, was the tide of golden-red hair which flowed down in frontier fashion almost to the shoulders of the white man. Never in all his days had Yellow Wolf seen such a scalp, and his eyes went bright and small with concentrated desire. He would give ten years, twenty years of his life, for the sake of enjoying the possession of that scalp. He could see it now, in fancy, glistening like a golden fleece from the central pole of his tepee, shining in the firelight, while the faces of the men were lifted toward it in awe and admiration. He drew a great breath, and reached for the Kentucky rifle, but still he hesitated. He knew his limitations with that gun, and this was a long distance.

At about the same time, the coyote decided that it would be safe to change his position. So he slid from his sheltering rock and stole down the hillside, with Yellow Wolf watching through the grass which he parted before him with his hand. He had often watched coyotes before, and never had he observed them without learning lessons of the greatest value upon the warpath, whether stalking for information or for scalps. Now he admired the perfect manner in which the little scoundrel glided from rock to rock and from bush to bush, sometimes, it seemed, walking straight into the eye of the big man with the flaming hair, but always unobserved.

The giant had led forth a span of mules, of such a size and build that the heart of the Comanche leaped in him again, for mules were infinitely prized among his tribesmen. There was nothing like a mule, indeed, for the weary miles of desert travel, when the chosen warriors rode south on the Mexican trail.

Now this white man, this white squaw, was harnessing the mules to a plow and preparing to labor again — a disgusting spectacle. More disgusting, indeed, because White Hawk had assured him in no measured terms that this man of the golden head was a warrior of tremendous fame and prowess! However, to see was to believe; and Yellow Wolf denied, in his heart of hearts, that a man could be both a hero and an earthworm as this settler seemed to be.

The coyote, it seemed, took somewhat the

same view of the case; for now it ventured to leave all cover for a matter of ten yards or so, and it leaped away across a narrow clearing toward the brush behind one of the sheds. After all, it was not taking a real risk. It was not taking more of a chance, say, than the man who lifts his head for a single instant above the stockade, to shoot an arrow at the encircling enemy. So decided Yellow Wolf, as he watched.

And he was very keenly alert, so that not a bit of the miracle that followed escaped him. What he saw was that the man of the red-gold hair turned the slightest bit to the side and then a gun winked in his hand at the hip, though the movement of that hand to draw the weapon was much faster than the eye of even Yellow Wolf could follow.

The same instant, the gun spoke — from the hip of the man, and not raised, and aimed! It exploded, with such a sure aim that it flicked up dust and gravel before the face of the speeding coyote. That cunning brute whirled about and darted for the covert from which it had just issued. The curling of a cracked whiplash could hardly have been faster. And yet, even as it spun around, fate overtook it. The gun spat again from the hand of the big man. The coyote leaped into the air with a screech, and falling, toppled over and over half a dozen times down the steep slope of the hill.

CHAPTER XIX
The Smoke Signal

The Indian closed his eyes, and he kept them closed for a long moment. He was telling himself that the glint of the metal at the hip of the gold head had not been the flash of a pistol at all; for who had heard of a gun which could speak twice as rapidly as one could snap one's fingers — or even a little faster? A coyote thinks a little bit more quickly than the whirring spokes of a carriage wheel revolve. And as fast as it could think that little wolf dog had stopped and whirled. And yet it had been struck dead.

Yellow Wolf did not want to think that there was magic in this. But, as he lay there in the grass with his eyes closed, he prayed to the Great Spirit that this might not be a fleshly man to whom had been confided the awful power of wielding the naked lightning flash. He opened his eyes and looked again.

No, there was Gold Head very plainly holding in his hand a species of pistol, stockier and rather shorter than the ones which Yellow Wolf had seen before. All the elements of magic, you will say, were instantly removed. No, not at all! For you must not forget that in the case of his saddle,

Yellow Wolf carried a rifle with which he only occasionally could strike the mark, and yet he was possessed with awe for the weapon. How much more so for those mysterious rifles of the trappers and the frontiersmen with which he had seen them perform uncanny feats! And then, how vastly more mystery was attached to this little pistol which spoke twice as fast as the rapid tongue of a chattering girl, and which killed with every syllable it uttered. It was magic, of course; for was it not apparent that the weapon had not been raised to the shoulder and sighted? It had merely been bared in the hand of the giant, and therefore it had worked its own mischief.

No, it was of course magic, but with a difference. For, in the first place, there had come to Yellow Wolf the dreadful suspicion that he was looking upon one of the chosen of the spirits; but now it was merely certain that this was a wise and fortunate man who had made the very biggest medicine that Yellow Wolf had ever heard of and had ever seen. To a certain extent, he could call himself blessed in that he had seen such a marvel. Only to recite it would make him a marked man, and Indians would ride many miles to sit in his tepee. And the wise men of the Comanches would become silent and raise their faces when they heard him tell this story.

For that purpose, he regarded the spot with keenest eyes, now. He estimated with a shrewd glance that the firing had been done at a distance of from twenty-five to thirty paces. He made sure that the white man's side had been turned and therefore that he had fired the bullets across his body, which made the impossibility of aiming doubly great. He would testify, also, that the mules, instead of bolting away as this miracle was performed under their eyes, had merely cocked their long ears forward and stood attentively watching, as though they, also, had fallen under the spell of this man's wizardry.

He observed, also, that as the big man now fell to work to skin his victim, his knife appeared to lack the cunning which lay, for instance, in the keen blade at the belt of Yellow Wolf. Only, with a prodigious force and comparatively few knife strokes, Gold Head seemed to draw the coyote from its hot pelt by sheer might of hand. The very inmost bones of Yellow Wolf ached as he saw this feat performed, for he knew all the secrets of how the pelt is neatly and snugly fitted to the body of a beast.

Then he saw the giant turn to the mules. Perhaps there were other and smaller miracles of big medicine to be attested, now, in the fact that he did not curse the mules as he drove them forth. No whip or blacksnake was curling and snapping in his hands. Neither did he roar at them; but with a word so quiet that it almost stopped in the thin air before drifting to the ears of Yellow Wolf, he sent the obedient team on its way. Through the gate they passed, through the lowered bars of the adjoining field; and now they were turning the mellow soil with the plow and adding new, shining, black furrows beside the whitening ones which already lay there.

Having seen these things, Yellow Wolf waited to see no more. He had ridden along this trail with the fixed determination of striving to exceed his orders, which were simply to learn if Gold Head were here and to send back instant word through the air. He had determined, if possible, to see the man and take his scalp, and come back to White Hawk with the trophy to make himself admired among his nation. But now he changed his mind completely. For it was plain that one who held in the hollow of his hand such medicine as this was not for the single attack of any one Comanche; rather, he was for the united assault of half a hundred of the best warriors.

So Yellow Wolf stole back from the hilltop which had screened him; and he reached his pony; and he rode hastily back up the valley, taking care to keep to such rocky and graveled places as would least plainly show the print of the pony's unshod feet.

He went up the valley a dozen miles to a tall eminence. There he collected the materials to make a fire. He struck a shower of sparks from flint and steel into tinder, raised a smoke, and then a fire; and, when the blaze was working satisfactorily, he heaped over the blaze a quantity of tender green trimmings from the boughs. This cast into the air a column of smoke as dense as a sculptor's marble and glistening in its whiteness as it rose. Over this column he cast his blanket, held it down for an instant, and snatched it back, releasing a big, fat, curling puff that sailed like a vast bubble into the sea of the air. He did the same thing again and again, and then annihilated the fire, stamping out the embers.

From the beginning to the end, the total time this smoke signal had lasted had not been more than two minutes. He could be sure that White Hawk would have watchers staring at that point upon the horizon. And, unless suspicious white men were scanning the sky with care, they would not have been able to detect any signal at all, except for that brief interval.

Having done this, he journeyed down into the wide valley beyond, where he had seen buffalo straying in a little group. For it was part of his duty, as a perfect scout, to have provisions in readiness, if possible, when the rest of his clansmen arrived upon the warpath.

He skirted down through the rolling hills, taking the greatest care in his approach, since this was only a small, detached company, flung out from the great central masses of the plains cattle. Since the group was small they were certain to be doubly wary and fleet of foot. Good luck favored him. A grove of young trees acted as a screen for his approach; and, lingering for an instant behind the outermost trees, he surveyed the band with burning eyes and picked his quarry — a strapping young male, whose meat was sure to be tender and whose bulk would supply a

plentiful body of viands for the coming Comanches.

Then he drove the sharpened butt of the lance
into the ground. With a thong that hung from
the edge of his heavy shield, he fastened it to the
upright shaft of the spear, and thus disencum-
bered, he drew forth his bow and prepared four
good arrows, chosen from the lot.

After that, he gathered the pony beneath him,
by working his heel cunningly and cruelly into
its tender flank; and, when it was quivering with
fear and pain, he released it, and burst into the
open with a wild yell. That inhuman screech
seemed to paralyze the buffalo for a moment.
With their shaggy heads raised and their tails
sticking straight out in fear, they remained as if
stunned until they were sure of the danger rushing at them. Then down went heads, up went
tails; and they were instantly at full speed across
the level.

The pinto was a sprinter. Now he whisked past
a slow-moving cow at the rear of the herd; now
he passed a heavy bull, which threw its head and
gave him a glance from red eyes. Now he was
closing on the chosen quarry. The buffalo, feeling
doom upon it, dodged like a cat. The brave followed on a pony not less quick-footed, and Yellow Wolf was beside his victim.

He drew his bow to the ear and sent the shaft
into the body; and, with such vast force was the
arrow driven, that it passed clear through and
issued upon the farther side. The buffalo still ran

a few strides, but the mischief was done. Presently it halted and stood with drooping head. Its hind legs sank to the ground, but still it braced itself resolutely upon its forelegs and shook its head threateningly at the man as he approached.

Yellow Wolf simply laughed. He seized one of the immature horns with a hand of iron. With the hunting knife in his other hand he opened the throat of his prey with a great, deep gash, to bleed the meat whiter. And then, standing by the dying body, he worked his heel upon its ribs to force the life away faster. There was no compassion in Yellow Wolf. But how could you expect such an emotion in him? He himself would not have known how to admire it. He would have regarded it as madness.

But, even as he worked at cutting up the body, he now and then cast a furtive glance over his shoulder as though he dreaded lest a monster with flying golden hair might appear over the edge of the hill and rush down upon him.

CHAPTER XX

In the Tower Room

The mules, turning at the end of a furrow, had moved slowly about; and the plow, swung deftly about by Oliver Tay, was beginning to flesh its blade in the turf once more, when he looked up and before him saw above Mount Loomis a little, round white cloud moving up past the trees. It was just like a thousand other clouds which spotted the sky on this day, except that it was a little whiter, if anything, and a little denser and more crystal-shining.

It changed, faded, melted, and was gone with a surprising suddenness. The mules came to the end of the furrow, and Oliver did not turn them. He was staring with a frown at the spot where that tiny cloud had disappeared. There was something wrong about it. What could it be? And then suddenly his mind cleared, and he knew. It was no cloud, for clouds are not breathed up in round puffs from the earth and past the trees. It was smoke, and what could have thrown smoke into such a neat bubble except the signaling blanket of a wild Indian, or a still wilder white man?

A moment later, the mules were turned loose in the pasture; and Oliver Tay was hurrying up the valley on a horse. He aimed straight at the shoulder of Mount Loomis; and so it happened that when he came over that ridge, his glasses ready, he was able to look down into the pleasant hollow beneath. There he perceived Yellow Wolf at the work of cutting up the dead buffalo. He looked more carefully, taking the Indian in the full focus of his glass; and then he was sure that it was a Comanche — and that meant trouble, particularly since it was a Comanche accoutered for the warpath. He turned the glass here and there and discovered a little scattering of buffalo in the distance, but certainly they were not in sufficient numbers to be worth sending the news of them on to a main body of these Indians. That floating bubble of white which had dissolved into the sky was a signal, and it was a signal of what?

Oliver Tay made up his mind quickly enough. There was danger being called his way, and what had he to meet the advance of a body of these marauders except his own single hand?

He turned his horse back, and headed in a bird's-flight line across country and toward Siddon Flat.

For Antonio Morales always said: "Whenever in doubt about Indians, call in your neighbors!" And Antonio Morales knew all about Indians. In fact, he was almost an Indian himself. Ah, to have the help of Antonio, now, together with great Carpio Vega, perhaps, and that little, wicked snake of a man, Capiño! However, they

148

were doubtless far, far south, working their evil, careless, joyous ways under the direction of Roderigo Venales. And this problem of Oliver Tay must be met by him alone.

His horse was dripping with foam as it made into Siddon Flat. He had come in, purposely, past the place of Samson Barge; and he had a glimpse of Marian in the garden. He reined in his horse and leaned across the garden fence to kiss her.

"I'll be back at once," said Oliver Tay.

"What has happened?" she asked him. "You haven't struck gold?"

"You're an optimist," said Oliver. "I'll see you again in half an hour." And he rode briskly on down the street, and through the town and toward the fort.

The fort of Siddon Flat was constructed in the simplest possible manner. The commandant's house was in the center. There was a parade space around it. Then came the barracks. And beyond the barracks another space which could be filled with the tents of traders, if need be, or turned over to the civilian population in case the Indians came down in a flood and swept them out of the town. And around all there was a tall stockade, loopholed, with a four-foot bank of dirt and stones on the inside, and a deep ditch on the outside. It was not much of a fort, and a single five-pound gun could have pounded it to pieces in no time at all. But against rifle fire it could hold out indefinitely, and therefore it was safe from the Indians so long as it could be effectively manned.

It had little watchtowers built at the corners of the parapets; and, since this was a time of peace, the commandant, Lieutenant-colonel Randolf Chisholm, was using the largest of these towers as an office. For, with the casements opened on all four sides, he was given more cool air and more view than from any other place in the fort.

On this day, Colonel Chisholm was in conversation with Peter Sydham, that gentleman trader, when the orderly brought in word that a farmer had just come in reporting danger from Comanches. Peter Sydham's brows rose, but Colonel Chisholm merely shrugged his shoulders.

"I've only been at this post three weeks," said he, "but in that time I've had a hundred alarms. They're Indian mad, the people out this way, Mr. Sydham."

Mr. Sydham agreed that they were. Still, he felt that the Comanches were enough to make almost anyone nervous.

"Stuff!" said the colonel. "Ten trained men could slaughter a hundred wild Indians any day!" He turned to the orderly. "Have Captain Alston question this farmer," he said.

The orderly saluted, but with a shadow in his eyes that made the colonel ask, "What's his name?"

"Oliver Tay," said the orderly. And he added with a glint of meaning, "It's *the* Oliver Tay."

"The Oliver Tay?" said the colonel. "Have you

ever heard of such a fellow, Sydham?"

"He's my cousin and my stepson," sighed the trader, looking down at the floor.

"Is that so? Why, I'll have him in, then — if you'll only explain why it is that a gentleman would take up farming in this part of the world!"

Mr. Sydham sighed again, in such a manner that the colonel stared at him. "As a matter of fact," said Peter Sydham, "I have to be honest with you. Oliver and I are not on the best of terms."

The colonel waited, and Peter Sydham continued, "As a matter of fact, Colonel Chisholm, my poor Oliver is a lad who was raised in the best possible manner and according to the very best methods. But all this would not do. There was a wild strain — well, I shall only say that his best friends are a rough lot of Mexicans, cutthroats, and what not; and now the poor misguided fellow has settled down, ostensibly to farm; though goodness knows what his real business may be."

The colonel smiled sternly. "A little farming on the side," he suggested, "and a good deal of lawless work as a real occupation. Is that your meaning, Sydham? I understand you, and I thank you for dealing so frankly with me. I'll soon send him about his business."

He sent for another orderly and dispatched a command that Mr. Tay should be brought directly to his own presence. Peter Sydham discreetly withdrew to the adjoining room very well pleased with himself; for ever since a certain day on which he had found that he was unable to face the scorn and the derision and the contempt in the eyes of Oliver Tay, he had been constantly waiting for an opportunity of doing harm to the young man. Now it seemed that the occasion had come.

So he tilted his chair back beside the window, and lighted a cigar, and hoped with all his heart that Oliver would recognize the scent of that brand of tobacco and guess that his stepfather was behind the reception which he was about to be accorded, as the fumes of that cigar floated into the room where the colonel was sitting.

A long swinging stride, a quiver of the floor that extended even into the adjoining chamber where Mr. Sydham waited; and Sydham knew that Oliver Tay was before the colonel. Colonel Chisholm allowed the big man to stand for a moment, while he eyed him. Courtesy was not one of the traits of the colonel, when he had to do with civilians. Inside the army, no one could be a stricter observer of the niceties of life than the colonel. But outside of the wearers of the uniform, the colonel evidently felt that every one was a private — and not a private in good standing, at that. He allowed no one to have a share of his consideration unless it were an occasional trader, like Peter Sydham, who carried a brand of whisky of a necessary excellence.

"You think that you have bad news about Indians," said the colonel. "Now let me have your proof." It was a very crisp and terse way of going at the thing. Mr. Sydham, in the adjoining room, waited for an explosion from Oliver Tay. But there was no explosion.

Oliver was merely saying, gently: "It's very well known that the big war chief of the Comanches — I mean White Hawk — has had it in for me for a long time and —"

"I'm not talking about ancient history," snapped the colonel. "I want the evidence that brought you hotfooting it into the fort and spreading an Indian alarm."

Very stern talk, colonel! Even Peter Sydham winced a little.

"Very well," said Mr. Tay. "The facts are that I saw a smoke signal up the valley from my house. I rode up to the place on Mount Loomis, and looking down into the hollow, I was able to see a young Comanche warrior rigged up for the warpath. He was cutting up a buffalo which he had killed. And I believe he was signaling to a band of his mates to come to his help so that they could loot the valley of everything that I have in it."

"Is that all?" asked the colonel.

"That's all."

"And the evidence of the 'raid' is confined to what you have just told me?"

"Exactly."

The colonel allowed an impressive pause to intervene; and then he murmured, "Interesting! I like to see a vigorous imagination at work."

CHAPTER XXI
The Challenge

In the next room Cousin Peter Sydham had grown so excited that a veritable cloud of smoke rolled from his cigar and now pressed through the doorway and into the colonel's room. And still there was no outburst from Oliver Tay. He was explaining calmly:

"You see, Colonel Chisholm, it may seem a sketchy thing to you, but I know that White Hawk most powerfully wants my scalp and that he's been waiting for a chance to get at me for a long time."

"And what has kept him away this long?" asked the colonel coldly.

"The fact that I usually have some friends with me — a set of fellows who are poison to the Indians; and White Hawk has never wanted to spend as many braves as he would have to in order to wipe us out. But now I am alone, and word of it must have been brought to him. Otherwise I wouldn't have seen that scout today."

The colonel raised his hand. "Now, young man, will you listen to me?"

"Gladly."

"The reason that White Hawk has not touched

you or any other person near Siddon Flat for a long time, is because of the troops under my command. And you may take it for granted that your group of 'friends,' whoever they may be, have nothing to do with his inaction. I know Indians. And I know what I'm talking about."

"I didn't know," said Oliver Tay, even more gently than before, "that you were an old Indian fighter."

"I have studied the situation thoroughly before being sent to this command," said the young colonel.

"Do you mean that you know the Indians out of books?"

"Yes," said the colonel.

"I thought so," said Oliver Tay. "So you know that I shall be safe?"

"Exactly! Now return and let me hear no more about this foolish matter. One swallow doesn't make a summer, and one Indian doesn't make a massacre; though to hear some of you westerners talk, by heaven! one would think that that was the case."

"I should like to point out a few things," said Oliver Tay. "The first is that I have taken every penny that belongs to me in the world and that I have invested it in my little ranch. I have bought up the best sort of cattle and stocked the grazing sections of it. I have bought horses and mules of the first quality. I've built a house and furnished it with all essentials. And I've bought tools for cultivation of the farm lands."

"I don't see," said the colonel, "what this has to do with the case, so far as I'm concerned!"

"I shall show you immediately," said Mr. Tay. "You are here to protect the lives and the property of the citizens of our country. Now, sir, my property is not something to be scoffed at. It's worth the protection which it would receive by the presence of a troop of cavalry for a few days. I'll pay for their food, and I'll give them shelter and lodging while they're with me. And I'll guarantee, besides, to show them more evidence of Comanches than they've seen in a good many days."

"I think that the matter is closed," said the colonel stiffly.

"Wait one moment," said Oliver Tay. "You have to remember that I have listed quite a number of things on my farm."

"Quite a number," said the colonel. "I shall have to ask you to leave me now, Mr. Tay. My time is not my own!"

The floor shook. Could it have been that Oliver Tay had stamped his ponderous foot? And now his voice rose and swelled to an ominous strength. "Colonel, I'm leaving the door open to you to protect me and my possessions. And if those possessions are destroyed by the Comanches, I give you warning that I am going to file a claim against you for criminal negligence."

"Hello, orderly!" called the colonel in a passion. "Take this fellow outside the fort, and do it at once!"

"Are you the orderly?" asked Oliver Tay.

"I am, sir," said the soldier.

"Don't 'sir' him!" shouted Chisholm. "Get him out of my sight."

"Orderly," said Oliver Tay, "be good to yourself and keep out of my way. Colonel, if you are worthy of the epaulets you are wearing, I'll have an answer from you later on about this matter."

Colonel Chisholm was struck dumb. Neither could he stir hand or foot; but, sitting in his chair, he gazed stupidly at the big man, as the latter turned upon his heel and strode from the room.

"I say, Sydham!"

Cousin Peter, very subdued and drawn of face, entered the room, turning his cigar nervously in his fingers.

"You told me something about this relative of yours," said the colonel viciously; "but if you had told me everything, I should not have consented to see him at all."

"One thing that I intended to say and forgot," said Peter Sydham, biting his lips, "is that Oliver is a very dangerous fellow in a fight, Colonel! Very dangerous indeed!"

"You think," smiled the colonel, "that because a fellow manages to knock over a buffalo or two and knife a Mexican in a barroom fight, that he is quite an Achilles. But if this rascal is enough of a gentleman for me to call him out, I'll soon show you the difference between a rough-and-tumble expert and a bit of pistol work!" The colonel nodded, with rather a secret satisfaction;

and he spread the mustaches upon his upper lip with thumb and forefinger.

However, he observed that Peter Sydham had not answered. Indeed, Mr. Sydham's color had not improved a whit. And now he advanced across the room and tapped a pink and pudgy finger upon the desk. "Colonel Chisholm!" said he.

"Well, well?" echoed the colonel, rather angrily.

"Let me assure you, Colonel Chisholm, that I value you too highly to permit you to throw yourself away. There is only one proper way of answering the insult of my stepson. That is to send a couple of sturdy fellows and have them give him a thorough blacksnaking."

The colonel sniffed with disdain. "I can't understand that viewpoint, Sydham," said he.

"You prefer to call him out?" asked Peter Sydham, rather crisply.

"Of course I prefer it. I've done nothing since I came here. I have to let people know that I'm a man able to take care of myself, sooner or later, and why not now?"

"Chisholm," said the trader, shaking his head with the solemnity of his conviction, "if you had the slightest chance, I tell you I detest that scoundrel so thoroughly that I should even encourage you to go ahead with the business. But upon my word of honor, if you stand up to meet him, he will kill you out of hand, with no more trouble and no more concern than you would use in shooting at a helpless pig."

The metaphor was not chosen with any particular delicacy, but at least it contained a certain innate vigor that gave the gallant colonel pause. He had plenty of courage. He had won his very early promotion to this high rank more by rash bravery in the field than by another way. And now he hesitated and stared wistfully at Mr. Sydham. For the whole heart of Chisholm was telling him that he should stand forth on the dueling field in this affair. And yet — there is really no wit or wisdom in throwing away one's life. And, from the conviction with which Mr. Sydham spoke, the colonel felt that to fight against the golden-headed giant would be equivalent to taking an overdose of poison — a swift and painless way of leaving this vale of tears.

"Is he so absolutely fatal?" said the colonel.

Mr. Sydham paused and cast about him for some illustration. Then he said, "You know that these fellows in this part of the world are lovers of battle, Colonel Chisholm?"

"I've been here long enough to learn that, of course!"

"Very well! I can tell you as an assured fact that there is not a man in the town and the country around it who would dream of crossing the path of my cousin. And at short range, Colonel, he has a trick of working at his revolver so that it chatters bullets faster than a woodpecker can tap a tree. And every bullet is aimed to split the edge of a shingle at twenty paces. And therefore, Colonel, I say that you surely will not be foolish enough to throw yourself away."

The colonel raised his gentlemanly hand. "Sydham," he said, "I believe that the code stops at certain reasonable points; and I fail to see any reason why a man should throw himself over a cliff for the sake of pleasing Madame Fashion. As for this fellow Tay, I shall simply forget that he exists. I believe that my record will permit me to do so."

Mr. Sydham breathed more easily. For he had arranged with the colonel to supply the soldiers at the fort with certain of the necessities of life at a rate which was very pleasant, to say the least. And Mr. Sydham would have been cut to the quick if the colonel had been snuffed out by the accurate revolver of his cousin. In fact, Mr. Sydham would have felt it to the very depths of his pocketbook.

Outdoors, the orderly had taken Oliver Tay down to the gate of the fort. "All right, Tay," said he. "You've had your money's worth out of the old man, and you've given me mine, too. He's a swine, and I'll see that the rest of the lads know about the talk that you made him swaller."

But Oliver Tay did not seem to hear. His head was too high, and his eyes were too darkened by anxiety.

CHAPTER XXII

Plunder and Fire

Through the town of Siddon Flat Oliver Tay went to accumulate a force of fighting men to ride back with him to the defense of his homestead. But he had very odd fortune. For the instant it was known that he was bound on a trip to fight the terrible Comanches, and above all that dreadful chief, White Hawk, there was a great deal of shaking of the head. Men told Oliver that they would be only too pleased to ride forth with him, and that they wished that they might be able to do some service with him against that foe to all men — White Hawk; but, unfortunately, that day they were very pressingly busy. But there was Neighbor Smith. No doubt his hands were free, and he and his two stalwart sons would go with Oliver Tay to the battle. But Neighbor Smith was in the very same case, yet he suggested that Neighbor Johnson would be sure to go.

And so Oliver was thrown from pillar to post until he at length reluctantly admitted to himself that these people would not take such risks for the sake of his farm. Had he been closer in, and his property been close to theirs, then they would have rallied at once around him and fought heartily, like the strong-handed men they were. But he had established a more or less distant outpost, and now he had to pay the penalty.

And, as half a dozen of the frontiersmen reminded him, "This here is the business of the troops. You better go to Colonel Chisholm."

Oliver Tay allowed himself a five-minute delay, and rode back past the Barge farm. Old Samson Barge, he knew, would willingly have gone with him. But Samson Barge hardly knew one end of a rifle from the other; and, besides, he was so rheumatic that he could hardly sit in a saddle. He would at least serve as a mouthpiece for a little message which Oliver intended to leave for the community.

When Oliver reached the front gate, there was Marian waiting for him, flushed with happiness; for he could come in to see her, these busy days, not more than once a week, at the most. He paused by Marian only long enough to frighten her with the cloud on his brow and to ask, "Where's your father?"

She had been raised on the frontier, and therefore she knew enough not to ask foolish questions. She simply ran on ahead and opened the door to the blacksmith shop, where Samson Barge was grunting with discomfort as he worked the foot lever of the bellows with his rheumatic leg and turned a heating iron bar in the whistling flames.

Then Marian Barge retreated in haste and left the two men together.

Samson Barge regarded the golden-haired giant with awe and in silence. He had never grown accustomed to the idea of such a Titan as a prospective son-in-law; and many a time he had almost wished that Marian could have chosen for herself a hero less magnificent, less beautiful, less famous — and somewhat more safe. Only for the last few months Mr. Barge had grown more contented with Marian's prospects in life, when he saw Oliver Tay settling down on the distant farm in the valley under the mountain. And his approval waxed to enthusiasm when he took note of the tremendous manner in which the giant approached his task, doing three men's work in every day, and running up fence lines, and building sheds, and heaving, and moiling, and toiling until in six months he had accomplished more than most men could possibly have done in two years. And so the farm was growing apace; and, before very long, Marian could go out to become its mistress.

Yet even as a farmer, Oliver Tay was not altogether reassuring. He was a span or two taller than an earth worker need be. And there was sometimes a flash of wildness in his blue eyes that frightened Samson Barge. It frightened him now. And those blue eyes were flashing doubly bright, by contrast with the darkness of the brows.

"Barge," said Oliver, "I've come to tell you that I think the Comanches are about to destroy Loomis Valley. Don't jump and shout. Don't ask what I'm going to do. I've been to the fort; and the colonel tells me that I'm wrong, and that the Comanches are so afraid of him that they wouldn't dare to come as close as Loomis Valley with a war party. I've been through the town, and I've tried to get them together to help me against White Hawk. But this seems to be their busy day. No, Barge, it wouldn't do any good for you to go out there, unless you want to plant your scalp in the valley and break Marian's heart. It wouldn't do any good. It'll be better for you to stay behind. And, if the word comes in that the Comanches have wrecked the valley for me, and left it in ashes, I want you to go to Colonel Chisholm for me and tell him that I believe the government owes me the price of what I've lost."

He left Barge stunned with this announcement and returned to his horse. After that, he turned his course straight across the hills and back toward Loomis Valley, guided all the way by the tall, bald head of Loomis Mountain itself. When he reached the valley edge, it was already too late. He sat in a clump of rocks and calmly smoked a pipe and watched half of his herd of cattle thronging down the pass through the golden light of the late afternoon.

Behind them came the Comanches; and leader of them all was White Hawk, with war feathers fluttering behind his head and shoulders, and his long lance brandished in his hand for very joy. The pace of the cows was not fast enough; and now there was a sweeping charge, and all went forward at a mad gallop. For, after all, the valley was a trifle close to the town; and, if the troopers came out from Siddon Flat, it would be well that the plunder should be well away among the hills.

Oliver Tay, from his place of vantage, with a glass of the first quality, counted them one by one as they rushed forward — seventeen stalwart braves. And, behold, from the farther end of the valley, a similar wave of cattle was being driven in, with more than a score of red men behind them. And the hay fields suddenly threw up red hands of fire as the Comanches set fire to the standing crop. The fire began to spread in a circle, while the wild men closed on the house itself. At such a distance, Oliver could not hear their shouting, but at least he could see them dancing with joy as they looted the house and poured their plunder forth in the front yard.

It was all done with amazing speed because these were experts at such labors. The house and the sheds were instantly emptied. The mules and the horses were gathered into one herd. The cattle were bunched closely in another, and then the whole procession wound rapidly away from the valley and soon were lost behind the smoke screen which they had thrown up behind them. For now the sheds were caught in the flames, and the long yellow arms of fire crawled inward through the evening shadows and reached the house itself, until it was mantled with a confusion of smoke and flames.

Oliver Tay waited until he had made sure of the destruction of all the thousands of his dollars, and the months of his labor. He was very young. And the time which he had expended in Loomis Valley seemed to him the irreplaceable portion of his loss. For nearly a year he had labored. Now all of that labor was snatched away from him. There remained for his portion the horse which he rode, and the rifle in the case, and the revolvers at hip and saddlebow. He had been stripped to the bone; and yet all of this might have been prevented by Colonel Chisholm, if the soldier had chosen. No wonder that Oliver turned his head and looked back in the direction of Siddon Flat with unspeakable rage in his heart.

He could not remain where he was. He would be very late, if he went in now to report the outrage. And so he chose to go forward along the trail which the Comanches were following, and he started at once.

Ah, to have had his three tried friends to help him, to say nothing of the great Venales and his band of thugs and warriors! But he had nothing to stand by him except the might of his own right hand and some remembered wisdom from among the many lessons which they had taught him. How would Antonio Morales have acted — that most famous of Indian fighters — in a case like this? Beyond a doubt he would have followed the marauders, also. But he would have followed them with the greatest care.

"An Indian fights best when he is running

away. He shoots straightest over his shoulder," Antonio Morales had been fond of saying; and Oliver Tay remembered that, now. No doubt, therefore, these Comanches would not leave themselves open to any sudden stroke from behind. But instead, they would throw out a rear guard to watch against a surprise attack, and other guards would be pushed out to either side and in front of the main body of warriors and plunder. How should Oliver Tay break through these guards? He did not even attempt it. But, estimating the turns and the windings of the cañon up which White Hawk had gone with his men, Oliver Tay decided that the great Comanche would undoubtedly keep drifting steadily to the left, for the very reason that toward the right and the east lay his natural hunting grounds. And if he kept to the left, he would be bearing along the outer edge of a semicircle, while a pursuer could gain vital ground by riding the chord of the arc.

That was exactly what Oliver did.

The moon was not yet up, but thick as sand on a beach, the sky was strewn with stars and whitened by their crowding rays, when Oliver rode over the edge of the southern cañon wall, and looked down into a thousand-foot chasm, deep in which weltered a huge fire like the red eye of a dragon looking up through the dark waters of a pool.

The Capture of Yellow Wolf

He left the horse on the edge of the cliff, because for the work which he had in mind a horse would be merely an encumbrance. Then he lowered himself down the face of the precipice. It was Antonio Morales who had taught him the greatest secret of mountain climbing.

"Look at the wild goats. They never hesitate because they know that nature never draws a line with a rule. She slopes in or out, and she has her jags and crags which will make fingerholds for you. So keep your body close to the wall, and never look down if you can help it."

It was a very simple rule, but it worked amazingly well. To keep one's body close in, so that there was less leverage against feet and hands, to trust a good deal to nature's rough edges, and to look down as seldom as possible — just often enough to keep the way clearly in mind and waste no effort! So he went down that staggering cliff and found, as usual, that once he was fairly committed to the task, it was easier than it looked. He came down and down until the voices of the redskins thronged up about him, and it seemed that they must surely be marking him as he climbed.

However, they had the glare of their camp fire to blind them; but he was fairly sure that, no matter how cautious they were, and though they might guard the valley, up and down, they would not be apt to take any precautions against an attack from the side, down one of these towering walls. He was right. He reached the bottom of the descent entirely unobserved and crouched to take note of all that was before him.

And the first thing of which he made certain was that in the looting of his house they had not failed to take along the little ten-gallon whiskey barrel which, like all frontiersmen, he kept for medicine and for hospitality.

The contents had been distributed through the party, and that was the reason that the uproar of a madhouse rose from around the fire. Half-naked forms leaped and pranced in the light of the flames, staggering and swinging their arms, and shrieking in a frenzy of excitement. Oliver wished, grimly, that he had Morales and Vega and Capiño with him; for he had no doubt, at first, that with their aid he could have routed the entire band.

But then he saw that a few of the entire crew were keeping themselves in hand; and, as he crept nearer, from bush to bush, he saw two drunken braves in vain attempt to press a drink upon a third of the gang. This was a stalwart warrior who sat on his heels at the very edge of the firelight, watching the revels but taking no part in them. And, when Oliver looked more narrowly at him, he made sure that it was the same solitary Comanche whom he had examined through his glass earlier in the day — he who had been cutting up the buffalo in the valley.

Whole shrubs and small dead trees had been piled near the bonfire; and, from time to time, great quantities of wood were thrown into the blaze — so that Oliver himself was half blinded, and that fact nearly cost him his life. For as he crawled forward, he put his hand suddenly upon warm human flesh.

The sleeping brave started into a sitting posture with a grunt of alarm and disgust; but, before he could make sure what had happened, Oliver struck him once with the butt of his ready revolver — sure that he would need to strike no more. He felt the bones of the skull crunch in beneath the stroke. Then, crouching behind a shrub, Oliver waited to see what might come of this.

There was only one in the band with ears sharp enough to hear the groan of the dying Comanche, and that was Yellow Wolf, who started now to his feet and strode toward the place from which the sound had come. And it seemed to Oliver Tay, as he watched the brave coming forward, with the firelight washing across his half-naked body, that he had never seen a more magnificent specimen of manhood than this copper-colored hero.

Yellow Wolf came close to the spot, but the

fire was too recently in his face for him to see clearly through the shadows. He screened his eyes with his hand and stared about him. Then at last he marked the crumpled body of the dead Comanche and leaned above him with a soft grunt of dismay. He laid hold on the shoulder of the dead man and turned him on his back. He had no time to straighten and give the war cry of alarm, for that instant Oliver was on him. A bone-crushing grip fell on the throat of Yellow Wolf, so that all sounds were stifled before so much as a whisper could be uttered. He reached for the knife in his belt; but, before it could be drawn, a fist as hard and rough as a craggy stone thudded against the base of his jaw — and all the strength and the cunning of Yellow Wolf was lost in darkness.

And now Oliver Tay crouched close over the fallen body, knife in hand. One stroke would dispose of this warrior, also, and leave him free to carry on his work of destruction until White Hawk should curse the day that brought him with his marauders to Loomis Valley. And yet he could not make up his mind to drive the cold steel home. He had seen this fine specimen of manhood in action, and the thought of snuffing out this life overcame Oliver. Another thought came to him — that it would be almost as well to take home one living Comanche as a prisoner as it would be to butcher a dozen here in cold blood. That was not the sort of work for which yellow-haired Oliver was intended. Little Capiño with his ever-ready knife would have been more at home on such an occasion. So he made up his mind, and retreated straightway, carrying with him the limp body of the warrior.

He reached the base of the cliff before Yellow Wolf recovered a little and began to groan and struggle. One grip of the mighty hands of Oliver Tay was enough to convince his captive that he was secured as thoroughly as though steel bands surrounded him. After that, there was no more struggling. A cruelly effective gag was thrust between the teeth of Yellow Wolf; and then Oliver herded him up a winding way which he could distinguish, now, along the face of the cliff — a sort of natural trail which turned and twisted many times but brought them to the top with comparative ease.

There he fastened the hands of the Comanche behind his back with his rawhide lariat and mounted into the saddle. Yellow Wolf made no protest but turned straight across the hills toward the trail for Siddon Flat, as though he knew the mind of his captor perfectly.

For half a mile they continued in this way. Then Oliver removed the gag and watched Yellow Wolf draw two or three deep breaths. That was the only sign which he made of his distress.

Said Oliver gloomily, in Spanish, for he knew that many of this tribe had learned that language during their raids into Mexico:

"What have I done to the Comanches, my friend, that they should burn my hay and turn my house to ashes and take away my cattle and my mules and my horses?"

The captive returned fluently enough: "An hour ago, I was a man and a Comanche. Now I am a sick dog. What does a dog know of the minds of the great Comanches?"

This seemed to Oliver a rather laconic manner of stating that his prisoner would not talk, and he could not help respecting the fellow all the more. They resumed their journey. A dull moon came up and shone faintly upon them through high-drifting clouds.

"What is your name?" said Oliver.

"I had a name," said the Indian. "Go ask the Comanches if they remember it. Ask the Apaches if they know me and how many of their scalps I took. But I have a name no longer."

Plainly, he was in a suicidal fit of despair; and Oliver murmured soothingly: "A man in his own tepee does not look for enemies, and neither does a brave beside his own camp fire. What has happened to you would not have happened if your friends had not killed their minds with firewater."

Yellow Wolf raised his head with a little snort of contempt and indignation. "That is true," he said, gaining a little of his old self-respect. "The white man always wins, either because he has big medicine or because he knows how to put a red devil into water and leave it behind him for the Indians. How many scalps," he added with a sudden irresistible burst of curiosity, "how many scalps did you take by the edge of the camp fire of White Hawk?"

"Not one," said Oliver, smiling in spite of himself. "There is only one dead Comanche there, and he will go to the happy hunting grounds because his scalp is on his head."

This was a patriotic youth, for he sighed with relief. He made no inquiry about his own fate, however.

"And how is it," said Oliver Tay, "that a drunken scoundrel like White Hawk can be the leader of heroes like you and send them to strike his blows for him and fight his battles?"

"White Hawk," said the young Indian gravely, "wears seven scalps and they are not all the scalps of Apaches!"

There was a grimness in his voice which kept Oliver Tay from asking what those scalps might be.

"White Hawk," went on Yellow Wolf, "has a great medicine. When he rides on the warpath, the young men do not die, but they come home rich and with scalps."

Oliver Tay said no more. For he saw that he could not extract information from this proud young man; and as for the exchange of interesting viewpoints, how could he expect to understand the secret workings of the mind of the Comanche and how could he hope that the Comanche could understand his? A million years of different ancestry forbade it. So they kept silently to the moonlit trail.

CHAPTER XXIV

The Feast

The moon had left the clouds and hung bright and high in the center of the heavens before they came to Siddon Flat. Oliver had not yet reached the edge of the town when the rapid hoofbeats of horses rattled down the road behind him; and he turned, half in fear lest a flying group of the Comanches might have hunted back toward Siddon Flat to intercept their captured warrior. But under the moon he saw now not the lean silhouette of Indians but men under broad-brimmed, peaked sombreros.

He laid his rifle across the hollow of his left arm and waited until, as they came closer, a shrill cry broke from one of them; and then a deep, ringing bass voice echoed the call. Oliver hastily thrust the rifle into its case and held out his hands as they swept around him — little Capiño, with his lean, wicked face lighted by pleasure, and big Carpio Vega laughing for joy and relief, and even that somber Antonio Morales smiling a little.

They told their tidings briefly. They had come to Siddon Flat, heard the rumor of Oliver's appeal for help which had not been granted; and then they had swept away to the valley to find what had happened and help if it were not too late. There they had found the smoking ruins of the house and the sheds and the stacks of hay, and they had come foaming back to Siddon Flat to report to Colonel Chisholm what they had seen and offer their services in guiding the troops. For they had no doubt that the flames which burned the house had consumed also the body of their friend, Oliver Tay; and they were hot for vengeance.

While Vega and Capiño related this tale, Antonio Morales was surveying the captive with his melancholy eyes that saw all things. "You have taken a prize," he said at last to Oliver Tay. "This tribe hasn't made a raid in the last three years without having Yellow Wolf in the thick of it. And this is Yellow Wolf in person."

So the eyes of the others turned back upon the captive, and the Comanche bore their scrutiny with a calm indifference.

"I've heard of Yellow Wolf," said Carpio Vega. "They say that he's so strong with a bow that he will shoot an arrow clean through a buffalo, now and then. And with a knife, he's a raging devil. And with a spear, he's a regular old-fashioned knight."

"He fought three Apaches two years ago," put in Capiño, who seemed to know of the prisoner as much as the others. "He was rushed by them. He killed one of them at a distance with an arrow. He took the second through the throat with his spear. And then, while the third was closed with him and running a knife into his body, this Yellow Wolf took the knife away from him and killed the last of the lot. But he was so weak from the wounds he had received that he barely was able to crawl away and nurse himself back to life, and so he missed all three of the scalps. But, Don Oliver, how did you get him?"

"I followed them up the north ravine from Loomis Valley, and I went down to the edge of their campfire light, to see what could be done with them. I put my hand on one of them by bad luck and had to knock him in the head when he grunted. Yellow Wolf, as you call him, came to see what was wrong; and so I took him away with me. I didn't have it in me to strangle such a fine-looking fellow, even if he was a Comanche."

Antonio Morales hissed softly between his teeth, and his eyes turned to balls of fire. "*Dios, Dios,* to have been there with you, brother! But there are enough left for our hunting."

"Speak to him, Antonio," said Oliver, "because you have their tongue; and ask the man why they came to raid me?"

Morales broke readily into the Comanche dialect. It was even said that, during his youth, he had been stolen away by these formidable people and had spent some years among them, which accounted to a certain extent for his skill on horseback and for his peculiar ability as a hunter and fighter. Yellow Wolf was so pleased to hear his own tongue, that he answered at once.

"He says," translated Morales, "that so far as he knows, none of the Comanches have any grudge against Don Oliver, except that White Hawk very much wanted to get rid of you, brother. And he offered ten of his best horses for the young brave who would bring in the scalp of the golden hair. And, finally, he sent out Yellow Wolf as a scout to learn what he could learn. But Yellow Wolf saw from a distance that you carried rapid lightning in your hand and were such big medicine that he saw you were not meant for him. He simply sent in his signal to White Hawk, in the distance; and so the lot of them simply came on to finish you off."

"Come in with me to the colonel," said Oliver Tay. "The sun is coming up in another moment. We'll have breakfast together; and then we'll take him to see the colonel, scalps and all. Now tell me about the rest of my friends. And what is Venales doing? And where is the band lying now? And is there any word lately of Diego Venustiano?"

He threw the questions at them with a gay abandon, and they answered them as fast as they could.

Roderigo Venales was not a day's march away, hungry to have Oliver Tay back with him, if he could get him; and for that special purpose he had permitted the three of them to make the ride to the town of Siddon Flat to try to persuade the new farmer to take a vacation from his cares. And the whole band was anxious to have him back.

As for Diego Venustiano, he had combed the mountains for them with a veritable army under his command. But still they had managed to escape from him. And they had dodged the officers of the law, and the rapid scouting parties of soldiers which were hunting for them steadily, here and there. There had been only one skirmish, when they were hemmed into a narrow, blind cañon by three score troopers.

"But the instant that we knew we were in a pocket," said Carpio Vega, "and before they could very well guess that they had trapped us, we whirled around and rode smash through them; and they fired at us as wildly as though they were blindfolded. We had no hurt at all."

"You forget Pedro, the Red," put in Capiño. "He was struck by a bullet that raked across his head. He died a day later, asking for red wine and a confessor."

"I said that we had no loss at all," said Carpio Vega again. "When we lose a fool and a drunkard, it is a blessing and not a pity."

Talking in this manner, they reached the edge of the town.

"Is it safe for us to show ourselves?" asked Carpio Vega.

"If it was before it is now. They know little about you here," smiled Oliver Tay. "They hear plenty about Roderigo Venales, from time to time; but he keeps his work well south of the river. If you're recognized here, it will be only by one of your own countrymen."

"That is a chance worth taking," said Capiño. "I smell roasting kid even as early as this. And I could eat an entire goat. I want wine, too, Carpio, in spite of what you say about drunkards. I want wine, and then I shall sing; for I am as happy to have Don Oliver with us as a wild horse when it sees its native mountains. Hello! Señora, here are four hungrier men than you can possibly have in your house, and a good wild Indian to pick the bones of that kid when we have finished with it. We shall pay you enough to buy a whole flock to take its place. Do we eat here, tell me? Or do we take good luck to that other house down the street which has a smoking chimney, also?"

"That is the Moreño woman," said the housewife eagerly. "She cooks no flesh except that of goats so old that it is like carving strips of leather. Come in, come in! I have a clean floor and goatskins for all of you. And may my tongue be withered if I charge you more for the cooked meat than the butcher would ask for it raw."

So they sat in the raw morning air inside the house of the woman, all in a circle, with the sleepy husband and two half-grown boys stumbling here and there, anxious to serve these unexpected guests, and pouring out raw Mexican red wine into cups for them. For they could see at a glance that these were not ordinary guests; and, if they had doubted, the sight of a real Indian as a prisoner would have convinced them that it was a great occasion.

It was pleasant to Oliver Tay. For he had spent so many months at hard labor that he had forgotten, almost, the cheerful ways of these men who lived outside the law, beyond the law. That other way, inside it, brought results, perhaps, in the long run; but it meant constant work, and a weary monotony of days one as like the other as twin brothers. But though these men toiled, they always had their eyes fixed on goals so rich and shining that their labor on the way seemed nothing.

"But when I left you, you were all rich," he said. "What has become of your money?"

Capiño made a wry face. "Tell the story of each of us, Carpio," he said, and covered his eyes with both hands, childishly, until the stories should be ended.

"Morales," said Carpio Vega, "went to Juarez and tried to double his prize with cards. And in two weeks he was naked. Capiño rode down to Vera Cruz and saw a pretty girl and decided that he would marry and become a householder. But he woke up one morning without a wife, without his money, and not even a trail by which to follow them. I went to Mexico City and for six weeks I forgot that I was Carpio Vega. But to forget costs money. However, I have no regrets."

That ended the story, and Oliver did not need to ask about the others in the band who had taken such treasure from Diego Venustiano; for he knew that their winnings had all gone much the same course. So he let the talk turn to happier things, while they feasted, all save the Indian, Yellow Wolf, who would touch nothing during his captivity but seemed to have his stern eyes already fixed upon his death.

CHAPTER XXV

Rumor

When one thinks how the strange destiny of Oliver Tay began to work, it seems as a matter of fact as though there had been a sinister conspiracy on the part of fate to defraud him of his just chances in life. For all who have read the history of Oliver Tay and considered it carefully, and all who have only had it by casual hearsay, must agree that there was nothing of the criminal about this man.

But he had developed certain bad qualities of temperament, rather than actual tendencies to sin. That is to say, the long quiet in which he passed the early years of his life, and the care with which his mother had shielded him had created in the manner of Oliver and to a certain extent in his mind a false calm. And a natural tempestuousness of disposition had been thoroughly masked. It was not until he began to live with Roderigo Venales and his men that Oliver, at length, was able to express himself freely. And there he found himself among circumstances and men so very wild that still there were more opportunities than he needed; and you might say that he never reached the bursting point.

But now matters had altered a great deal. Oliver Tay had been placed in such circumstances that he had finally lost his temper completely and had expressed his opinion of a colonel of the United States army in a ringing voice and in very broad language. And that outbreak was only a sign of more that was to follow. Still, there is little doubt that had nothing untoward happened, Oliver Tay would have confined his outbreaks to language alone. It was only the singular misfortune of Oliver that placed him in a situation where deeds were more to the point than words. Where words, as a matter of fact, were of no value whatever. So we come to the point where this odd tangle must be explained. We go back to the time when the companions were breakfasting on roast kid in the very early morning, in that humble house in Siddon Flat.

In the middle of the feast, little Capiño, hearing hoofbeats swinging down the street, glided to the door and looked out — suspicious little snake that he was — and then turned at once and said to his friends: "It is Pedrillo. What can have brought him here? Has he come to call us back? Hello, friend" — this to the woman of the house — "if we are asked for, there is no one here except your family. Close the door."

"It is too late," said Carpio Vega, who scorned such foolish and rather unmanly stratagems. "Keep the door open. If Pedrillo has a message for us, let him deliver it."

A moment more, and a dashing figure of a man

pitched out of the saddle and landed running. While the trained mustang was checking itself on braced and sliding hoofs, the *caballero* had turned in at the door of the house and stood suddenly panting before them — covered with dust, and a dust cloud still about him, but nevertheless brilliant through the mist as a sun, almost. Flaming gold buttons, and a golden scarf with a vast crimson fringe, and silver work here and there, and a radiant shirt of blue silk, and a closely fitted Mexican jacket, and even, on his heels, long arched Mexican spurs of gold, and a hat banded and heavy not with gold only, but with jewels also — such was the vision that flashed upon the eyes of the men in the shack. He took off his sombrero and waved it in cheerful greeting.

Said Carpio Vega sternly: "Do you know what men on this side of the river will say of you, Pedrillo? That you are too beautiful to be good." And he smiled a little.

But Pedrillo paid no attention to this remark. He had crossed the room with long, quick strides, and now he clasped with both his hands one of the big hands of Oliver Tay.

"Don Oliver, Don Oliver, do you remember me after almost a year? I am Pedrillo. Do you remember? When Venustiano's —"

"Hush!" said Oliver Tay smiling. It is easy to say too much and very hard to call the words back. I remember you perfectly, Pedrillo. I am very happy to see you."

He looked at the man and the woman of the

house, but they held up their hands and smiled. They could guess that such finery as Pedrillo wore had not been bought with honest money; but nevertheless, they admired his magnificence just as much — or perhaps a little bit more. For what is inherited money? Many a fool has it to spend, to be sure.

"We have no ears, friends," said the householder and his wife.

However, Pedrillo had been sufficiently warned, and now he rounded into the ear of Oliver Tay: "Venales is not two miles away. He sent me to find you. He cannot show himself in Siddon Flat, he might be known. Too many people have seen his face. He begs you to come out with me to visit him."

There was a flash in the eyes of Oliver Tay. He knew well enough what Venales would want of him. And now he was foot free and hand free, to be sure, and ready for a new start — no matter in what direction. But an instant of thought made him shake his head. There is no folly like placing oneself in the way of temptation, and the eyes of Oliver darkened again. "I must stay here, Pedrillo," he began, "for —"

"Listen, listen, Don Oliver," pleaded the youth, biting his lip with anxiety. "Venales has a five-year-old gray horse. He is wonderful. He climbs a mountainside as though he were flying it with the wings of an eagle. And Roderigo has promised him to me if I only so much as bring you out to talk with him. What harm is there in

186

talking, Don Oliver? What harm is there in that?"

This naïve appeal made Oliver laugh; and, when a man has laughed, half of his wisdom is tossed over his shoulder. "Very well," said he. "I'll go along back with you."

"God bless you, my kind friend," said young Pedrillo. "I shall have the gray. And I shall laugh at Roderigo, who swore that you would never come." He was fairly dancing with joy.

"Listen to me, Carpio," said Oliver Tay, turning to handsome Vega. "You can guess where I am going. Tell me, are you three safe in Siddon Flat?"

"We're safe enough. But you, Oliver, are you going —"

"Hush! I shall be back inside of the hour. Do not have any fear of that. In the meantime, look to Yellow Wolf. Take care of him as though he had a white skin because, no matter what deviltry he may have been up to in Loomis Valley, I have an idea that he has a heart as white as any man's. *Adios, amigos!*" And he was gone through the door with young Pedrillo.

Carpio Vega turned full upon the Indian brave, and he found that Yellow Wolf was staring after the departing figure of big Oliver Tay with a strange mixture of awe and wonder. And Carpio raised his finger. "Watch him, Antonio," he said to Morales. And Antonio Morales merely smiled, with infinite wickedness and infinite patience, like one who knew this business that was in his hands.

Now that they were left with the Indian on their hands, and Oliver Tay had gone to see the leader of their band, if all had gone well nothing should have happened while Oliver was away. But all did not go well, and that was owing to the prime creator of trouble in this world — rumor, which has a thousand tongues. For rumor had heard a whisper in the house of where the three waited; and how could it well be otherwise, seeing that there were two children and a woman in the place?

Rumor flew out of that house and sped across the village, and her tidings ran through ears like quicksilver and passed from tongue to tongue. She started as a mere whisper, she ended by being a shouting voice that reached the fort of Siddon Flat and hummed at the ears of the sentry at the gate, and passed instantly from him to his sergeant, and ran in haste from the sergeant to the lieutenant of the watch, and sped from the lieutenant to the captain of his company, and now behold rumor, in the gallant person of the captain, standing at the colonel's door. He was admitted and found the colonel at breakfast with his crony, the polite trader, Mr. Peter Sydham.

The colonel was not pleased with this interruption. His temper was never good before noon, and now it was very touchy indeed; for he was in the midst of certain busy plans with Mr. Sydham concerning contracts for supplies at the fort.

For instance, there were certain ways in which

cheap beef could be bought, from certain people who brought in cattle from the range without examining with too foolish a scrupulousness into the identity of the brands and the owners thereof. And the wise young colonel saw no good reason why some of that cheap supply of beef should not be diverted to the fort as a market. In that case, he could take part of the profits; and Mr. Sydham could take another part. So both parties would rest contented; the soldiers would have their beef, and the government would not have to pay a whit more for meat than it had ever paid in the past.

This was a line of thought so flawless that Mr. Sydham could follow it without the slightest difficulty, and he freely expressed his admiration at the clear-mindedness of the colonel. For his part, he declared that he knew exactly in what quarters to look for such beef. And, as a matter of fact, the same brilliant idea had occurred to him. Except that he felt a more equal division of the spoils would hardly be equitable. For all the colonel had to do was to see that the quartermaster accepted the new contract. Whereas Mr. Sydham incurred all the unpleasant necessity of dealing with the rustlers who brought in the beef — low fellows who soiled the ears of a gentleman with their profane conversation. So that Mr. Sydham believed that if he took two parts of the spoils of war and the colonel accepted a third portion, it would be eminently fair.

"I understand you perfectly," said the colonel.

"And besides," said Mr. Peter Sydham, "you must know that there is a great deal of danger, really. You can't trust thieves. And if these fellows let the word come out that I have been buying rustled cattle, why, it will not be well for me. It would ruin me as a trader in this part of the world forever and a day."

"That is sad," said the colonel, sympathetically. "But as a matter of fact, I am pressed for money. I have certain obligations in the East — family to keep up, you know. And besides, as the matter stands, though I understand exactly how you feel, perhaps I could find some other person who would think that he could undertake the job on a fifty per cent basis." He leaned back and spread out his palms in a gesture of regret.

Peter Sydham blinked a little and nodded, also. It was a bitter pill to swallow; but, as the colonel had so gently suggested, there probably were others who would be most willing and even anxious to meet his terms. Mr. Sydham was considering, and on the point of surrendering, when the summons came at the door; and the captain was brought in.

The latter saluted like a perfect model of a captain, which he was. And with his heels clicked together, and his chest thrust out, and his neck as stiff as a ramrod, he made his report: "Bad news from the town, sir; so serious that I thought I had better bring the immediate report of it to your ears."

"Another gun fight, I suppose, another gun

fight," said the colonel angrily. "I am not the undertaker and professional brother to the ruffians in this community, Lodge. I thank goodness that I have no interest in them. So let them bury their dead and have done with it. I shall not order out a single man."

"I beg your pardon, sir. Not gun fights — not in the town, that is to say. Indians — the Comanches — have been raided by night."

CHAPTER XXVI
Four Prisoners

The colonel had his faults, but he had his virtues also. He had a mind that worked as rapidly and as accurately as a steel trap, and he had enough presence of mind to have commanded an army on a field of battle. He said quietly now: "That is a different matter. The Comanches are a friendly tribe nominally. What fools have dared to raid them? Mexicans, I suppose?"

"I hoped that it would be that," said the captain, "but it seems that there is an American citizen mixed up in the affair and that makes it our business also, I presume."

"An American citizen? Some infernal renegade!" snapped the colonel.

"A fellow named Oliver Tay, I believe," said the captain.

The colonel looked at Mr. Sydham, and Mr. Sydham looked at the colonel. There was a mutual understanding of great depth between them.

"And I believe," said the captain, "that he is not a renegade but has seemed to be an honest farmer."

"That will do, Captain," said his commanding officer. "You have a grave fault, Lodge. You don't keep your eyes and your ears open, and that's what you must do in a frontier community. I know Tay. A ruffian with a gentleman's manners — up to a certain point. Absolutely capable of conducting a raid on peaceful Indians! Eh, Sydham?"

"Frightfully sorry to say so," said Peter Sydham. "But the fact is, a very violent nature — and he was here talking nonsense about Comanches only yesterday."

"There's nothing to do, Captain," said the commander of the fort, "except to seize the entire party and bring them before me at once. Can they be found?"

"They are in a house in the town, now."

"Excellent. I'll be glad to see this fellow Tay again, face to face. A little happier to see him than he will be to see me, I take it! Take your company —"

"There are only four in the entire party, sir."

"Take plenty of men, Lodge. When you are dealing with desperadoes, numbers are never foolish. You can not play too safe. Have them here as fast as you can. I'm glad that you've brought this news to me promptly, Lodge. National complications are apt to rise out of those raids. The entire Indian tribe is likely to take the warpath on account of some such outrage. What did Tay do?"

"How many he scalped, no one knows. But he has brought a prisoner back with him."

"Some chief to hold for ransom, I suppose,"

said the colonel. "Very well. Have them here at once. I'm impatient to see them. Be sure that you use the Indian well."

And Captain Lodge straightway marched out an entire platoon and doubled them down the village street at full speed. Rumor had roused them, and rumor led them straight to the correct house; and all in a moment armed men with fixed bayonets flooded around the little house. A window was kicked open by Morales — behold, the whole garden was packed with brown-faced soldiers. Carpio Vega tore down the rear door, and recoiled instantly before half a dozen leveled bayonets. They were surrounded and pressed against the wall instantly. But they were not yet down. There was a pair of pistols in the hands of Capiño and of Morales, also. And Carpio Vega carried a pair of his famous revolvers. They covered the invading riflemen.

"Now," said Carpio Vega, speaking his perfect English, "let's see this game start, my friends. We have done no harm in this part of the world. We have nothing to answer for. If you have come to arrest us, you've come to arrest the wrong men. And I want to ask you, at once, to bring forward your officer in command for an explanation."

"We'll explain afterwards," said the sergeant, pressing through the back door. But he stopped when he saw these three faces, ranged sternly in a semicircle in front of the impassive Comanche, Yellow Wolf.

"Captain Lodge! You'd better come in here to talk!"

Captain Lodge came in haste. "You'll only be held for an investigation," said the captain soothingly. "All that we want is the freedom of the Indian, of course —"

"You can't touch him," said Carpio Vega. "We are holding him here on our promise to a friend."

"You'll have to forget that promise," said the captain. "I have orders to set him free."

"That's a thing which we cannot do," said Vega.

"I have power to make you," said the captain.

"It will cost you ten men to kill the three of us," said Vega; "and you shall be the first of the ten, depend upon it."

Captain Lodge, for a moment, wished that he had not blundered so hastily into this crowded little house. But then, he was a brave youth; and he recovered his presence of mind at once. He said, "I have been sent to bring you to the fort; and I'll do it, if I have to die and half my men with me. If you can suggest any compromise that will get you to the fort I'm willing to listen. I don't want to be unreasonable!"

"That's very kind," said Carpio Vega. "Tell us, why we should go to the fort at all? What have we done?"

"Raiding a friendly tribe —"

"We've raided no friendly tribe."

"My colonel has sent me here to take you," said Captain Lodge, "I've waited long enough.

195

It's my duty to warn you —"

Carpio Vega looked into the face of the captain and saw two important things — that this youngster was in the first place perfectly brave, and in the second place that he was very excited. And, putting the two together, Carpio Vega knew that it was time to surrender — but not unconditionally.

He said: "I'll make this agreement with you. I'll go with you to the fort, and you can take the Indian with us, so long as you'll agree that Yellow Wolf is not to be set free until Oliver Tay agrees to it. We'll stay there willingly until our conduct has been examined into. Is that entirely satisfactory?"

The captain hesitated. "That seems a fair statement of terms," said he. "I ask you, Sergeant Berry, if you see anything wrong in accepting this offer?"

"Kind of looks to me, sir," said the sergeant appealed to, "that there's six reasons for it, and not one ag'in it!" And he glanced with a sour grin at the steady guns in the hands of the three Mexicans.

"I agree with you," said the captain. "I'll make that agreement."

"Will you shake hands on it, with each of us?"
"Of course."

Three strong, quick brown hands caught his and in another moment the procession started for the fort. The weapons of the three had been taken from them, with the exception of Capiño's

196

knife; for he swore that sooner than give up that knife, he would part with his right hand. The captain did not think it worth while to insist on the point. So they marched toward Fort Siddon; and, first in the procession, escorted rather than guarded by the soldiers, with his hands now free, and his head as high as ever, was Yellow Wolf.

Just what had happened, he had not the slightest idea, but he was fully able to comprehend that a turn for the better had taken place in his affairs due to the arrival of the soldiers. And now he was more highly regarded by them, apparently, than were the three Mexicans who stalked behind him, each closely guarded.

They reached the fort, they passed through the gate, and they were brought before Colonel Randolf Chisholm in his office. And Peter Sydham, still in the next room, listened with a beating heart and a hungry ear and a soul of malice, hoping to hear the voice of Oliver Tay. There was no giant Oliver among them!

"How is this, how is this, Captain?" demanded the colonel. "Have you missed the worst man of the lot?"

"Oliver Tay was not with them, sir!"

"Set out and find him. Mount fifty men and scour the country for him. I must have him. These others are nothing, compared with him; because, when you get to the bottom of the business, you'll find that he was the root and source of all the trouble. Go at once!"

And the captain went.

CHAPTER XXVII
Waiting

It left the young colonel facing the three Mexicans and the Comanche. He felt himself swelling with virtuous wrath. And so he began simply, in a small way, as one sure of the enormity of the crimes of those who stood before him.

"What harm," said he, "has this Indian ever done to you?"

"None," said Carpio Vega, who was always the spokesman.

"And with no harm done," said the colonel, "you seized him by force."

"We did not," said Carpio Vega; "but Oliver Tay took him, out of a whole war party."

"Oliver Tay? Oliver Tay?" echoed the colonel wrathfully. "And can you tell me what possible excuse that young man could offer for such an act while we are at peace with the Comanches?"

Carpio Vega was a man of much self-control; and, while Antonio Morales and little Capiño showed their teeth like angry wolves, Vega said merely, "Perhaps Don Oliver was hasty. But he grew a little impatient. It irritated him when he saw his cattle and horses driven off."

"Ha?" echoed the colonel. "Does he accuse

198

them of that? But I tell you, I know that most of the cattle rustling is done by the white men themselves, and then blamed upon the Indians. Is that all?"

"Not quite," said Carpio Vega.

"What else, then? What else, man?" snapped the colonel.

"Why," said Carpio gravely, "it is a matter of fact that this same Comanche and the rest of his war party burned the sheds and the barns and the haystacks and the plows and tools of Oliver Tay, and finished off by plundering his house and setting fire to that, also. So that up in Loomis Valley there is only a drift of ashes and blackened timbers where there was once a fine farm."

The colonel listened with a flushed face and with startled eyes. For he could not help remembering that this was the very danger which Oliver Tay had feared, and which he had brought word of to the fort. His mind flashed back to army headquarters, and to a court-martial for neglect of duty. "What proof? What proof?" asked the colonel. "What proof that the Comanches did this thing?"

"Oliver Tay saw it with his own eyes," said Carpio dryly; "and, to get a witness of the fact, he followed the Comanches, and took this man alive and brought him back."

The colonel was stunned. Mr. Sydham had warned him that young Tay was dangerous; but the colonel could hardly conceive of a man foolhardy enough to approach, singlehanded, the campfire of marauding Indians, and actually to bring off a living prisoner as a proof of what he had done. So he straightway ordered the three Mexicans and the Indian into confinement.

"We will investigate this matter to the roots," said the colonel. "Now where is Oliver Tay?" He called in Peter Sydham.

"You have put me in the wrong, Sydham," he said. "This Oliver Tay we think to be a scoundrel, but even a scoundrel may have the right on his side now and then. It seems that his farm was raided and burned to a cinder, and these Comanches have done the trick. I am horribly in the wrong, Sydham, owning to your advice."

"Wait a few hours, and you'll find that Oliver Tay has put himself far more in the wrong than you," said Peter Sydham with a faint smile.

"It is a time for action," said the colonel, "not for waiting. There is nothing more deadly than to do nothing when things are going wrong." It was an old maxim which he had inherited from his father.

"However, you should wait," said Peter Sydham. "I tell you that I know the blood of these Tays. There was his uncle who came west and lived like a wild man and became a great trading agent. There was his father who loved a duel better than a dance. There was his grandfather who captained a privateer in the war of 1812 and finally was blown out of the water because he insisted on fighting a man-of-war at half-pistol shot! And the further you go back in the history of the Tays the deeper you'll find them dipped in fighting. It's the sign of the clan. And now you have sent the captain for Oliver, but the captain won't come back with him."

"Ah," said the colonel, "you take a great deal for granted." But, nevertheless, he was impressed by the surety of Mr. Sydham.

"I take a great deal for granted, because I know these people perfectly. All that you need to do is to keep the Mexicans and the Indian in captivity for a few days."

"And then?"

"Oliver Tay will come to get them out."

"Snap his fingers in the face of the United States army? Tush, Sydham! Impossible!"

"You will see," said Peter Sydham. "I tell you, I know this fellow. Now at the present time he is in a position to make a complaint against you to your commanding officer. But if he tries to take the law into his own hands — that would remove a burden from your shoulders, Colonel Chisholm?"

"Gad," said the colonel, "you are a clever fox, Sydham! Tell me why you hate the boy so thoroughly? Is it because, as the rumor has it, you've slipped his inheritance out of his pocket, and married his mother so that he wouldn't sue you for what you took?"

Peter Sydham started to grow indignant. But then he thought better of it and leaned back in his chair with a shrug of his shoulders. "I don't pretend that I'm disinterested," said he. "He's a poisonous rascal, Chisholm. I'll never be better contented than when I hear that he has gone to his long account. And I begin to think that you have the same attitude toward him."

The colonel began to frown. Then he, also, changed his mind; and the two smiled at one another in a sinister agreement that boded very ill for Oliver Tay.

But Oliver had no thought of the colonel and Peter Sydham at that moment, for he was in the act of dismounting with his guide at the narrow mouth of the cañon whose boulder-strewn floor angled sharply up into the mountains, some two short miles from Siddon Flat. He had no time to take a single step when a man with a nervous step and keen, impatient eyes came out in front of him and then hastily toward him with a shout. The call brought a swarm of a dozen men from the boulders and they rushed about Oliver Tay — wild, unshaven, fiery-eyed fellows who wrung his hand and called his name as though he were the brother of them all. Oliver Tay of flawless ancestry, brother of these casehardened outlaws and cutthroats and robbers! A year dropped from him. He could see the other days when he had ridden with them, and camped with them, and learned their ways. And it seemed to Oliver that that had been the one happy and free time in his life.

Then Roderigo Venales waved the others away. He took Oliver aside and they sat together on a broad-backed stone. "I have heard everything," said he, "what White Hawk's war party has done to you and your farm. And I've come to ask you again, Oliver. Are you ready to join us?"

Oliver sighed. And he looked around him at the brown, sun-brightened faces of the mountains near at hand, and the more distant peaks looming through tender mists of blue. Then he shook his head. "To be a free man — that's very well for me," said he. "But to hold a gun under the nose of a man and ask for his money, to stop a train, to raid a pack line of mules — could I do that? No, Venales, I couldn't — though there is much that calls me to be a border bandit."

The other merely smiled. "We are not fools enough to ask you to," said he. "Nor even to want you to. Would I use my hunting knife to chop wood, or my ax to break stone? Every man has his particular use. And we have a need for you. I can plan the work we have to do. With Vega and Morales I can lead the men to the work I lay out.

"But, after that, there is the duty of dividing the spoils. And in the camp there are always a thousand disputes arising. We need a judge. Last month I lost three of my best men through knife fights. It's what ruins us. We no sooner have a strong band together than fights break them up. We need a judge and there's only one man in the world whose honesty we know and trust, and whose courage we have proved, also. We mean you, Oliver. And that is why I have come back here again to ask for you. We don't expect you to ride with us in our raids. We don't wish you to stop any man with a filled wallet. The more honestly you treat the world, the more we can honor your judgments over us. What do you answer to that?"

Oliver took out his hunting knife, long-bladed, heavy in the handle, balanced to perfection. There was a young sapling with a three-inch stem some paces away; and, as he juggled the knife thoughtfully up and down in his fingers, he suddenly spied the little tree, its silver bark glistening in the sun. His hand darted forward, the knife slid from his fingers and became a bright streak that ended abruptly. Yonder stood the knife fixed almost to the hilt in the trunk that was shaking there with a sharp, shrill, humming sound, like that of an angry hunting wasp. Capiño had taught him that valuable trick.

"It is all very well," said Oliver Tay with another sigh. "And, if I could trust myself as much as you trust me, I think that I might go with you."

He brought a revolver into his hand with a lightning gesture. It spouted a sudden cloud of smoke, jagged across the lightning streaks of red fire. And the hunting knife suddenly loosened and fell from the tree to the ground. So accurately had those shots been placed that they had torn away the wood and literally blown the knife loose without touching it.

"But," sighed Oliver, "I have learned some things too well to trust myself. And suppose that

I got tired of throwing knives and bullets at trees, Venales? Have you thought of that? Suppose that I grew interested in living targets? No, at heart I, too, am a border bandit."

CHAPTER XXVIII

Cousin vs. Cousin

If Roderigo Venales had been a little more of a rascal and a little less of a man, he might have tried persuasion; but, as it was, he could not help remembering that if ever a man had owed his life to another, he, Venales, had surely owed his existence to Oliver Tay.

And therefore he did not strive to persuade. He merely said: "Wherever we are, Oliver, we are waiting for you and hoping to have you with us. *Adios*, then, *amigo!* Go quickly before the others see you going, or they will try to hold you with their hands and keep you with them. For a fortnight, now, there has been no talk except of how we may get you back to us. We have ridden five hundred miles for nothing."

So Oliver went slowly back toward Siddon Flat, filled with regrets — not regrets, surely, that he had given up the life of an outlaw, but deep regrets that he could not use the kindness which he felt for these wild fellows and which they felt for him. He went on, as I was saying, at a slow pace, with his head down, when he was suddenly confronted on the road on the outskirts of the village by a squad of four of the hard-riding cavalry who were under the command of the colonel at the fort; and now they had that same weather-bitten sergeant at their head who had presided at the taking of the three Mexicans.

So he simply threw his cavaliers in a loose semicircle; and when Oliver Tay looked up, he found himself thickly surrounded, just as he reached the mouth of a little alley.

"Put up your hands!" the sergeant was saying.

Oliver obediently raised them above his shoulders and looked with his fearless eyes into the face of the sergeant. "And what is all of this about?" he asked calmly.

"Nothing of importance," said the sergeant, "except that you'll go along with us to the fort, my hearty, and join up with your greaser pals, there."

"My greaser pals?" echoed Oliver Tay calmly.

"The three that was taking care of the Comanche," said the sergeant. "They're all waiting for you, old-timer. Are you ready to come along peaceable? The colonel'll be glad to see you. Fall in behind him, Murphy and Jones. Take his bridle, Griggs. Harrison, you might take his guns."

They closed in on Oliver Tay with the assurance of men whose duty is just about accomplished, and certainly the idea of resistance had never occurred to one of them. For they had five guns to cover Oliver Tay; and he was a lone man, with his hands above his head. But the mention of two things had vastly disturbed him. In the first place, he was stung to the quick to know that, on account of him, the Mexicans had been taken into the fort with Yellow Wolf. In the second place, the mention of the colonel was like a knife thrust to him, for he knew that after the manner in which he had parted with Chisholm only the day before, there would be no tender treatment in store for him at the fort.

"I'd like to know what I'm accused of," said Oliver Tay.

"Accused of messing up half of the Comanche nation and getting them ready for a war rampage in revenge," said the sergeant. "Come alive, Smith!"

"All right," said Private Smith, "as soon as I can —"

The rest of his speech remained unuttered, for Oliver Tay had dropped his great hands from the air upon the unlucky sergeant. That gallant soldier had not even a ghost of a chance to defend himself before he was torn from the saddle, twisted over in the air; and, before his first yell of alarm had begun to ring through the air, his body was being securely gripped, and he was held as a sort of shield between Oliver Tay and the guns of the cavalrymen. And Oliver, with the pressure of his knees, turned his horse into the alley mouth. "Keep back your men, Sergeant," he said, "and there'll be no harm done you. But if they close on me, I'll wring your neck first and then wring a few of theirs."

"Keep back, boys!" screeched the sergeant.

"I'll be all right if you don't rush him. Larry, for goodness' sake hold off and keep away."

There was a snarl from the soldiers; but they would not disobey these pleadings, and so Oliver reined his horse into the momentary security of the alley. There he flung the sergeant to the ground, not hard enough to stun him, but hard enough to make him groggy on his feet for a moment, while Oliver turned his mount and sped away. He doubled straight back on the next street, turned again, and presently he was riding boldly down the main street of Siddon Flat while a hue and cry went crashing away through a far corner of the town. He went out of Siddon Flat, and he went straight back into the hills. There he paused to think the matter over.

From every angle it was a most disagreeable affair. If he moved in this matter, he was directly offending the majesty of the government of the United States. And if he did not move, then three of his friends would be left to rot in prison, or, worse still, they would be kept until someone recognized them as members of the gang of international criminals led by the celebrated Roderigo Venales.

So, with these thoughts bothering him, Oliver Tay grew gloomier and gloomier.

At length, he turned the head of his horse across country; and, turning down the first gulch, he came crashing straight into the view of none other than Mr. Peter Sydham. That gentleman, riding a dainty-stepping high-blooded horse, was returning after a little morning fishing expedition to secure the trout for his own lunch; for he was a fellow with a most fastidious appetite. He had a full basket under his elbow; and his heart was very high, when he unluckily came upon Oliver Tay. Mr. Sydham was not a coward; but now he gasped, leaned over the pommel of his saddle, and spurred for safety.

"Come back!" called the mellow voice of Oliver. "Come back, or I'll shoot your horse from under you."

Mr. Sydham turned and looked back, obediently; and, as he saw the long rifle that glimmered at the shoulder of Oliver, he knew that this young man could verily live up to his word — every letter of it. Therefore Mr. Sydham reluctantly reined in his horse and returned. He sat the saddle biting his fat lips. "You startled me, Oliver," he admitted.

"That's why I want to have you back here, Cousin Peter," said Oliver Tay. "If you had stopped willingly for a chat, I would never have thought of bothering you; but, when a fellow turns pale, it begins to look as though something is on his conscience. When he deliberately runs away, why, Cousin Peter, that would be taken in any court as a direct proof, wouldn't it? You're something of a lawyer, I believe. Tell me if I'm not right!"

Cousin Peter had turned from white to red. "As a matter of fact, Oliver," said he, "you've become such a rough-handed fellow that I'm rather in doubt of what you might do; and you haven't been very friendly."

"The point is," said Oliver, "that I want to find out what could have been bearing down on your conscience so heavily, just now. And could it, by any chance, have had anything at all to do with the quarter of a million that Crossman Tay left to me and which you manipulated away while I was in Mexico?"

"Good gracious, Oliver," said Mr. Sydham, "does your mind still turn on that?"

"When you married my mother, Cousin Peter," said Oliver, "I thought that I must keep my hands off you. But the more I think of it, the more I feel that an investigation of what happened to that money might be a very good thing."

Mr. Sydham made a gesture of bewilderment. "If I had the fortune you speak of," said he, "would I not be back in the East, enjoying it?"

"Unless," said Oliver, "you decided to send my mother back there out of harm's way, while you stayed here and tried to make that money grow and multiply? That's rather logical, isn't it? You knew that this country produced that quarter of a million, and perhaps you thought that you could stay on here and invest it properly."

"Oliver, Oliver," sighed the older man, "is there no faith in you?"

"None," said the cold young man. "And I have heard, besides, of various investments you

211

have made in cattle and in a fur-trading company."

Mr. Sydham began to perspire freely, "My own capital!" he exclaimed. "It had nothing to do with your own money, my dear boy. I have showed you the accounts by which I very foolishly made many mistakes and finally lost all of your money." He added hastily: "Not that I ever intended to cut you adrift, Oliver. No, no! I have always intended to make some sort of provision for you. But, as a matter of fact, you have been so very high-headed that I could not get you to listen to reason, in these respects or so much as take a penny of what I should very gladly have given."

"There, you see, is the rub," said Oliver. "I need money, of course, but I don't want charity even from Cousin Peter. But as for those accounts — why, accounts are simply figures written on a sheet of paper, and anyone with a pen and a bit of imagination could construct them, eh?"

"Heavens, Oliver, would you accuse me of stealing from you?"

"You're a clever fellow, Cousin Peter," said Oliver. "However, I've made up my mind that when I get a chance I'll have to start an investigation of that old affair. I give you warning now — so that you'll have a chance to get your accounts in even better shape."

"Oliver, Oliver, what will your mother think and say?"

"She is a trump card, I admit; and she is in your hands," said Oliver grimly. "But we'll have to see how the game is played. Good-by, Cousin Peter!" And he turned his horse away.

CHAPTER XXIX

The Face at the Window

Every man with any intellectual kingdom likes a bit of leisure, now and then, to explore for undiscovered country, or wander again through twice-traveled regions; and so it was with the colonel who, unless he was on active service, usually managed a quiet evening with a book and an occasional sip of whisky and water. He had those comforts now; and, with his heels hanging on the edge of an extra chair, and a fire in the open hearth banishing the evening chill, he looked now and again, lazily, through the open window across the room, toward the haze of blue beyond.

He knew that that haze represented the night sky, infinitely distant; but, to the eye, it seemed in touching distance of the hand. And it reminded the colonel of other things which seemed close and were not — such as a higher grade, for instance. He would have traded all of those stars in the heavens for just a small one of golden threads to sew onto his collar; but he knew that to become a brigadier general needs great luck or a great war — plus brains.

So he banished his own problems, and re-

214

turned to his book at the very moment that the tender blue of the night sky beyond the window framed a looming bulk of head and shoulders. Like a panther, the stranger slid through the window. One foot was already on the floor when the colonel looked up into the face of Oliver Tay and the steady muzzle of his revolver.

He started to rise, but thought better of it and leaned back in his chair, while his eyes flashed to the two doors of the chamber through which help could come. Indeed, footsteps were constantly going up and down the corridor, and the orderly was surely due to make his report before many moments. That comfort was instantly removed.

Mr. Tay, without a word, turned to secure those doors one after the other. I say that he "turned," and that is the only word. Only from the very tail of his eye did he keep the colonel under observation, and Randolf Chisholm was terribly tempted to reach for the pistol on the chair beside him. But he resisted that temptation; for something in the very negligence of the manner in which that other gun was held made the soldier feel that the hand of Oliver Tay was as sure as death itself. So he made no move while the key was turned in the lock of each door. Almost instantly there was a gentle rap.

Oliver Tay motioned across his shoulder. "You can't be bothered," he murmured softly.

"Busy," called the colonel in echo. "Can't be bothered with the report now."

"Very good, sir," said the faint voice of good discipline which does not recognize in this world such a thing as disappointment. And martial heels tapped rhythmically away down the hall.

"You have four men that I want," said Oliver Tay, "the three Mexicans and the Comanche. I'll have them here. Quickly, if you please!"

"You'll have me order the four of them here and turn them over to you?" said the colonel gently.

"Yes."

"By what authority, Tay?"

"By an authority with six voices," said Oliver Tay. And he twitched the muzzle of the revolver upward as he rested on the arm of an easy chair.

"That," said Randolf Chisholm, "would be treason!"

"Treason," said Oliver Tay, "is a very strong word; but death is a stronger one."

"Do you mean that you would shoot me down like a dog?"

"I think that you have a right to that name," said Oliver Tay. "Yes, Colonel, I would shoot you down like a dog. So send for them at once. I am in a hurry, as you may guess."

The colonel leaned a little forward in his chair. "Do you know that the Chisholms have served in the army of our country for three generations?" he asked.

"I trust that the service will not end tonight," said Oliver Tay coldly.

"Perhaps," said Randolf Chisholm. "But not

because of cowardice, Tay; I shall not send for the men."

Oliver Tay looked at the other with new ideas, as though he were seeing in him a veritable continent of unexpectedness. "Do you think that I have been bluffing?" he asked.

"I do not care to think about you," said Chisholm.

"Is that final?"

"Perfectly final," said the soldier.

"I am sorry," said Oliver; "but you are about to die. You have hounded me like a dog. You have seized four men over whom you have no authority. Chisholm, are you ready?"

The colonel sneered and set his fine, fighting jaw.

The revolver rose and steadied, and the terrible eye of Oliver Tay looked straight down the barrel and into the heart of his victim. "Have you any last message, Chisholm?"

"Not to be delivered by you," said the colonel. Little beads of perspiration had gathered on his forehead; and he leaned a trifle forward in his chair, as though to meet the tearing shock of the bullet.

Suddenly the gun fell to the hip of Tay. "I never knew before that a scoundrel could also be a brave man," said Oliver Tay. "*Adios*, Colonel; I give you this last piece of advice. When you come hunting for me don't ride at the head of your men." He stepped back to the window, slipped gracefully and smoothly through it and was suddenly gone.

The colonel stared after him for a heartbreaking half of a second. He felt that he had been so close to death that he still could hardly consider his life as being sound and safe. Beyond that window, he knew, the roof of the barracks commenced; and therefore he did not attempt to see where Tay had gone. Instead, he rushed for the doors of his room, shouting as he went. The key had barely turned, and had flung the door open when he saw the orderly and two barracks servants running down the hall. He met them with a blasting shout: "Oliver Tay is in the fort. He still hasn't had time to leave, perhaps. Spread the word! Call Captain Dickson! Turn out the guard!"

And, as they sped away like frightened rabbits to do his business, he himself rushed after them to lead in the hunt.

In the meantime, Oliver Tay had remained crouched outside the window of the colonel's room; and, the moment that he saw the room empty, he slipped back through the window. He was standing beside it when he heard three guns fired in rapid succession and, at the same time, a rapid fire of orders called and repeated, and the rush of men getting hastily into line. It pleased him immensely, to be able to stand here and watch by the starlight the search for himself. He found the colonel's box of cigars — fine, long, black ones; and he lighted one and began to smoke it carefully, with due enjoyment. He puffed that blue-brown smoke through the window and saw the gathered soldiers disperse in groups — some on rattling horses, and some on foot. And yonder he could distinguish the very tones of Chisholm's clarion voice.

It would not take them long to make sure that he was not within the walls of the fort, he felt; and therefore he waited while the cigar burned shorter. He waited, and picking up pen and paper, he wrote:

Dear Chisholm: Courage is a splendid attribute, especially in a soldier. I could not help coming back to let you know that there is something in you which I admire.

Oliver Tay

He left the paper, picked a few more cigars from the box, and then glanced out the window again. It seemed to him that the uproar was rapidly leaving the fort and passing away through the town, though there was plenty of bustle within the stockade, still. Now he went out of the window again and ran in his stocking feet across the roof of the long barracks. He knew what section was given over to the use of the confinement quarters, and he made straight for that portion of the building.

He dropped flat, his head projecting over the eaves so that he could look down into the arcaded passage which passed before the cells. Of the two guards, one had been called away to join the hunt, or else he was not at his post. The second man wandered up and down with his thoughts far more on the other events of the night than on the prisoners whose barred doors were behind him. Now a sudden crackling of musketry made him run a pace or two into the open parade ground and look wildly about him.

That instant Oliver Tay sprang from gathered feet and hands like a beast of prey, and all the weight of his body struck the guard. The luckless soldier collapsed and lay in a jumbled heap to be picked up by the back of the coat and carried by Oliver back into the shadows. There his hands were tied, and a section ripped from his own shirt was fixed in his mouth. The guard's keys were taken from his pocket; and now, sitting up in the darkness, the bound and gagged man watched the figure of the giant go down the line of doors.

"Carpio!" called Oliver softly.

And a voice just as guarded answered: "Here, brother!"

One key after another gritted in the lock. Then it opened, and suddenly three men flooded into the passage.

That bound and gagged guard knew Spanish; and he heard the rescuer say, "Where is Yellow Wolf?"

"In this next room. Let him stay there, or do you want to let him —"

"He comes with us."

Another moment, and the next door was ajar; and Oliver called, "Yellow Wolf!"

The tall Indian stepped to the entrance. "I am ready," said the Comanche in his broken Spanish. And he straightened and stiffened a little, as a good warrior should when his death day has come.

But Oliver Tay was saying: "Here is a knife. It's the only weapon we can spare, now. Keep close with us, Yellow Wolf; and no harm will come to you, unless we all go down. Carpio, the stable is yonder." And he headed the fugitives in that direction.

CHAPTER XXX
Bought and Paid For

They crossed the parade ground, running at full speed. But though Oliver Tay was proud of his sprinting powers, he found Yellow Wolf running lightly and easily at his side. And with Yellow Wolf beside him they darted around the corner of the stable and came straight into a jumble of seven troopers in the very act of swinging into the saddle. Straight at the leader went Yellow Wolf with a yell of demonic fury. That wolf cry alone would have done the business of the trooper. The flash of the knife quite finished him. He forgot all about the pistols in his holsters and the saber at his side and saved himself from the knife thrust by toppling backward on the ground. Yellow Wolf, leaping into the saddle, whirled the horse about, and charged into the center of the little knot of troopers and horses.

But there was no resistance. They had started out as a belated group of searchers after skulking fugitives. They had not keyed up their nerves to meet the attack of five desperate fighting men. Two or three guns went off, and the bullets whistled aimlessly into the air while the refugees

222

seized the horses and mounted.

"Straight through the main gate and down the street," cried Oliver. "That's the last place that they'll look for us." And off they flew like five arrows from one string.

That gate was guarded night and day, as a matter of course — but guarded against danger from the outside not from within. And, as they rushed through, there was only one wailing voice that cried after them: "Hey, what the devil? Guard! Guard!" And a bullet hissed past their heads.

They paid no heed to that. They had put the fort behind them; and the only danger was what lay before, and that made peril enough. For Siddon Flat was now alive with hunters. Nearly every soldier had been sent out from the fort, some in squads on foot, and some on their horses. The foot men hunted through the houses, and the riders scoured the streets; but only one body of men appeared before the fugitives, and this was a group of a dozen troopers led by the colonel in person.

Even these were taken at a tremendous advantage. Oliver, urging his horse on with heels and the quirt which he had found at the saddlebow, saw a stream of cavalry issuing from a byway; and in front of the men he recognized the erect form of Randolf Chisholm. But Oliver and his four companions were that instant upon them and through them, without firing a single shot; and then, as Chisholm discharged his pistol and shouted to his men, the troopers darted off in pursuit.

A stern chase is never a long one. It is partly because the fastest horse may break his heart in the first wild effort to overtake the fugitives in the first burst, and partly because the keenest hunter has not the same desperate energy as the hunted. There were some fine horses in that troop of the colonel's men; and Chisholm himself was soon in front, overtaking the five riders with every stroke of the long legs of his Kentucky gelding.

But one man cannot ride down five and expect to beat them in hand-to-hand conflict. The colonel was sharply reminded of this when Antonio Morales, turning in the saddle, marked the distance by which the colonel led his men; and then unslinging the cavalry carbine, which he found in the case beneath his leg, he tried a snap shot. If he had had his own rifle, it would have been Chisholm's last moment on this earth; but, even from the strange gun, he sent a bullet hissing so close to the colonel's head that that courageous warrior drew rein a little. His cavalrymen came up with him, but riding at their pace they could only gain inch by inch or not at all upon the fugitives.

They were out in the hills now, when little Capiño, with two fingers between his lips, sent a long whistle and then another screeching through the night air. And then two guns were fired.

"Are they sending signals to friends ahead?" asked the colonel suspiciously of the sergeant who kept beside him.

The sergeant shrugged his shoulders. This whole affair was so confused and so jumbled that he could not make head or tail of it. They had come out to hunt one man. Instead, they found that the one man had pierced through the guards at the fort and had liberated prisoners to join him; and so the sergeant said: "Goodness knows what'll come of it, sir. Anything is possible, it looks like."

He had no sooner said it, than the colonel and all of the rest saw a dozen shadowy horsemen pour out from the mouth of a boulder-choked ravine, and, with them, the fugitives turned tail and fronted the soldiers, while a long-range rifle fire sent bullets spatting upon the stones around them.

The colonel called for a halt at once and filed his men off into the shelter of a rock mass as large as a house. There had been enough guns fired to serve as signals to the town, and already he could distinguish the beating of hoofs as riders hurried toward the sound of the guns. But until they came up, Chisholm had no intention of letting his men be butchered by the superior numbers of fellows who could shoot as cleverly as that same renegade who had recently put a bullet within an inch of his cheek.

Far in front of them, the men of Venales were swinging off up the rocky cañon and disappearing into the deeper shadows of the valley. And never was there a more joyous crew, for they felt that they were taking with them a richer prize than any they had seized in many a month.

Yellow Wolf, marking all this with wonder, drew back his horse beside Carpio Vega. The latter had regarded the Comanche for a long time with interest.

"Look, Yellow Wolf," said that stately gun fighter. "Yonder is an open way for you. No one is guarding you now. And why do you hesitate? Two seconds of heels and whip, and you are a free Indian once more."

At this, Yellow Wolf tilted back his head a little, so that the big cords of his neck thrust out, and the draggled feathers in his hair drooped, as he stared up at the stars of the sky. He seemed to find among them a means of explaining himself to his companion.

"I am not a child," said he; "and I am not unknown to the Comanches. The Apaches, also, know me a little," he added, with a grim note in his voice. "And when a man is sure that his tribe will not forget him, and when he has scalps at his belt or on the head of his spear, then it is time for him to think of dying well. No man dies well while he still owes a debt. I could have been left in that dark little room to die like a mangy wolf, prowling up and down before the iron bars. But the great chief came and spoke, and the door sprang open. I stood in the entrance, prepared to feel the knife thrust into my heart. But the great chief put the knife in my hand and said, 'Come with us. You will be safe.' Now, when the heart of a man has been bought and has been paid for, will an honest Comanche refuse to give what is no longer his?"

To this, Carpio Vega listened with the keenest attention. Then he nodded, and he said, adopting his language to the style of the Indian: "This is as true as the flight of a hawk is straight when it sees food."

Said Yellow Wolf, after a moment: "I was afraid that even such a man as the great chief did not have followers among the white men. But I see that he has his friends, even if they are not of his own tribe."

"I'll tell you this," said Vega. "Every man with a clear head and steady nerves, and a little grit belongs to the same tribe as Oliver Tay. And that, Yellow Wolf, was why he did not cut your throat. It was because he knew that you are a man like himself. You suspect that he saved you from the prison for the sake of butchering you later. But you are wrong. You are safer in his hands than in your own tepee in your own village."

So they rode on through the night. And now the darkness grew visible, like rolling smoke; and the vast mountains were seen rushing up from the earth toward the heart of the sky. Then granite slopes began to glisten with the light of the dawn. A dim clamoring below could be seen now, through a thousand feet of blue shadow, to be a little river, splintered to white against the rocks in its course.

Said Roderigo Venales to Oliver: "Do you remember, Oliver, when we climbed the rope ladder and turning our heads all that we could see beneath us was the line of the climbing slaves with the ore baskets at their backs? It is better to turn and look down on this, eh?"

"It makes the back of my legs ache," confessed Oliver, with a smile. "And there is the sun."

There was not a heart in that column so brutal and calloused that it felt no awe when the sun rose from a well of gold and orange flames and went towering up the sky, touching faces and hands with an instant warmth.

Little Capiño was the first to turn from that sight. He stopped his horse on the dizzy edge of a pinnacle of rock along the trail and pointed down. The others followed suit; and Oliver, seeing a long troop of riders winding up the valley beside the white waters, put his glass to his eye and examined the men more closely.

"I should have known it," said he. "I should have known that whatever was trouble for me must be game for him."

"For whom?" asked Venales, scowling.

"That fellow," said Oliver, "who rides beside the colonel at the head of the troopers, down yonder. There are other people who wish me no luck, I suppose; but there is only one who would be actually happy if I were to fall off a cliff. And now that I see he actually has a hand in the business of hunting me, Venales, I tell you that I would give my right hand to charity, if I could have my left hand in his throat. It's Peter Sydham."

CHAPTER XXXI
Yellow Wolf Pays a Debt

The troopers were traveling abreast of them — but a thousand feet lower down; and that thousand feet meant weary miles of traveling before they could come to grips with the fugitives. As for that, Venales did not worry. He had his men not on picture horses but on seasoned bronchos capable of traveling through these difficult mountains almost as easily as though they had been on a plain. And so they wound along their trail until the chief decided on a breakfast halt, and accordingly a brief pause was made.

It was then that Yellow Wolf was missed. No one could remember having seen him leave the line of march. Little Capiño, at that, showed his teeth in a grin.

"That's a true Indian!" he said. "They can make themselves disappear like something in a fairy story. You'll never see Yellow Wolf again. What nonsense were you telling me about that good Comanche, Vega?"

Carpio Vega hung his head, ashamed, and could not answer. They breakfasted. They rode on. Far ahead of them, and high, high on a rock against the blue of the heavens, they saw a magnificent mountain sheep with the sun flashing on his coiled horns. A long shot, perhaps an impossible one, it seemed, and therefore the call was instantly, "Morales! Antonio Morales! Now for your rifle!"

"You remember me now," said Morales with pretended sourness, though in reality he was as pleased as a child with a toy. "You remember me now that you want fresh meat. You that have not more than one eye to divide among you! However, there is someone else here that can do this business as well as I." And he handed the rifle which had been proffered to him to Oliver Tay.

Every day of his life, revolver and rifle had been sedulously practiced by Oliver, in the recent months. And yet, under the critical searching of these many eyes, he changed color a little; and he had to set his teeth hard to bring back some of his courage. He gave a single glance at the gun, weighed it for half a second in his hand; and then, shaking back his flood of golden hair, he placed the butt in the hollow of his shoulder.

"In a long shot," his teacher, Morales, had told him a year before, "sight above and below, and then split the difference, leaning for the wind. And shoot when you have to."

So Oliver waited until his nerves had gathered a sort of explosive force. Then he pressed the trigger. So great was the distance that there seemed an appreciable instant after the spurt of smoke before the mountain sheep on the pinnacle reared like a horse, and then toppled down from the height.

There was not much of the shape of the sheep left by the time it had finished falling into the narrow level of the trail. But it meant meat for the entire crew; and a few cunning hands and sharp knives instantly divided it into portions, while the rest of the horsemen rode on.

"Was there such hunting in Loomis Valley?" asked Venales.

"Hush!" smiled Oliver. "Loomis Valley is a place that I have heard of too often. I wish to forget it. Gregorio!"

"Yes, Don Oliver."

"That is a magnificent horse you are riding."

It was a glorious black, beautiful as a panther, and with a panther's marking almost invisible in the hide.

"It is a fine animal," said Gregorio. "Shall I tell you how I happened to catch him?"

"You have told it a thousand times," said Venales. "Why should we hear it again when —"

"I wish to hear it, Gregorio," said Oliver gently.

The outlaw flashed an ugly glance at his commander. "I shall tell you, then," he said to Oliver. "The others need not listen — may they all be confounded for throat-cutting thieves! Only honest men should hear about honest horses. But I tell you then, Don Oliver, that I went into a town in the Sierra Madre, no matter where, to look for something to do; and, while I lay behind a knot of brush, I saw a *caballero* ride by on his horse.

"The instant I saw him, I knew that he was mounted by the wrong man, and I saw another in the saddle. I saw, also, that this was the matter on which I was sent to this village. I jumped up and sent a bullet past his nose. And, after he had stopped, I took the horse and rode away; because you see, señor, that I could not allow such a fine horse to have a coward in the saddle. I did not like the saddle, either; and so I waited for a chance to get this one with the silverwork, which is almost worthy of him. Ever since that time I have been waiting to find the man who is really worthy to sit on his back in this same saddle. And at last, Don Oliver, I have found him. He is yours." He jumped from the stirrups as he spoke; and, with a bow, he placed the reins in the hand of Oliver Tay.

"What, Gregorio!" exclaimed Oliver. "Do you think that I could rob you of such a —"

"It makes no difference, really, on what I ride," said Gregorio, half bitterly and half smiling. "I can rob from one beast's back as well as from another. But the black was intended for you. He will never fail you, night or day. He will answer a feather's weight on the reins. He will lift his ears whether you curse him or praise him. And he will grow fat eating thistles and run a hundred miles a day even under your weight. Take him and thank the mare that foaled him, not Gregorio!"

So Oliver, seeing that the man was in earnest, accepted that princely gift, and suddenly found his weighty body carried as though on the back of the wind.

As for Gregorio, it was plain that he had made himself an important member of the gang by that stroke of policy and generosity combined.

"I thought that he was no better than a hired man," whispered Venales to Vega; "but you see that he has a heart. This will help to tie Oliver to us. That Gregorio is a jewel of a man."

And Gregorio himself, as he had promised, seemed as content and as much at home on the back of Oliver's old horse as he had been on the black stallion.

They made a long march that day, and sighted the troopers no more. So they came out on a little plateau and camped there to eat the mutton which Oliver's trigger finger had presented to them.

The moon rose and lifted the many ridges of the range into misty view, when the patrol was heard calling a challenge; and a moment later there was a shout of recognition. Presently they saw two riders and a man on foot coming rapidly toward the fire. One rider was the patrol. And when they came closer everyone could recognize the half-naked body of the other rider as that of Yellow Wolf. By a rawhide lariat he led a prisoner stumbling behind him, a weary, down-headed, dusty, footsore fellow whose clothes were torn to rags, he had stumbled and fallen so often on the terrible trail over which he had been passing that day.

They carne closer to the fire. Yellow Wolf, dismounting, took the lariat and placed it in the hands of Oliver Tay. And then, for the first time, Oliver recognized the prisoner, for it was none other than Peter Sydham. Peter Sydham with a noose around his neck! Peter Sydham, sick with fatigue and with terror and with despair, who now fell at the knees of Oliver and groaned:

"Oliver, Oliver, keep the red devil from murdering me! I have been walking half the day not an inch from death. I have had his knife at my throat a dozen times. He has taken me here to rip off my scalp and kill me. But you, Oliver, dear lad, you'll save me?"

"Stand up!" said Oliver.

Mr. Sydham rose to his feet. He cast a wavering glance around him at the circle of watching, silent faces, as one in the hope of finding pity as a beggar hopes to find a crust of bread, however wretchedly small. But there was no token of softness. Their eyes turned curiously but calmly from Oliver to the prisoner, and it dawned upon Mr. Sydham that these fellows looked to Oliver Tay with the perfect confidence of men who felt he could do no wrong. And it seemed to Peter Sydham that he had never before seen formidable men so utterly in the hand of another as these were. In Oliver, therefore, was all his trust.

"Oliver, dear boy —" began Sydham again.

"Be quiet a moment," said Oliver Tay. And

he turned to Yellow Wolf. "Brother," said he, "this morning I saw this man in the valley and was willing to give my right hand to have him. How did you take him?"

Yellow Wolf allowed the faintest trace of a smile to appear upon his features. "They went like fat cattle," said Yellow Wolf. "Their eyes were filled with dust when they looked down, and with the brightness of the sun when they looked up. They went slowly. Their horses melted with sweat. And the men turned red and gasped in the heat. Three Comanche boys could have herded them into the river."

His nostrils quivered fiercely for an instant; and in his eyes there appeared a spark of fire, as though he still tasted in afterthought the plentiful crop of scalps which might have been reaped. "However," said Yellow Wolf, "I followed them. I watched their trail and their dust and heard their talk and one after another strayed for a little. And I let them go." He took a deep breath. Surely the patience of the Indian in his man hunt had been sorely tried on this day! He said at last: "Then this fat steer who kept with the bull all day" — such was his definition of the young colonel — "stopped to drink at a little stream; and, as the others rode past him, he stayed a moment kneeling by the water and bathing his face. I waited until he was done, and then I touched him on the shoulder." Another smile of savage delight crossed his face. His story was ended.

CHAPTER XXXII

Cousin Peter

The style of Indian talk was well known to Oliver. He said now, briefly: "I understand now why the Apaches run like sheep when they hear the Comanche war cry. It was well done, brother. Look! Here is a rifle which has been charmed by the greatest of all hunters, Antonio Morales. He has given it to me, and now I give it to you. It will not miss when the fight is hottest."

Yellow Wolf, trembling with pleasure, perhaps more for the compliment than for the value of the gift, took it with both hands and stepped back with a shining face.

And Oliver raised his head a little so that the golden hair fell back again. "Now, Cousin Peter," said he, "I have heard the entire story."

"Oliver, Oliver," said the other, attempting playfulness as he shook his finger at the big man. "Did I see you rewarding that rascal for the trick that he played me? However, I understand. You have had hard feelings about me, Oliver. Erroneously, to be sure, but you could not keep from sending that red tiger to play a joke on me! Rather a practical joke, but I forgive you, Oliver, with all my heart! I am really glad to see your clan, Oliver. Astonishing lot, on my honor! But now for a touch of brandy before my knees shake away under me. I'm so tired — dragged along through the dirt and over the rocks — my neck raw with the cutting edges of that infernal lariat. By heavens, Oliver, and all the while —"

Oliver smiled. And there was something in that smile that silenced the other utterly. He bit his lip and looked again to make sure that he was right; and, in fact, the eyes of Oliver Tay were just as cold as chilled iron.

"I don't suppose that I need to point out," said Oliver, "exactly how happy Yellow Wolf would be if I told him that I was through with you, and that he could do anything he pleased with you."

"Merciful heaven!" breathed Mr. Sydham. "Oliver, your mother —"

"There is mercy in God. Look for it in Him but not in me," said Oliver, "except under conditions."

He paused, and Sydham clamored trembling, "Whatever you wish, Oliver, dear boy! Whatever you wish! I am in your hands entirely!"

"We'll have the whole truth, then," said Oliver Tay. "We'll begin with the money and continue with that point. But in the first place I'll test your power to tell the truth by asking you one thing to begin with. Did you or did you not influence the colonel to treat me more like a dog than like a man?"

Mr. Sydham's eyes started from their sockets.

With all his heart he wished to dodge the truth; and yet he feared that, if he lied, he would be turned over instantly to the grim red man who was now handling the rifle with such significant fondness in the light of the fire. "Heaven forgive me, Oliver. We all have our sins. And I am no better than the rest. But the fact is, I was afraid that you might be dangerous; and the colonel — in short, I advised him to be just a little watchful."

"That's enough," said Oliver, controlling his voice. "I can guess at the rest. And now, the matter of the money. The quarter of a million, Cousin Peter!"

"Oliver, I swear on my knees that only place me safe again in reach of Siddon Flat, and you shall have every penny restored to you."

"Ah, you did not waste it all, then?"

"Will you believe me, boy?" pleaded the miserable Sydham. "I had your interests at heart all the while. But such a vast sum in the hands of a mere lad! I had the handling of it at first, you know, when we all grieved to believe that you were dead. And, while I was handling it, all of the investments turned out almost ridiculously well. I discovered that I had a sort of genius for finding out the good spots to place that money; and from farms to fur trading, whatever I backed panned out wonderfully.

"And then you appeared, Oliver; and I feared that if this big business were turned over to you, being young, you might dissipate it — all of the work of Cousin Tay, and my own work, also.

And therefore, for a little while, I thought it would be better to let you carve your own way until the wild oats — forgive me if I call them that, dear Oliver — were completely sown, and then to make you a wonderful gift of — all of your property back and immensely increased!"

"Why, Cousin Peter, would you have done all of this for me?"

"Is not your mother's child mine, in a way? Who should I work for, except for you?"

"Good!" said Oliver Tay. "And now we'll have this little story all written down in black and white. And you'll mention the amounts of the investments, and the companies they have been placed with, and how much they have increased; and you'll be very specific, Cousin. And if you should make an error, though it might be no more than the slip of a pen, I shall let Yellow Wolf do the correcting. But if you do all of this — I shall set you free."

"Do I have your signed promise of that?" asked Cousin Peter, white with rage and grief at this sudden turn of events.

"My word is better than my bond," said Oliver. "Now sit down and write."

So Peter Sydham had paper and pen furnished him by Venales, who kept such commodities always in a pocket of his saddle in case of odd emergencies somewhat of this very nature.

Carpio Vega drew Oliver aside. "You will be able to go back to riches, then, Oliver," said he. "And just when we thought that we had won you back to us, we'll lose you!"

"Do you think that?" smiled Oliver. "Tell me first how I shall be able to return? I think that this confession might possibly insure my property to me — though I doubt it. But when I go back to claim it, what shall I do? I have done worse than murder."

"Worse than murder? Oliver, you have never murdered a man."

"No, thank goodness! But in the eyes of my country, I have broken open jails, insulted the dignity of the army and therefore the flag which flies behind it. And now I've fled from justice; and I've been consorting with armed bandits, Vega. So tell me what would happen when I tried to return?"

Carpio Vega bowed his head. "Shall I tell you honestly?"

"Yes," said Oliver.

"They would put you in prison for half your life or else a mob would hang you to a tree."

"Exactly," said Oliver, and his smile was steadier than ever. "But the truth is, Carpio, that I think I may be happier living a free short life as a border bandit in the mountains with you, than in cities living a long life where all men are more or less slaves. There — he's finished. I want you and Venales to be witnesses."

"And the girl?" said Vega, suddenly.

"What one man misses another man takes," said Oliver; and he stepped grimly forward toward Peter Sydham.

PART THREE

THE PRIZE

CHAPTER XXXIII
The Rodeo

In the first place there were ten thousand black-eyed señoritas who would have been glad to marry Diego Venustiano, and why, therefore, did he have to look north of the river for a wife? Some people said that it was because, from the day he left Old Spain, he had always had to take the hardest way to every one of his successes. The very silver which he took from the earth in such vast quantities at his mines had only been found by systematic efforts which would have killed off the strength and the patience of ordinary people. And he had filled all his life with such enormous labors that it had not been possible for him to find a spare moment in which to marry and raise a family.

No, not until he had reached the iron gray of middle age — the hard years of a very hard man — did Diego Venustiano finally stop one day in the midst of a stride as he was walking up and down the long hall which served him as a living room in his house. He had been turning over in his mind certain methods newly discovered and which, applied to his mines, might increase the huge river of his income by perhaps fifty per cent.

And in the midst of these cogitations he suddenly had said: "What will become of this mountain of wealth after I am dead? And with ten thousand enemies, such as I have, who can tell when death will come?"

So mused Diego Venustiano. He sat down and remained for an hour without moving. For he felt trapped, as though life, having been defeated by him in hand-to-hand combat all his days, had finally resorted to this cowardly method of crowding him to the wall. Yes, magnificently as he had worked, all of his labors would go for nothing. He had no relative worthy of this inheritance. He had only one real friend. And that friend, perhaps, was only devoted to him for the hope he had that one day Venustiano might remember him in his will.

At least, this was the suspicion that flashed across the mind of the rich man. And, though he immediately defended Andrea Rulliano in his heart of hearts, still he could not help feeling that a shadow had fallen across his very soul and would leave a stain there forever. He decided, before that hour ended, that he would marry as soon as possible.

But wait! Do not think that even then, so late in life, he really hurried. No, he began his quest for a wife by rebuilding his house. That is to say, he enlarged it until it was entirely another structure.

There were ten flat acres on the top of a mountain which might have had another name in the olden days; but it had been known for many years, now, as Mount Venustiano. And, in the center of this rolling land, he had built himself a house. Now he used his mansion as storage space and for servants' quarters and called up a host of builders, architects, masons, stone blasters, stone hewers to rough face the mighty blocks, and deft-handed workers to give the massive rock the finish of glass. For Diego Venustiano decided that every inch of his new house into which he hoped to welcome his bride should be built enduringly and founded as deeply as the fortunes of his family — which he trusted might run on forever.

So, first with powder and drills, they cut the massive rock away and ripped out the deep and solemn chambers which were to serve as cellars in which the treasures of a king and the wine of a pope could have been stored with ease. And then — for all this time the stone was being quarried for the walls — the house rose with wonderful suddenness.

And as it was built, it was finished with the care of a jeweler; and, while it was being finished, furniture of all kinds and rich hangings were brought to fit out the interior; and the huge water wheel in the valley, which operated the never-ending cables that dragged cars up and down from the top of the mountain, was constantly raising precious burdens for the house of the *señor* — so that, as the house spread, all men wondered. But, for the first time in his life, Diego

Venustiano found that he had embarked upon a task in which the expense was to him the item of least consideration. All that he wished was to make sure that the place was such as would overwhelm the imagination and charm the heart of a lovely woman.

It was not a lofty structure. No, it was a simply a single story, though that story was wonderfully tall and spacious. And, after the fashion of the adobe houses of Mexico, it rambled here and there with a delightful carelessness, and inclosed little gardens and cool courts arcaded with graceful columns. Diego Venustiano watched the progress of the work with a swelling heart. He began a new life. For hitherto he had made nothing in all his years save money, and now he saw that money was only a means to an end.

When this mansion was completed and furnished, only then did he think of finding the woman to place in it. But that was not to be done in a moment, and first he went north of the Rio Grande to look into the possibilities of certain hardy but fine cattle with which to help stock the beautiful valley at the foot of Mount Venustiano.

On that journey he rode through Siddon Flat; and, on his way through Siddon Flat, he saw a girl's face, pale, beautiful, and sad. He stopped his horse, just as he had stopped on another day in the pacing of his living room. For he knew that this instant he had seen the woman who must be his wife.

In three hours he knew all that was necessary

to know about her. She was the daughter of a simple and poor farmer on the edge of the town. Her name was Marian Barge. And, if there was sadness in her face, that was because she had a good reason for it. She had been engaged to a wild young giant who had disappeared a year or so before into the mountains. Perhaps the wolves dined off his bones long ago; but she was still true to him, and would not look at the young men in the town, and spent her time caring for her father's house — which was work enough, seeing that Samson Barge had been badly broken in an accident some months before, and ever since had kept to his bed.

So Diego Venustiano had himself introduced to Samson Barge, and to the sick man he opened his heart. He told him the truth with brevity and with warmth. He described his wealth and his house, both waiting for a mistress.

And Samson Barge said in the end: "All these here things would be enough to turn the heads of most girls. But I dunno about Marian. She's in the next room. You ask her."

It seemed wrong to Diego Venustiano. He suggested that there should be time for a courtship, first of all.

But Samson Barge shook his head. "She'll never marry you for love," said he. "Because all the love that's in her is for another man. But if you want her anyway — why, talk to her. It ain't in me to try to persuade her, though she leads a dog's life here, slaving for me."

So Venustiano went to Marian and sat before that pale girl — and he was pale himself, you may be sure — and laid his proposition before her in grave, cold words, just as he would have outlined any business proposition. Only his eyes were somberly eloquent. She told him with equal gravity and coldness exactly what her father had said before. She loved another man. And she did not think that her heart would ever change. But she knew — who did not in that country — of the wealth and the name of Venustiano. And, if some of that wealth could be used to give her father the care which he needed, to lift him from this abject poverty —

"There is no need to buy my help by marrying me," said Diego Venustiano, his heart freezing with grief. "I shall make your father comfortable."

"That would be something for nothing," said the girl. "We cannot take charity."

He went away to think it over. It was very unromantic. To take to that magnificent house a girl with no love for him and so mismated in age! And yet, as he thought of it, and as his mind grew more fixed upon her, he was sure that no other woman could ever take her place. And there was enough passion in him, finally, to waken love in her at last. It would come, say, with the first child. Ten thousand better men than Venustiano have argued with themselves in the same manner, you may be sure.

So they reached an agreement; and Venustiano

went hastily back to his home to prepare, leaving behind him in Siddon Flat such provision for Samson Barge that that honest man heard of it with a burning face.

"It ain't right!" he told Marian fiercely. "Honey, ain't you selling yourself for my sake and not for your own happiness?"

She managed to talk him out of that. And, as for the future, a married life — why, this world is not for dreams and dreamers, she had come to believe. There is very little that happens as we would have it.

Back in his own country, Venustiano had mounted to a seventh heaven of expectancy and hope and joy. He went straight to the old house of his one friend, Andrea Rulliano. To Don Andrea and to the Señora Rulliano he opened his heart. He would send for this girl. He wished to let her see the country and the people before the marriage. And would the señora be hostess to the girl and keep her in her house?

Señora Rulliano would be delighted.

So, with that decided, Venustiano went ahead to the next step. This girl must be introduced to the country in such a fashion that the people who looked upon him as the king of the countryside would be prepared to welcome her as the queen, also. She must step upon this new stage in a proper setting, and so Don Diego arranged a ceremony which would fittingly fill the eye of the country folk.

It was to be such a rodeo as had never been

seen before in all of Mexico. There would be enough cattle barbecued to feed ten thousand. And at least that many would ride across the mountains to enjoy the ceremonies. There would be prizes, too, sufficient to bring every capable young man in Mexico to the games. And, to crown all, Marian Barge, who distributed the prizes, would be announced at the close of the festival as the betrothed bride of Venustiano.

But, ah, Diego Venustiano, who will summon the whole world to come and look at a jewel before it is really his? Are there not thieves?

CHAPTER XXXIV
Flinder

When I think of Diego Venustiano, I am amazed. For it is a proof that if a man grows very old and wise in some ways, he will remain a child in others. This miner had learned how to follow a silver vein almost by instinct. He had made enough money to buy out a national mint. And he had shipped his bullion safely by mule train through regions infested with outlaws but who dared not touch his goods — except for that one wild exception of Roderigo Venales, of course.

But here was Diego Venustiano, whose mine was a precise and well-oiled machine in most respects, now become a veritable child in regard to his marriage. Let me give one example. It occurred to him, as a sort of afterthought, that at a marriage there must be a priest to officiate. Well, for that matter there were plenty of priests in the community. And it would be a simple matter to bring a dignitary to his house.

But that would not do. It did not fit into the fairy picture which Venustiano was painting for that marriage, for the future life he was to lead with his bride. He wanted to be married to

Marian Barge by a priest who would stand to him in the position of the archbishop to the king — in the days when the archbishop was appointed by the crown.

So he stamped his foot, as you might say, and a fine church sprang up in the valley. It was built only of adobe; but then, adobe churches will last five hundred years if they are the right kind; and this was distinctly the right kind. But was it to be a ghost of a church, surrounded by the empty fields?

He stamped his foot again, and a village sprang up around the knees of the lofty church, for Venustiano had chalked off a section of his rich valley lands, fenced them in from the cattle, and allotted half interests in the patches of ground to those who cared to farm. Instantly the agriculturalists swarmed in to take advantage of that generous offer. And, in a month, with the help of the patron, their pleasant, simple houses had been built, their little vegetable and flower gardens laid out; and the rain and sun made the village bloom. And the great Venustiano let his will be known to the priesthood.

Of course, he was listened to with awe and reverence, as a holy man. For is not that man holy who builds churches in a wilderness and surrounds those churches with worshipers by the villageful? An able, gentle, young ascetic came to rule this new flock — a youth with a starved face and tender eyes like a saint, who could tame the worst outlaw in the mountains with a single glance.

So this part of the ceremony was prepared for. But what could have been less like the work of a man and more like the way of a child? However, Diego Venustiano was not attempting to be logical or sensible. He was only being happy, spending money by the hundred thousand, and spreading his elbows at the board of prodigality.

It had an effect, too, this change in the great patron. For the mountaineers had looked upon him before as upon an eagle, sitting on a mountaintop, or as a gloomy miser, living in a castle with his wretched wealth. But suddenly it appeared that in some miraculous manner his heart had been touched. And many people attributed the miracle to the gentle young priest in the valley in the new church, forgetting that the cause must come before the effect. However, it was plain that the patron was transformed. He had been one who took. He was now one who gave. And suddenly a thrill of wonder and of affectionate awe spread through their hearts. It was the coming of spring for the fame of Venustiano.

And, no matter how childish you may call it, these were good things, and in a sense rather great things, that Diego was accomplishing. Even the rodeo which he planned with such care was a harmless affair. If it was a mistake, it was because he was too confident. But that is to be shown afterward.

In the meantime, it became known that an

American girl had entered the country. She was a friend of Señor Rulliano, it appeared, for she was living in his house; and she was being introduced by his wife, busily, to the few great families in the mountains — overlords of valleys, of forests, of thronged domains of cattle. But no one, except the Rullianos, knew that there was any relation between the arrival of this girl and the great works of Don Diego. No one would have been able to guess it, seeing her pale face and her unassuming ways.

Least of all would anyone have connected her with this wonderful preparation for the rodeo. And what a rodeo it was to be! For Don Diego had prepared prizes to be dreamed of, but never to be matched. To the best rider, a fortune in pesos! Silver money, so that you will know that you have received your full price! And for the best roper, another fortune! And for the best trick rider, also money! And Indians will be allowed to compete. Then there will be killing before the affair is over, you may be sure of that! And, for the best hand at bulldozing grown steers, a great reward!

What, is the money never to cease flowing? The price of a thousand, two thousand days of work for a little exhibition of skill during five minutes? Men will come from the ends of the Americas for the sake of such an affair!

"Ah, let them come! Let them come!" said Don Diego. "Goodness knows they shall be welcome. There will be food and shelter for everyone. I have bought canvas. There will be a white field of tents put up around the village. Whole herds of fine young, fat cattle are ready for the butcher. And there are trainloads of sweets in preparation, and tons of bread and vegetables and beans, and all that the heart of man can wish for, and great tuns of wine and vats of beer."

Tush, you cannot keep good news. It will slip away like quicksilver and course through the veins of the world. And the tidings of the preparations in the valley of Venustiano spread like oil over water! Mount your horses and pull the cinches tight. Get to the valley. You may be sure that you will never regret the going if it be only to watch, eat, drink, sing, listen. To say nothing of those who can join in the feats of skill!

But still, though all these mighty movements were going forward, Don Diego could not quite be sure that he had a proper crown for the celebration. And he cast about him daily in the search for a climax. Not easy to find a climax! You cannot readily balance a mountain on top of a mountain. However, he did not cease hoping, and finally he heard by chance of what he wanted.

Flinder was taken at last, the great white horse which had coursed like running fire through the mountains, which had broken into a hundred corrals and run off with the stock, which had captured whole herds of saddle nags with the magic of his free-ringing neigh. Flinder had been taken, that great, white shooting star of the mountains!

Oh, and he had been paid for! Thirty men had ridden on that heroic quest. And a score of tough mustangs had been ridden to death. And then, in the struggle to master the giant, a man had been killed and another man maimed. And after that, in the attempt to ride this thirteen-hundred-pound monster, the first rider had been crushed to death and the second had been almost kicked in two.

Three men killed, and the injured make a grisly list! They would hang a dozen men for such murders. But Flinder is different. He is only the more admired, the more desired, for his dreadful deeds — fighting for liberty, and willing to kill himself while he strives to get it. But, at last, by starvation, by patience, by craft, by wisdom, by might of hand from a dozen men, he is mastered. He is taught to answer the bridle. He can be ridden — not easily. But, at least, it is possible for a fine horseman to stay in the saddle!

"I have it!" cried Diego Venustiano. And he laughed and struck the shoulder of Rulliano, who happened to be with him.

Rulliano looked at him askance. "You have what?" he asked. For his old friend daily amazed him.

"I have the crown for my rodeo. I shall buy Flinder and offer him as a prize for the best marksman. Eh?"

"Buy Flinder?" cried Rulliano. "Buy what you

258

will, but you will never be able to buy Flinder
— not for three thousand pesos!"

"You shall see — you shall see!" He called to
him a most trusted emissary. "Take six of the
best riders on my range," said Don Diego. "Here
is gold. Bring me back Flinder."

And so Flinder was brought. And even the
stern heart of Venustiano leaped when he saw
the horse. But still his purpose held. It should be
a mere prize in this rodeo. Men would speak of
this generosity. And perhaps — who knows —
'this would be the white lightning stroke that
would open the heart of pale and lovely Marian
with awe and wonder, and let love come slipping
in.

And Don Diego began to look upon the stallion as a gambler looks upon an ace. For what
would Marian think, then, when she saw her
betrothed give away as a prize in an entertainment in her honor a gift which an emperor might
have valued more than the most precious jewel
in his crown?

But, alas, Diego Venustiano, the honey which
calls the bees to you will call the hornets also!
For the word has gone forth. And wild and desperate men have heard that Flinder is indeed to
be the prize. And if you fear thunderbolts, then
fear the powers which this magic of yours is
assembling, Don Diego!

CHAPTER XXXV

The Gunmen Come

But in fact poor Venustiano had no fear. He lived in a rarefied atmosphere. He walked above the clouds of doubt, at this time; and, therefore, any cowardly and base suggestions of gloom he would have shrugged away as in duty bound. Not to be happy and confident, he felt equivalent to a criticism of his lady.

And the longer Marian Barge remained in that country, the more certain he became that she was perfect. She was not witty; she was not very gay; she was neither wise nor eloquent. But she was simple, kind, and pure; and those three qualities, in the eyes of Don Diego, were worth a whole ocean full of accomplishments. She had no artistic gifts. She could neither draw nor play German music. But she could sit at the piano and sing folk songs of the West and the South of her own country in a way that brought the tears to the eyes of the proud Spaniard and made his breast swell. He knew that she was not happy. But she never complained, and she never repined; and, with a courage worthy of a man, she lived up to the letter of the bargain she had made.

Sometimes, when he looked at her gravity and

her gentleness and her sorrow, Don Diego was overwhelmed with a sort of religious awe. He used to rush away and find Padre Ricardo, the young priest, and pour out his heart to him. Or else Don Diego would suddenly make a vast resolution and set about carrying it into effect.

It is hard to believe that these impulses of compunction could lead to such great results; but, as a matter of fact, a fine hospital was built in Mexico City and endowed for the poor. And this was the effect of Marian Barge on the Spaniard. And he did other things, like an emperor, or a madman, or a lover. Or like all three rolled into one person!

And, in the meantime, people were flooding into the valley long before the rodeo. Your Mexican is either a day late or a day early. And, in the case of such an event as this, they did not care if they were a fortnight beforehand. They came in droves — men and women and even children, because whole families had left their flocks and their little farms and come down to see the festivities. And they wanted, as you might say, places in the front rank.

Don Diego made all welcome. The city of white tents grew steadily larger outside the village which had been built. The market place was thronged. And in the great eating rooms which he had built, and where the inside of these barn-like structures was made alive and gay with sinuous colored paper streamers, long tables were laid out thrice a day; and he who wished might come here and dine. Do you wonder, then, that the thousands were trooping in.

Señora Rulliano walked with her young guest in front of her house, which stood on a hill on the farther side of the valley. Time was when the Rullianos had owned all of that valley. But that was before the coming of Don Diego. Now, in the middle of the plain, they could see the white-walled houses of the town and the snowy tents circling about it.

"Look, Marian, my child! It is all for you! Everything that you see is for you, alone. And doesn't it fill you with awe, a little?"

"It will be such a show," said the girl thoughtfully, "that, even if one of the principal actors were to fall out, certainly another would simply be brought in, and the play would not be stopped."

At this, the señora looked sharply at her companion and frowned; and that evening she said to Andrea Rulliano: "I tell you, Andrea, that slip of a girl does not understand. She thinks that Venustiano is amusing himself like a child. And these tremendous preparations don't seem to move her. As a matter of fact, it's plainly to be seen that she doesn't love poor Diego a whit; and it's your duty, my Andrea, to tell him what he must expect from his wife."

Don Andrea was a man who had been in politics for a certain time. He had not remained there very long, for the very good reason that a bomb had been cast at his feet one day. A devoted peon picked up the bomb and ran out of the room with it, and was blown to heaven as a reward for his devotion. But Don Andrea, though he never became important politically, learned some truly political lessons, and, among the rest, he knew that all men will eventually do exactly what they wish to do, and that nothing which we attempt on our part can really change them without leaving a feeling of malice toward us.

Don Andrea knew this; and so he replied to his wife, "I think you don't understand, my dear, that Don Diego is in love."

"I have reason to forget," she exclaimed bitterly, "that there is such a thing as real passion in this world!"

"I love to see you moved, my bird, my pet," said Don Andrea. "Flutter your wings again. It is immensely becoming."

"You detestable —" breathed his better half, and left the room.

But that was the end of the warning which Don Diego should have received, and which might have had some influence upon him, though that is rather doubtful. And all went marching forward triumphantly toward the great opening day.

The center of everything, however, was not Don Diego himself, but the white horse, that creature winged with speed — Flinder! The animal was kept in a circular fifty-acre field surrounded with a strong ten-foot fence. There he sported every day and drank the water of the little brook that crossed the meadow, or grazed upon the good grass, or enjoyed the shade through the heat of the day beneath big trees.

And all day people watched him with hungry eyes — men and women and children who had been raised to the important knowledge that the most important of all the treasure which can fall into the hands of a man is a fine horse; and here they were seeing, as they felt, perfection. So they stared and gaped and hungered. Everything that was known about him was repeated around the ample margin of that fence. And a thousand untrue things were attributed to him. He was worth a great deal of talk.

When he grew tired of the lazy life in the meadow, after the wild days of freedom which had so robed his body with iron strength and beauty, he would break into a gallop and swing round and round the inclosure almost too fast for the eye to follow the action of his legs. For he was standing on four dark stockings; and, when he began to move rapidly, then his legs seemed to disappear; and he was simply a white streak supported by invisible legs. And beneath him there was seen merely the winking of the sun upon the polished ebony of his flying hoofs.

And, when he had finished his rounds at full speed, he invariably ended his little race by plunging to a halt in the exact center of the inclosure, where there was a low hill. There he would stand with his glorious head thrown high, his tail flung into a grand arch, with the love of freedom trembling in his body and lightning in his eyes.

Such was the stallion whom the thousands came to see, and, as time went on, and as the days for the rodeo grew nearer, people began to feel that all that went before really hardly mattered at all. Even the magnificent prizes for roping, for riding, and the rest, seemed nothing. And all the other lesser prizes, for boxing, running, leaping, wrestling, throwing the weight, were hardly worth the attention of the crowd. There were hosts to contend for all of these prizes, of course; but the heart of the crowd had nothing to do with them. Their interest was centered on the great stallion and the contest which would be held for possession of him.

Presently, as the hour drew nearer, men of a different sort entered the raging, boisterous, wine-flowing city of Don Diego Venustiano. You could pass down the street and pick out these men with casual glances, for they were different from the rest. They would be seen standing in obscure corners, with preternaturally active eyes surveying all around them. Or they would be sidling down an alley, but always you could be sure they would have a stout stone wall at their backs! These men wore two guns very low down along their thighs, where the tips of the fingers were continually brushing against the handles. And the holsters were sure to have a worn look.

Or else, perhaps, there would be no gun at all showing, but you would see these pistol experts wearing very open, loose coats; and then you could be sure that the weapons were carried under the coat. And there were double-barreled pistols, and single-barreled, and long ones huge enough to throw a bullet that might knock down a horse, and long ones, slender and delicate, intended to strike a small mark and kill by delicate precision rather than by size and mere violence. And there were even, here and there, a few models of that new fashion of short gun which was becoming more and more popular with the passage of every year in the western mountains — the revolver. And yet only a few had appeared this far south. The gun remained a good deal of a mystery.

But these fellows with the rather reserved manner, fond of lurking in corners, and always sure to have their backs guarded by a strong wall — these fellows were most apt to have the new-fashioned revolvers, because it was their business to keep distinctly up to date in such matters. They either kept up to date or they died young. And the crowds which circulated through the town of Venustiano knew who these fellows were. They were the gun experts who had come into the valley to contend for the possession of the white stallion. A quiet, soft-spoken, silent-stepping lot they were; and people avoided them as animals avoid poisonous snakes. But Diego Venustiano was delighted, and he said:

"I have gathered the deadliest lot of gun fighters in the history of the world. And the rodeo will be famous forever!" He had become mad, you would say. He was now rejoicing in the strength of the explosive which he was trying to manipulate with his bare hands!

CHAPTER XXXVI
In the Arena

Even the buzzards in the sky were excited and gathered by the dozen, hanging in the air on tireless wings above Mount Venustiano to tell one another that never before had there been so many living creatures in the valley; and Don Diego, looking up into the air, seemed to feel his fortunes menaced by the living circle which these birds of ill omen kept in the heavens above him. He fell into a fury and ordered them destroyed, but even his oldest retainers merely gaped at him. For does one go gunning for birds that hang half a mile up in the sky? Such a silly superstition troubled Venustiano for a moment only. Then he turned his face forward to the other events of the day.

The rodeo was to begin. Lists had been set off behind barriers as if for the contests of chivalrous knights. Great bleachers had been built all around it. And the air above the bleachers was sure to be filmed over with a thin mist of dust which was constantly rising from the great corrals near by, where the wild horses — the fuzz-tails — were kept for the riding contests. And there were the corrals for the steers, also, which were to be roped, thrown, and tied. And there were the stout yearlings, to be handled in the same manner.

They not only raised a dust with their constant milling, but they also kept a constant clamor in the air, with the bawling and the booming of the cattle and the shrill squeals and the brazen trumpetings of the fuzz-tails.

Don Diego looked upon this slight confusion with a pardonable satisfaction. It was the aura of excitement which should properly surround an affair such as this one which he was creating.

The time came for the opening ceremony. It was a solemn parade, which began on the broad top of Mount Venustiano and wound down the sides of the mountain and across the narrow strip of level, and through the little new town by the river, and into the arena.

At the head went one band. At the rear went another. There was need of that much martial music, for the cheerful and loud tunes which the first set of musicians sent thrilling through the air were soon trampled out and drowned by the stir of trappings, the squeaking of saddles, the roll of voices, and the stamping of hoofs. And there was need for the second band at the rear; and, even so, half way between the two, in the very center of the procession, there was a region in which one would be very conscious of confusion, but of no music whatever.

Behind the first band came the "quality" of the mountains, representatives of the oldest and the best families, many of them descended through the centuries straight from the conquistadors to whom little principalities had been assigned out of the vast domain of Cortez. And they were a little less proud, perhaps, than archangels, and a little less haughty than hot-blooded steeds. They came to smile at this rude festivity. And they came to shrug their shoulders at the *nouveau* rawness of the wealth of Don Diego. However, he was not the son of a nobody in Old Spain. And he could be forgiven for having made his millions by the labor of his own brain and hands, though they, for instance, were much too good to envy him such occupations.

But secretly they had been eaten up with curiosity to see the new house of this palace builder. And they had been struck chill with awe as they strolled through the great halls and the flowering courts and the fountain-cooled patios of the Casa Venustiano. There was certainly no other residence in Mexico like it. They felt really more wonder than envy. They had seen such a place of beauty!

And more than one young, dark-eyed beauty felt a secret leaping of the heart at the idea that some woman, some day, was sure to become the mistress of all of this magnificence. Such thoughts were rapidly communicated. And Don Diego, who certainly had never been much of a social favorite in the years that went before, even after his wealth had been mounting into the complicated millions, now found himself suddenly showered with invitations. He was wanted here, and he was wanted there. He found that, in building his house and arranging his rodeo, he had made himself a necessary part of the "better" people of the mountains.

And he did not even smile, for he understood these things. He was too seriously bent on watching one face in all that crowd, moving always at the side of Señor Rulliano, a little less pale than usual — yes, actually clapping her hands together as she passed breathless through the magnificence of room and court. After all, Don Diego was not an entirely unwise enchanter! And even if this girl were the least mercenary and the most self-sacrificing soul in the entire world, still she could not help feeling that life with *any* husband in such a mansion would perhaps be tolerable.

And so they had passed out and joined in the procession, the Rullianos and Marian Barge with the rest, with Don Diego following the "quality," as a king might follow his nobles. And all of Don Diego's household rode around him and before and behind him.

You would have been astonished to see how many of them there were. Don Diego himself had been amazed when they were mustered — all the gardeners and house *mozos* and stable boys and grooms and hunters and cooks and a whole corps of mechanics, to say nothing of a select bodyguard of fifty fine shots and expert riders. Many would take part in the competitions who habitually rode with the silver trains which he

271

dispatched now and again across the mountain trails.

After the great household of Don Diego came the columns of the competitors, light-footed youths who would run in the foot races, and heavy-shouldered men who would box with bare hands, and ponderous wrestlers, and mighty weight throwers. And then there were the contestants for the riding prize, most of them fellows that sat just a trifle askew in the saddle, they had so often been battered and beaten and smashed in their dangerous business in life. Then came the bulldozers of grown steers, men both daring and mighty. And there were the expert ropers, men of all kinds, young and old, thin and fat; because dexterity with a rope is a gift and may have been bestowed upon the youth or the old man. And there were many men of all kinds following for the other prizes.

But last of all came a silent legion of dark-faced, solemn men, each keeping a good distance from the other, never hurrying their horses. And what horses! Looking at those mounts, one could not help wondering why any of these fellows should ask for a different charger, for each was more beautiful than the last and more earmarked for speed. But then, looking more closely at the faces of the riders and their restless eyes, one could realize that in horseflesh only the very best could satisfy them. For a difference of a second in a mile might, on many occasions, mean life and death to them.

When the procession reached the village, where the women and the children and all the men who were mere spectators were grouped, then there were respectful cheers when the head of the columns passed. Wild shouts and rejoicing greeted the great "patron" and his household; and there was noisy excitement, also, as the various contestants passed, until it came to the contestants in marksmanship — the gentlemen who would match their skill with one another for the sake of that greatest of prizes, Flinder.

Silence fell on the crowd. They drew back a little and looked upon these men with wide, frightened eyes, knowing well enough that most of these faces were not meant to be exposed to the light of day except when sheltered by a black mask, and guessing, perhaps, that there was hardly a gun in any of those holsters that had not a notch or two filed into its handle.

So the procession went on; and, at its end, like dust after a wind, came a trailing, whirling march of little boys.

In the meantime, the head of the long files had reached the arena. And the band marched in, blaring forth its noisiest music. On the southern side of the lists, where the sun would not shine in the eyes of the watchers, there was a large dais; and there the gentry of the mountains found comfortable chairs awaiting them, and plenty of room for each, and cushions to put them at their ease, with ushers to show them to their places and then wait upon them when they were seated under the canopy which had been raised here against the sun.

They had fine European wines served them. But for the multitude which swept among the benches looking for a front-rank place there was other entertainment, beer and, above all, the favorite pulque, fresh-made, cool and with a taste which the Mexican loves above all else in the world! From long booths that refreshment was served to them; and up and down the aisles in the bleachers, all day long, sweating boys carried the beer and the pulque busily — all free of charge.

In the meantime, the arena was filling rapidly. Some men had laughed when they saw the vast extent of ground which Don Diego had fenced off for his lists; and they openly laughed when they saw the crowded rounds of the benches. But now they laughed no more; for a veritable ocean of humanity was pouring into the place, and benches filled in whole sections at a time, and the shrill voices of disputants over favored seats rang and re-echoed across the field. Indeed, it was found that not enough seats had been built; for, after all the benches were filled, there were still ranks which had to be content to stand on the parapet at the rear.

But it was a splendid spectacle, that bowl of people waiting for the good things which Don Diego had arranged for their eyes. What excitement! Even the gentry from the mountains — even those oldest descendants of the famous conquistadors — could not contain themselves, but broke forth into whispers and murmurs.

However, Don Diego looked at only one face. He watched Marian Barge, to see whether or not she were stirred. And, for the first time, he saw that she had discarded all grief. She was like a happy child, looking here and there. And now, at last, he was sure that he should be able to win her love.

Alas, Diego Venustiano, do not forget Flinder and the strange men who have come to join the contest for which he is the prize!

CHAPTER XXXVII
"Before the End of the Day"

Aside from the Rullianos, no person in all the assemblage had the slightest idea that the festival had anything to do with the presence of the "gringo" girl who sat there on the dais among the great folk of the land. But they began to suspect that she might be a person of eventual importance when it was learned that she had been chosen for the graceful task of presenting the prizes. And, for that purpose, she had a special place in front, like a little throne, to which each victor was escorted and where he received his due reward.

For three days they came up to her one by one, slender foot racers, brawny wrestlers, grim-faced riders, and all the rest. But even Marian Barge was taking these matters casually, for the fever which gripped the rest of the crowd had taken her, and she looked forward only to the contests with weapons which were to close the last afternoon of the great rodeo. No matter what heroic deeds and what feats of skill, knife and gun would eventually fill the eyes of the spectators.

There had been a sanguinary suggestion made to Señor Venustiano that the knife contests should be arranged as actual fights — perhaps with somewhat blunted weapons. But he would not listen to that. For five hundred pesos, he knew that some of those savages would find a way of driving even a blunted point into the heart of a rival. So it was all a contest at targets.

And what a group stepped forward to try their fortune at the game! Young and old, big and lean, there were half a hundred fellows, each of whom had a deadly fame in his home community for his skill with the naked steel. And they were ready to gauge their prowess against that of the rest of the world. Take them north of the Rio Grande, and they might have found sundry Texans who would have yielded to no man in their ferocious willingness to fight out a battle by means of the big bowie knives. But these experts could use a knife as a hand sword or javelin. They had grown up with the steel in their fingers, and the tricks which they performed with it were wonderful to observe.

There was an elimination contest, in the first place, in which the contestants threw three knives in succession at a round target with a bull's-eye; and, from the first trial, there emerged six champions to dispute the final struggle.

And, as they threw, a lieutenant leaned beside the chair of Don Diego and whispered at his ear, "Señor, one of the men in the field now is a member of the gang of Roderigo Venales, and it is said that Venales himself has come to the rodeo today!"

Don Diego stirred like a lion in his chair. "He would not dare," said he. "I know that Venales is a slippery and daring rascal, but he would never dare to put himself within the reach of my hand after robbing me as he has done."

However, he added suddenly, "Which of the knife throwers is said to be of the band?"

"The little man," said the informant. "He who is taking his stand just now."

"When I saw them all," said the master, "I recall none of them being as undersized as that. I don't think that Venales would have such a little man in his crew."

"Look!" said the lieutenant. "He has struck the very center of the target!"

It was true. The goal had been removed to almost twice the distance at which the first shots had been thrown; but the first knife of the little man landed fairly in the middle of the bull's-eye, and there was a shout of appreciation from all who could see.

"It may have been a chance score," said Don Diego calmly. "I don't think that such a fellow —" He paused.

The second knife had glanced from the hand of the little man, and it quivered in the target at the very side of the first.

"It may be," said Don Diego. "He has skill enough to be wanted by Venales. By heaven, you are right; and that, most probably, is one of Venales' murderers!"

For, as he spoke, the third knife was flung; and

it landed so close to the other two that the palm of a man could have covered all three. There was prolonged shouting and cheering at the sight of this. For the knife, after all, was the weapon cheap enough and common enough for all to possess, whereas the pistol, and particularly the new-fashioned revolvers, cost a small fortune. And so all the common herd were delighted to see the effectiveness of their national weapon vindicated in this fashion; and many a boy, as he watched, set his teeth and swore that he would practice hours and hours a day, until he should be able to do just such a thing as this and even before so many people.

"For a clever rascal like that," said Señor Indorno, a great cattle king, turning to Don Diego, "what is the use of a gun, which makes noise and cannot kill any more effectually than a heavy knife placed like that."

"It is a light throwing knife that they are using," suggested someone.

"Tush!" said Indorno. "I heard the thud as it struck home! And those three blades are buried half their length in the soft wood."

The knife-throwing contest ended suddenly. The rest of the candidates for the prize seemed unnerved by the uncanny skill of the little man, and presently he came to receive his award.

"Go down and look closely into his face," said Don Diego. "I wish to make sure. If he is really one of Venales' men, he will have his neck stretched from the tallest tree on Mount Venustiano before the morning comes."

So the spy of Don Diego stood close, very close, to Marian as the little man came before her. He was an ugly, dark-faced fellow, with rather wide shoulders and very long arms; and, when he came before her and lifted his sombrero to salute her, he stared straight into her face with a boldness that made her own eyes waver. It almost disconcerted her in the little speech which she had to make with the bestowal of each reward:

"This prize is given to you by Señor Venustiano, because you are worthy of it, and because he hopes that you will wish to remember this as a happy day."

The little man, in reply, murmured something so very low that none could make out what he had said except the girl herself, unless it was the emissary of Don Diego, who had pressed up close to the very back of Marian. Even he could not believe the thing he thought he heard. He stepped hastily to the side, so that he could scan her face; but all that he saw in her eyes was question and bewilderment. He hastened back to Don Diego.

"And what did you see?" asked Venustiano.

"I saw a man who looked ten times more formidable at close hand than from a distance. I saw enough to make sure that he was hardy enough to have been selected even by Venales. Yes, and even as one of Venales' best men! But that, after all, was not the strangest part of the affair."

"Not the strangest part? Not strange that out-laws who have plundered me should come to take part in this rodeo? Have him watched through the crowd."

"I have sent two men to trail him constantly. You shall have him the moment that you wish."

"You have a reasonably good head on your shoulders," admitted Venustiano almost grudgingly. "Now, tell me, if you can, the part of the affair that was more remarkable."

"It was this," replied the other. "I stood at the very back of the señorita, as you commanded. And so my ear was hardly farther from this little man, the prize winner, than her own. And I heard her make her little speech to him as she gave him the gold — a whole handful. He replied in a rapid voice, pitched very low; and he was looking into her eyes, not mine, which made it easier for her to hear than for me. And yet I thought that I made some sort of sense to his words — and very strange sense, at that!"

"Continue," said Venustiano kindly. "If it was merely an oddity at which you guessed, I shall not be harsh about it. What do you think that you heard?"

"I thought," said the fellow, "that I heard him murmur rapidly, 'He will come before the end of the day!' "

" 'He will come before the end of the day!' " echoed Don Diego.

"Yes," said the other, "that was exactly what I thought that I heard. I couldn't be sure."

" 'He will come before the end of the day!' "
repeated Don Diego heavily.

And he looked down at the dusty floor of the
arena in dismay. He could have ventured his life
on the truth and the purity of the girl. And yet
who could tell whether or not she might have
buried in her heart the recollection of another
man — this same giant lover of hers about whom
he had been warned in Siddon Flat; and what
was more likely than that this very man might
have come to the rodeo about which half of the
world must have heard by this time!

He looked slowly back to the face of his lieutenant. The latter was a trusty creature of his, a
sort of extra pair of legs who for fifteen years had
scampered on errands for Venustiano, and who
had by this time no wits of his own and no desire
for anything except to please his master.

"You have probably heard nonsense, Federigo," said the master as calmly as he could.
"And what was the bearing of the señorita at that
time?"

"I stepped to the side where I could look at
her as closely as possible, and it seemed to me,
señor, that she appeared baffled and surprised;
and she looked after the man as though she
would have called him back to her and asked him
to explain. However, he went straight away. I
merely paused to send two men to follow him
and keep him in view. And then I came to you
to report."

"Your ear has played you a trick, and that is

all," said Venustiano. "However, keep on the alert. Send for young Warne. It is said that he has seen the faces of half of the band of Venales. And, if the scoundrel has actually dared to bring his men down to this rodeo — Go, send for Warne at once!"

CHAPTER XXXVIII
The Blond Giant

Anxious only to execute each mission in turn and execute it well, Federigo was off like a ferret. But he sensed a bit of a mystery in this affair; and, being not quite a machine, but something of a man as well, he could not help hoping that he might be able to unravel it.

In the meantime, he found that everything was happening to make any calm investigation almost a matter of impossibility. For the time had come for the beginning of the shooting contest which was to decide the ownership of Flinder. That white beauty was now led into the arena, with a magnificent gold-worked saddle upon his back, and the flash of real jewels setting off his bridle, and his mane woven into twenty little braids, each braid finished off with a golden tuft of great richness; and he looked like a charger out of the Arabian Nights, such as Aladdin might have ridden.

There was a wild uproar when he first came in. He stopped on stiffly planted legs, and instantly a wave of silence followed, which lasted all the time that he pranced around the inner circle, while all eyes followed him in a frenzy of desire and wonder and joy.

"There will be bad shooting today," said Señor Rulliano. "There is always poor shooting when it is for a great prize. Some of those rascals out there, I tell you, would have calmer nerves if they were shooting at a fighting man rather than against others for the sake of Flinder. By the way, where did he come by such a name?"

"From the Indians, perhaps," said Señor Venustiano, his mind too filled with other problems to heed this.

"It's not an Indian name."

"Whatever it may mean," said another of the gentry, "it seems to me to fit him perfectly, for it suggests to me a sort of wildness, a carelessness, like a thrown spear or a flying bullet. And that's the look that Flinder has, as though there were no fear in him, eh? And enough speed to make himself vanish if he really chose to use it! I feel that there's the devil behind that horse."

"He has killed men enough to give you that idea. But that was before he was tamed."

"Tamed, do you call it? He's like a striding lion!"

"Ah, that's high spirits only. He can be ridden. He is ridden every day. Hello! What a roar! And see the smoke. It looks like a battle!"

The contestants stood in a long line, each man firing his three bullets at one of a line of targets; while his score was being marked down, he stepped back and the next set of marksmen stepped into place.

There was little or no air just now. And the heavy black powder soon raised a cloud of smoke that lay thick along the field like a very dirty fog and half obscured the firers. The first rounds were completed and the second elimination ended; and finally there were three contestants. Three, that is to say, remaining with the rifle! And following that there would be an equal struggle with pistols or revolvers. And the grand climax would occur when those who had qualified either for rifle or revolver were to meet in the concluding contests, which would be for any sort of firearms, at the pleasure of the marksmen, fired from the back of a running horse and at moving targets. That would be, after all, the real test — the battle test, as you might say.

A lucky breath of wind cuffed the fog of smoke back and showed the contestants, one a typical *vaquero* and another a lean, tall man with a very dark skin and eye — a somber figure. But he who took all eyes at once was a splendid young giant with golden hair that flowed down around his shoulders — a man dressed in all the brilliancy of the Mexican gala day costume, and yet apparently not a Mexican at all, if golden hair and blue eyes had any meaning.

He had an effect upon everyone in the arena, it seemed, and chiefly upon Don Diego himself, for the latter half started out of his chair and exclaimed: "Andrea! Andrea! Attend! Do you hear?"

"I hear you," said Rulliano. "What is wrong?"

"This is a miracle such as I never expected to see with these eyes of mine. I want you to believe me, Andrea, when I tell you that — and yet I cannot believe my own eyes!"

Rulliano leaned forward and scanned the trio of marksmen with close attention. He made no comment, but calmly waited.

"I have often told you," went on the host, "about the day when the scoundrel, Venales, and his crew held up the silver train?"

"Of course, of course," said Rulliano. "There is no doubt that I have heard that story enough to know the details. What of it?"

"You remember that I have spoken to you about the crisis when it looked to me as though my men were surely rallying to beat Venales? Yes, in another thirty seconds we would have butchered them or driven them over the cliff, I am sure."

"I remember, I remember," nodded Don Andrea. "As a matter of fact, what happened then, according to you, has always seemed to me like something borrowed from a storybook. Because a magnificent, long-haired giant leaped up from the shrubbery and charged down on your line, with guns spouting fire and death from either hand; and his singlehanded charge turned the tide of battle; and, in another instant, instead of driving the outlaws over the cliffs, your men were scattered, and even you yourself had become a prisoner! Isn't that the point in the story?"

"Yes," said Don Diego calmly. "You remember it perfectly. And I see that you smile at it a little!"

"I cannot help it," said Don Andrea. "Not that I think you would exaggerate, but even a Venustiano can become a little excited in the middle of a battle. Tush, man, I respect you all the more for what happened — to your imagination. But, really, do not ask me to believe that any one man could have done so much."

"It is very well," said Don Diego. "Now I ask you what would you say if I were to point him out to you?"

"Point him out to me? Here?"

"Yes!"

"It would be an amazing thing, Diego, if such a rascal dared to show himself at this rodeo!"

"Yes, it is a thing not to be believed easily. But at the same time I wish to have you remember a detail in my description of that giant. He had long golden hair, did he not? And he was young?"

"That is true, and what of it?"

"Look yonder, at the third of those riflemen — that man upon the right. It is he."

"Impossible —" gasped Don Andrea. But he stood up, in his excitement, and he stared. "You cannot tell, Diego!" he exclaimed. "Not at this distance, where the man's face is just a blur!"

"Distance makes little difference with him," declared Don Diego. "If he were barely discernible on the edge of the horizon, I think that I should be able to tell him, by something lordly in the turning of his head. It is the same man. I

288

tell you, Andrea, I have no doubt whatever. I would wager ten thousand pesos that that is the very man."

"But to put his head into the lion's mouth in this manner!" cried the other. "Is that a thing to be believed, unless he's mad?"

"Mad! Perhaps he is a trifle mad. I think that every one of the outlawed fraternity who have ever laid eyes on Flinder are a little addled in their wits, as a matter of fact. They cannot keep away from him. They are mad to have him, and that is the reason that he has come down here to take his chance that I shall not remember him."

"What will you do?" exclaimed Don Andrea. "By heaven, when I look more closely at him I really believe that the scoundrel could do the thing that you ascribe to him in the battle. He seems to have the confidence and the courage and the strength of any ten men!"

"He has," said Don Diego; "and to see him in battle is worth a year of life."

"But now what will you do?"

"What do you advise?"

"Send a dozen picked men, of course, and capture him at once, without waiting!"

"Consider, Don Andrea, that this rodeo is given by me, and this ground is really, in a way, my own place, my own house, where I have invited the rest of the world to come and make merry and be contented at the games which I am giving. And if I make an arrest in the midst of the games —" He paused.

"But consider, also," went on Rulliano, "that this rascal really cost you the price of a vast treasure — the cost of the entire train of silver!"

"Do you think that I forget that?" murmured Don Diego, with a strange smile. "But there is another thing which I have never dwelled on with you to any extent, and that is the manner in which I made my escape from the band of Venales."

"I guessed, rather, that it was the speed of your horse and the confusion of the fight."

"I tell you that it was none of those; and I should have been hanged from the edge of the trail without mercy, if this man, this golden-haired giant, had not given up all of his shares of spoil for the sake of a gift which the band was to make to him. When they agreed, he asked for me. They grumbled, but they gave me to him; and, when he had me, I thought that he intended to keep me for a high ransom. But he merely took me aside and told me that he considered me a hardhearted scoundrel; but that he felt I was a brave man who deserved a better death than hanging by thieves, and he set me free to go on my own way without a penny of ransom paid."

CHAPTER XXXIX
"At Midnight"

To this anecdote Don Andrea listened, speech-less with interest. "I understand," said he, "and therefore this big man has come down to the rodeo, trusting that you will do him no harm, because a long time ago he set you free."

"I don't think that's in his mind," said Venustiano. "He must know that law-abiding people keep no faith with outlaws. And what has drawn him down is the hope that he'll not be marked in the crowd or that I'll do no harm on the day of the festival. And I think, by heaven, that that is exactly the manner in which I should act, Don Andrea. I am going to let the word go round at once. All men are free here, and no officers of the law shall touch any person for offenses in the past. Federigo! But look again at that giant, Andrea, and tell me if I have exaggerated. Have you ever seen such a man before?"

Rulliano stared again. "I never have," he admitted. "And I can almost see him, Diego, plunging down the hillside with his revolvers spouting smoke and fire. If I had been among your men, I think that I should have turned and run for safety, also. Look, they are shooting for the final rifle prize!"

It was quickly over. These men knew their business, and they were soon through with it; and, when the contest was ended, it was found that the tall, dark, ominously handsome member of the three had won the first prize, and the golden-haired giant was second.

So the winner came to Marian Barge to take his prize from her hands; and honest Federigo took advantage of his semi-official position to stand very, very close, from mere curiosity to see such an expert rifleman at close hand. He saw the dark-faced man take the prize without any acknowledgment except a faint murmur which certainly could have reached no ear other than that of the girl, unless it were Federigo's. Back to Don Diego went his emissary, all in haste and in excitement.

"Did you see him closely, Federigo?" asked the master.

"I saw him as close as I see you now. And now I can almost swear, sir, that I have seen him before, and that the place where I saw him was among the band of Venales. Consider, señor, that the last two prize winners have both been from that crowd of tigers."

"Let them be!" said the patron, though his face had darkened. "Let them be. For, after all, I am the host and they are in a sense my guests. They shall not be touched while they are here — the impudent scoundrels! But I pray to heaven, Federigo, that none of them carries away the main prize of the day. This last was a surly looking fellow!"

"He had a message for the señorita, nevertheless!" said Federigo.

Don Diego was fairly raised from his chair. "What is that?" he asked sharply. "A message from another of that scum?"

"Señor, I heard him more clearly than I heard the little man. Goodness knows how it is managed, but I have always been able to gather in whispers. And I heard him most distinctly."

Don Diego drew back a little, scowling; but then he said gloomily: "Continue, then. What was the message that he brought to the señorita?"

"Ah, señor," said Federigo, "I fear that no good will come to her and that you should have given the great honor of prize distribution to one of our own people."

"Be quiet! You speak like a fool when you give advice that has not been asked for, Federigo. Tell me what you heard and not what you think about it."

"Then, señor, I tell you faithfully and simply all that was heard. It was not much, but very strange." He simply said, 'He wishes to know if he may come.' "

Don Diego changed color. "Speak again, and slowly, Federigo. You heard him say: 'He wishes to know if he may come!' "

"Those words, exactly. I know that they make

very little sense, but they are exactly as I heard them."

"It is a mystery," said Venustiano. And he added grimly: "Whatever else you may do, keep this matter a secret between you and me. Do you understand me?"

"I understand," said Federigo.

"And did you observe her face?"

"I did," said Federigo. "And, though she is always pale, still at that moment I thought that she became so white that a mere candle ray would have shone through her like the sun through a translucent stone. As though she —"

"It is enough," said Don Diego. "There is no more to say. But go back, Federigo. You shall understand before the day is over why everything that touches this girl touches me, also. And I beg you to look well and closely. With the ear of a rabbit and the ear of a fox as well, Federigo!"

Federigo needed no further encouragement, but still he was called back.

"You are sure that she made no answer?"

"I had my eyes fixed on her lips. I should have known if she so much as breathed. But she did not. She returned no answer whatever, but her glance wandered out toward the field and remained fixed there."

So he left Venustiano and went back to his listening post, while a cold wave of fear and suspicion passed through the very soul of Don Diego. After all, what Federigo had said might turn out to be true enough; and he would have done better had he trusted to a girl of his own people, rather than to the daughter of a strange race. And yet he could not doubt her long.

A haze settled upon the heart and upon the mind of Don Diego; and, when it cleared, he heard a great shouting. The whole arena was ringing with it, and he looked up to see three men standing in the center. One of them was the giant of the golden head. It occurred to Don Diego that it might be a prolongation of the rifle contest. No, that was ended. They held revolvers.

He recovered from his unpleasant daydream to hear Don Andrea saying eagerly: "I have never heard of such shooting, Diego! I have had no faith in the new pistols. But now I begin to think that they are magic. Good heavens, how can they be made to fire six shots as if in a single breath — six words in rapid succession? And yet aimed shots! Did you see, Diego, that your golden man and the other big fellow did not lift their revolvers much higher than the hip?"

Don Diego had not seen, but he nodded his head. "Now I remember how he charged down the hillside," he said. "And he came firing a gun in either hand and making the shots chatter out. And he was sighting down neither gun. I thought he was merely firing wildly. I did not dream that they could have been placed shots."

"It is the other man who wins, however," said Don Andrea. "Your golden man is a close second twice, however; and, if luck goes well, he should press the others for the final contest. By heaven, Diego, he would make a picture on the back of that Flinder, would he not?"

Venustiano did not answer. He was watching with an abstracted eye while the winner of the revolver prize strode across the field and came to Marian Barge for his prize; a man with the face and the bearing and the stride of a lion. What would happen now? Was some mysterious stranger sending in a message by each of the winners in the competitions? And who could the man be who dared to open such a bold correspondence with her? There was murder in the heart of Venustiano as he thought of these matters. And yet he could hardly believe his eyes and ears when Federigo presently came breathless before him.

"It is the third time!" said Federigo.

"Not another?" echoed Don Diego.

"Another — and another message to the señorita!"

"It is not possible!" said Don Diego through his teeth.

"The third man — the third man from the band of Venales! And I have gathered much news, in the meantime. I have circulated the word that all men are safe with you as their host until the end of the rodeo, and even afterward, so long as they do no wrong here on the field. And that news opened mouths. We began to hear talk freely. And, in the first place, I have learned that we are right about these men. For all of the last three winners do actually come from the band of Venales."

"I have guessed as much. That last big man, especially."

"He is called the right hand of Don Roderigo."

"It is Carpio Vega, then," suggested Don Diego.

"It is that great Carpio Vega, who should be leading bands rather than following a leader, except that he has no ambition. And the winner of the rifle shoot was that other famous fighter — that man who killed four Apaches in a single day! It was Antonio Morales."

"The devil has given them courage, to bring them down here under our eyes!" said Venustiano savagely. "Morales and Vega in the very flesh — and here! Tell me, who is the little man, then?"

"He was Capiño. The thief and knife fighter!"

"I know. Why, all of these names are in the nursery stories of children. But, while you were hearing other things, what did you find out, by any chance, of the man who is sending in these messages, and what message did he dare to send by Vega?"

"I do not know who the man may be; but I know that Vega said only one word, which was: 'When?' "

"And did she answer?"

" 'At midnight!' " replied Federigo.

CHEER XL
The Gringo

Wait!" exclaimed Don Diego. And then he paused and let his head fall, in the intensity of his thought.

For three days he had been living on a sort of pinnacle of glory; but now, on the last day of the great festival, a cloud had grown suddenly until it was blackening half of his sky. For it was perfectly clear, now, that someone well known to the outlaws, and perhaps one of them, was seeking an interview secretly with this girl. And it was equally clear that he was to obtain it, if she were able to grant the favor. And though he told himself that there was nothing miraculous in the desire of a man to see a girl, or of a girl to see a man, and though he vowed to himself that there could not be so much as a single shadow upon the soul of Marian Barge, yet the doubt persisted. He could not argue himself out of his gloom.

And a sudden shame possessed Don Diego that at the close of this day he was to announce to the world that he was betrothed formally to Marian Barge. A shame that even such a man as Federigo should know that there was the slightest finger of suspicion pointed at Marian.

"Federigo," he said suddenly, "what this all means I cannot tell. Come close to me."

Federigo, trembling to find himself suddenly become a person in whom his terrible master could repose an actual confidence, bowed his head close to listen, and he heard the voice of Don Diego murmuring: "The truth is, Federigo, that this girl is to be announced as my betrothed bride before the end of this day. What these messages to her mean, I cannot say. There is no other person in the world who guesses, except you. Federigo, you must help me to solve the riddle; and you must work with sealed lips. Your very thoughts must be dead to everyone in the world except to me. Do you understand?"

"I understand!" said Federigo faintly. He stood up, a little giddy, and wanted to rest his hand against one of the pillars that supported the canopy against the sun, for he felt sure that to be trusted so deeply by such a person as Venustiano was a most perilous matter.

"There are three of the men from Venales who have brought word to her," said Don Diego, "from another man who wishes to see her; and they have kept at her until at last she has consented, as you know. Now, then, the first thing is for us to guess the name of the man. Have you any thought on that subject?"

"Venales himself?" murmured Federigo.

"Venales? Never — and yet why not? Perhaps Venales! We close our eyes against nothing. Most probably it is some member of the gang, and therefore why any member other than the leader? You are right, perhaps. And I hope that you are correct, for there could be no harm in him."

He checked his thinking aloud. At least, in the sallow, unhandsome face of Venales he told himself that there was nothing which could stir the heart of a romantic girl. He sighed with relief.

"There was a former lover of hers," said Don Diego earnestly, "who left Siddon Flat a year ago and disappeared into the mountains and was never heard from again. But perhaps — who can tell, — he may have joined with Venales. That, I think, may be the clew. And now she will be willing to see him again — to say no." He bit his lip. "You understand, Federigo?"

"I understand, señor."

"Surround her with watchfulness. Be ten men in one. If this matter is brought through well and safely — do you hear me?"

"I hear you, señor."

"I shall make you rich, Federigo. I shall make you one man in ten thousand. That is a faithful promise. Never forget it!"

"I shall not!" said Federigo, beginning to tremble again; and with all his heart he wished that this girl had not been so dreadfully important, for then he thought that he might have been able to spy upon her far more easily and with quieter nerves.

"Take yourself away. Come back instantly when there is anything to report. And, first of all, tell me who is that yellow-haired giant in the field. I already know that he is one of Venales' men."

"I have heard everything," said Federigo. "And it seems that the young giant is the very greatest of them all."

"Except Venales himself, you surely mean?"

"Greater than Venales. They obey Venales because he leads them to money. But they love Don Olivero."

"Olivero. He is a Mexican, then?"

"Not with that hair, señor. He is a gringo."

"With a Spanish name?"

"They have changed his name, perhaps. He is Olivero Tay. And the men of Venales love him like a father or a brother. They would die for him."

"How did you learn this?"

"From a shepherd, just now, who has been drinking too much pulque and cannot keep his tongue in order. When he sees this Señor Tay, his head begins to nod; and he goes through the crowd telling how he was hurt by a fall, and how some of the men of Venales found him, and how this giant, Tay, picked him up and carried him half a mile on his shoulder, as though he were a light parcel, and then put him down and took care of him and bandaged his wound. And the fellow says that Don Olivero sent the great outlaws of Venales running here and there to do his errands for him. He swears that that is the case, and that this Olivero Tay is the very greatest of them all. Greater than Venales, and greater than Carpio Vega even!"

"Great enough to stretch a hangman's noose, some day," said Don Diego gloomily, "or great enough to stop a half-inch bullet! Now go back and find out what more you can. Forget the gringo. Learn if Venales himself is here."

But if the mind of Don Diego was anxiously taken up with such reports and with such ideas as this, the rest of the crowd was not troubled in the same fashion; and, for them, there existed nothing of importance in the world except the wonder as to who would be successful when all of the preliminary contests were over and the last struggle for Flinder had been concluded.

Those preliminaries were ended at this moment. Six men had been weeded out from the scores of contestants. The disappointed heroes fell back along the edges of the arena, filled with the bitterest grief, for it was known that many of them had ridden hundreds of miles, and one man had taken his horse more than three hundred leagues in an overland voyage to make his try for Flinder. He was a failure with the rest, and only six could match wits and skill in the last struggle.

Even Don Diego showed more excitement and forgot some of his worry as he watched the men lined up for the work. They were mounted, every one of them, for it had been decided that the decision was to be made under, as nearly as possible, exactly the same conditions that a man might meet with in his normal life; and in normal life all of the mountaineers, of course, were on their horses or their mules. What horses they had, these six! One might have said that they had been selected from their compatriots not for marksmanship but for the excessive beauty of their mounts. A splendid spectacle they made as they reined in their chargers and looked carefully to their guns.

And there were three of the men who were said to belong to the band of Venales. What greater tribute could have been paid to that outlaw than to know that three of his followers had won through to the finale on such a day as this! Carpio Vega on a gray horse, and Antonio Morales on a roan, and Oliver Tay on a gleaming black covered with panther mottlings, and the three other men on a cream, a chestnut, and a pinto!

They stood their horses in a row at the foot of the arena. The audience was quiet. It was not known even what the target would be, when suddenly from some boxes in a corner of the field a well-grown jack rabbit was turned loose and darted across the opening, with the shout of the crowd to give it wings, heading straight for the opposite gates.

Have you seen a jack rabbit run? No, nothing will qualify except the jack of the mountain desert. He has not a multitude of hedges to dodge through and tall glass to squat and hide in. He lives in a wilderness where it may be fifty miles to the nearest covert and where all things pursue him — wolf and coyote with wits and speed both, and all the cat family with the subtlety of their craft and the lightning of their spring. So he has to develop the speed of a sprinter and the endurance of a bird, and like a ground-skimming bird the jack rabbit runs.

So this lanky brown creature, when it was loosed into the rodeo grounds, gave one high spy-hop, to make sure where it was and what the noise meant. Then it scooted for the farther gate, while the voice of the marshal rang out, "Shoot that rabbit, Oñate!"

Shoot Oñate did. He had his rifle across the hollow of his left arm; and he swung it instantly to his shoulder, drew aim, and fired. Alas, at just that instant the rabbit swerved. He fired again and knocked a cloud of dust over the darting creature. He sent his third shot through the jack from end to end, and the big bullet crumpled the body against the farther end of the arena.

Very good shooting, indeed, and the crowd shouted its appreciation. It doesn't sound hard, perhaps, but try it at a jack rabbit which has dissolved itself into a dusty streak across the ground. And now everyone, understanding what was to be expected, stood up in their places, climbed upon the benches, and a trembling excitement lived in every face.

CHAPTER XLI

Won!

In the meantime, Oñate, grinding his teeth with mortification because he had needed three bullets in order to put the rabbit out of the way, was half unnerved; and when a second rabbit was loosed, and he was called upon by name, he missed it utterly with the only two attempts which he had time to make with his shaking, fumbling hands.

That disposed of Oñate. He did not have to be told that such shooting would not do in this company, and he fell back with dropped head into the crowd that edged the field. Other jacks were being turned loose in rapid succession. A stolid, swart-faced man was next in line — Martinez was his name — with a double-barreled rifle in his hands and another at the side of his saddle, loaded for use.

There was no need to call upon the second weapon. The instant his name was shouted, the butt of his rifle tipped gently, unhurried, to the broad face of his shoulder, and the rabbit made its death leap before it had jumped thrice. Martinez calmly reloaded the used barrel; and, in the midst of that reloading, his name was called again, a second rabbit was loosed, and this time he finished his preparations with the same perfect calm, and the rabbit was a hundred yards away before the rifle rose to his shoulder. It was the same thing. The instant his eye caught the rabbit in the sights, the little beast was dead. There was no delay. And there was a screech of joy through the stands at the sight of such marvelous snapshooting.

The dark Morales came next. He knocked over the first rabbit with the first shot; but the second was a dodging, twisting, elusive streak, and it ran to safety. Morales was out of the competition.

"No one will ever beat Martinez!" was the general comment. "That man is a genius. He thinks with his rifle!"

The rider of the chestnut was next. He missed on his first rabbit and got the second. Carpio Vega also tried and took one out of two, and then it was the turn of the golden-haired fellow.

A rabbit darted out, a zigzagging streak of a creature. The first shot of Oliver Tay missed; and, suddenly dropping his fine rifle, he snatched out a revolver. The first shot kicked dust over the speeding jack. The second dropped it dead.

And there was a wild uproar. That was beautiful work! Very fine shooting, indeed. But was the revolver allowed?

Certainly, announced the judges. Either revolver or rifle. The thing is simply to drop the creature dead!

Four men have been snuffed suddenly from

the picture. There remains only the swart Martinez on his pinto, and the golden-haired gringo.

"Look!" said Don Andrea to his host. "That giant of a fellow is good-natured. Did you see him shake hands with Martinez?"

Don Diego answered with a burst of enthusiasm, "Now that he is in this final struggle, you will see him win!"

But Rulliano shook his head. "That Martinez is simply cold death," he declared. "The man has no nerves. For did you notice? The second rabbit was loosed to him while he was in the middle of loading his weapon. But he shot and killed, just the same. Did you think, Diego, that in the entire world there were six such shots as we have just been watching?"

"I did not," admitted Don Diego with unction. "I have heard of men who could occasionally strike such targets. But these fellows are inspired. Now, look! Do you see Morales and Carpio Vega drawing up to Oliver Tay and giving him their good advice?"

"I see it. Martinez will beat him, nevertheless. And yet his long hair would fly out very well behind him, if he were to ride the great white horse."

"You will see him do it. I think you will see it."

"I have five hundred pesos that say he will not."

"You are betting on Martinez?"

"Of course. I raise my bet. A thousand on that dark-faced genius with the rifle."

"The rifle is very well, but the revolver is the new weapon. I believe in the future and the present. Martinez is from the old school. And so I take your bet, Rulliano! Halloo-o-o-o!" He gave a hunting cry with great excitement.

Two rabbits had been loosed, and darted down the field like mad things, their ears flagging back with the winged speed which they were using.

With perfect unconcern the rifle tilted to the shoulder of Martinez. He dropped the first; he missed the second. No, the rabbit was not safe. One had proof now that the motions of Martinez were deceptively swift. He had time to drop the discharged gun, and, snatching up his second rifle, he planted a bullet fairly in the body of the jack, just as it was darting across the margin of safety.

The crowd, which had been watching with held breath, screeched with satisfaction.

And now Oliver Tay?

They were instantly silent again, listening, watching, breathless.

Another brace of rabbits — and away they went, dodging like inspired devils. But what was this? The revolver leaped from its holster into the hand of Tay, and the double report was like one sound and its instant echo. And there lay two dead jack rabbits in the very beginning of their race for freedom.

The crowd was stunned. There had never been

shooting like this before. And they stared in silent amazement toward the man with the flowing golden hair, mounted on the tall, black horse.

"He did not shoot like this at the target!" cried Don Andrea, bewildered and excited. "Good heavens, Diego, he was even beaten in both rifle and revolver work! But now the devil is in him!"

"He was shooting at a lifeless target before; but these are living and running creatures, which makes a difference to him. Trust me, Andrea! If there were fighting men down there, he would be shooting even straighter. I shall take your money from you, Andrea."

"I am amazed, but still I think that Martinez will win. He is a dead shot. Will there be more rabbits? Hello, what's that?"

A pigeon had been loosed from a trap near the riders; and, as it rose, the rifle of Martinez spoke, and the bird fell. Another — and it was torn to tatters by the bullet from the revolver of Oliver Tay.

"Ride!" called the judge.

And the pair of champions started forth, trotting their horses, then cantering them. A yell of frantic applause broke from the crowd, and the noise was as instantly hushed, so that they might use all of their faculties for the observation of whatever might happen.

"Martinez, both for you!"

The swarthy man twitched his head around, and straight behind him he saw a pigeon tilting upward in the air and a rabbit loosed along the ground. With the pressure of his knees he turned the horse sharply; but, before the active pinto was cleanly turned around, a rifle bullet had found the soaring pigeon, dusted feathers from it. A second smashed the life from its shining body. Then, dropping the gun and tearing out the other rifle with anxious speed, Martinez fired at the flying rabbit — once — and again; and the rabbit was seen to stagger, and then it dragged itself beneath the gate.

There was pandemonium in the rodeo grounds. That rabbit would die, but undoubtedly it had not been struck by a center shot, for otherwise its life would have been snuffed out instantly.

What decision would the judges make? It is a score and a half for Martinez.

Now, Oliver Tay, will you match this performance? Sooner or later one has to fail entirely. And certainly a revolver is no fitting weapon with which to do long-distance shooting. He must knock down his targets at the beginning of their flight or else not at all. And shooting against birds in the air and rabbits on the ground —

Once more he and Martinez were cantering smoothly on, side by side, the golden-haired gringo smiling and cheerful and the Mexican as somberly calm as ever.

"Tay!" shouts the voice from the marshal's stand.

He rears the fine black horse on its hind legs and spins it around with unbelievable suddenness. And there is a pigeon just gathering headway — The revolver leaps out, flame and smoke spurt from it; but the pigeon, in that instant, has swerved sideways, and the bullet is flying toward a mark that seemed no thicker than the edge of a knife and glistening illusively in the sunlight.

A miss for Oliver Tay, and the pigeon, thoroughly frightened, is scudding away with thrumming wings that thrust it off at redoubled speed every instant. Another shot; feathers fly from the bird; it turns with a sharply angled dodge in mid-air and flies straight into the face of death. The third shot brings it to the ground, turning over and over, beautiful white feathers brightly stained with crimson.

And Oliver Tay swung back his horse and tried a flying shot at the rabbit, which has now covered half the distance to freedom. The bullet cast a shower of dust into the air and dimmed the target for the fifth bullet, which also missed completely. Not a yard away, now, lies freedom for that jack rabbit, which means the white stallion for Martinez.

No, head high, smiling, calm, at ease, Oliver Tay has fired again; and the rabbit rises into the air and, spinning head over heels, strikes the bar of the gate and flops heavily back into the rodeo grounds.

Flinder goes to the gringo!

CHAPTER XLII
The Award

If Oliver Tay had congratulated Martinez and wished him the best of all sportsman's chances before the contest, Martinez now made no such return of courtesy to his successful rival at the conclusion of the fray. He went to the judges to protest. With three bullets he had done his work. It had cost Oliver Tay six.

The judges were deaf. "Your rabbit still lives. Perhaps it will not die at all!" they told him. Flinder was not for him. It was for the giant.

A giant for a giant, in fact! See him now as they lead him in, two men conducting him. Half the time they are dangling in the air, as he rears and prances in acknowledgment of the uproar which greets his majesty. And the other half of the time they are tugging and straining vainly at the lead ropes to urge him forward. He goes forward as he pleases. He stops when he pleases, and sometimes turns a little and pricks his ears toward the distant horizon, as though asking himself if it would not be very much worth his while, after all, to dash these miserable, clinging humans to the ground and streak away over the edge of the sky line to eternal freedom? But he had absorbed enough lessons to make him realize that there was more in man than met the eye.

Don Andrea, paying over the money which he had lost with a good grace, murmured, "But now, Diego, will you bet again?"

"I think I shall," said Venustiano. "What is it this time?'

"Flinder will be entered in the race, will he not?"

"If there is an ounce of spirit in his new owner, Flinder will be entered!"

For, as the very last act of the rodeo, on a course laid out all around the rodeo grounds, there was to be a two-mile horse race.

"I think he will be entered, well enough," nodded Rulliano. "And I will wager another thousand, Don Diego, that my thoroughbred beats him."

"Perhaps, for your horse is a racer. And you will be having a lightweight rider against the bulk of this Oliver Tay. But, at the same time, I tell you that I am going to lay the bet, and without asking odds from you. Because I think that on this day Oliver Tay will take a great deal of beating."

"I take you, then, for another thousand. See the crowd! They are mad over this white horse. I'm a little mad over him myself, Diego. There was never such another creature in the history of the world."

"See him dance and scorn them, even if they are his masters!"

"How could this Oliver Tay manage him for a race?"

"He will find a way, and my bet stands. Now he comes closer to his horse. Look, Andrea, are they not matched? Are they not of the same soul stuff?"

For, as the crowd poured out from the stands and surrounded the horse, at a distance respectful to his heels, Oliver Tay came striding through them, looking as much larger and as much more magnificent than the other men in that assemblage as Flinder looked like an ideal horse when compared with the other mounts of that day.

To the place where Marian Barge stood the stallion was led; and there he paused, shaking his head at the noise of shouting all around him. Up to his head came Oliver Tay; and, taking the splendid Mexican sombrero from his head, he raised his face to the girl who stood above him, giving him with a gesture, in the name of Don Diego, this splendid prize. But what she said, if she tried to speak, could not be heard. For there was a veritable din around them.

Oliver Tay, replacing his hat on his head, touched the pommel with his hand; and, vaulting lightly into the saddle, he rode off from the field toward the course for the race which was to test what horse and rider could perform together after so brief an acquaintance. A lane was made for him; and Flinder went dancing through it, sometimes rearing on his hind legs and walking and sometimes trying to lunge away, but held by a powerful curb and a mighty hand that bowed his head down against his broad breast and held him in check.

The whole interest of the crowd was in this magnificent horse and his no-less-magnificent rider. There was only one little counter-whirlpool of excitement, observed only by a few; for, as Don Diego left his place and went toward Marian Barge he saw that her face had lost all color. It had become, as Federigo had described it a little time before, as white as translucent stone; and, at the sight of Don Diego, she dropped her head and sank to the floor. He reached her with a leap; she had fainted away.

"It is the sun. She has been standing too long under that hot sun, with so much to do — poor child!" So said the ladies who tended her with much sympathy.

Don Diego waited only to make sure that she was not seriously ill but that she was recovering instantly from a fainting spell. Federigo had come to him, and he drew that sharp-eyed spy to one side. "Now tell me, Federigo, what you noticed, if anything, that could have caused this thing?"

"That made the señorita faint?"

"What else could I mean?"

"There was no chance to hear what she tried to say, and Señor Tay made no attempt to speak back to her because there was a wave of shouting all over the field."

"Very well. But you have eyes, Federigo. Did you see anything?"

"A man's eyes may deceive him, señor —"

"I am not asking you for absolute facts, fool. Even a chance guess would be welcome to me now, I tell you!"

"Then I may say what I thought I saw. Which was that, when Señor Tay came toward her, the señorita stood up and then sat down again quickly, as though she had grown suddenly weak. I thought that she would faint then, instead of later. However, a bit of color suddenly came back into her face. She stepped forward quite boldly again. And at that time, as Señor Tay came before her, it seemed to me that her whole appearance changed, señor, and she looked down at him with a sort of joy."

"Wait!" interrupted his master. "Do you understand, Federigo? If you are wrong in this, you had better never have had a tongue to speak at all."

"Señor, I think that I understand. But what I saw with my own eyes I may believe. What was in the mind of the lady I cannot tell, but I know that for an instant she seemed happy. And then —"

"And Don Oliver, on the ground beneath her — what of him?"

"I was to watch the lady, señor, and not other people. Besides, when I looked at him, just then, he was surrounded by a whirl of the people; and I only saw the golden flashing of his hair as he turned toward the stallion."

"Then tell me, Federigo," said the rich man,

"what you can make out of all that you have overheard and seen?"

"Señor," said the spy, trembling, "I had rather be the eye and the ear of Señor Venustiano; I do not wish to try to be his brain, also!"

"Nevertheless," exclaimed Don Diego, "you have some thought! I tell you, Federigo, there is no other man in the world to whom I dare to open my mind at the present moment, and therefore I shall be glad to have your opinion freely. Speak out to me!"

Poor Federigo looked rather wildly about him; but then he said desperately, "It seems to me, Señor Venustiano, that all I have seen points in one direction."

"So it seems to me, also," said his master. "Let us see if I agree with you."

"In the first place, I hear it said that 'he' is to be here. And shortly afterward we see the man with the golden hair in the field. And then another messenger comes and says that he will soon come to her; and a third arrives asking when he may come; and she answers that he is to come at midnight. And, after that, the man with the golden hair himself arrives before her; and I see her start up, and her color change twice, and a sort of joy comes into her eyes."

He paused, looking curiously into the face of Don Diego, but the latter maintained his nerve with a great effort and bowed his head a little. "And then, Federigo?" he pressed.

"And then, as Oliver Tay turns away from her,

she falls in a faint, señor."

"Ah!" groaned Venustiano, his face suffused with sweat and his skin turning gray.

"So that I should say, Señor, that Oliver Tay is the man who will be expected by the señorita at midnight this same night."

Having delivered this opinion, he bowed and remained with his eyes fixed on the ground. In the meantime, the two were left totally alone, for there was a great bustle all around them as the people hurried away toward the race grounds to get the best posts of observation.

At last the master said: "Stay by me, Federigo. Before long I shall have other work for you to do, connected with this same matter, I'm afraid. Be constantly near me, and — one thing more: Those fellows, Oñate and Martinez — what do you know of them?"

"I know very little, señor, except that —"

"Tush, Federigo, you have at least heard a rumor about every human being in the universe. Tell me what you know."

"Only that it is said that they shoot too well to be entirely honest!"

"I thought as much. I want you to go to them. Tell them that I was pleased to see such fine work with rifles and revolvers even by men who were beaten — by luck. And let them have something to retain them — two or three hundred pesos apiece, or more if you think it necessary. Understand, Federigo, before the end of this day they must be my men."

CHAPTER XLIII

Murder!

Preferably Federigo was one who would neither think nor know. He would simply observe and report. However, he had by chance been thrust so deep into the confidence of his master on this day that he could not help guessing a single step ahead and arriving at a strange conclusion. There would be a use for Martinez and for Oñate, both. Was it so very difficult to imagine, therefore, what use Don Diego might be able to make of two expert fighters and wild men — a use that very day, perhaps, say at about midnight.

Now, Don Diego turned his back for a moment upon the dark ideas which had thronged up into his mind. In the first place, there was much else for him to do. The happy faces of his guests showed him that even the elect of that wild mountain land had enjoyed themselves to the uttermost through the three days of the festival, and he must mix with them. Then he had to speak again to Marian Barge and to ask her if she would not retire and rest. Her eyes were already wandering far before her toward the place where the riders for the race were gathering. No, she would not go. She felt well. She felt very well.

It was only a passing dizziness which had troubled her. And now she would stay, of course, to see how the race might turn out.

Don Diego heard her with a sinking heart. It might be that he was utterly wrong in all that he surmised, but he felt that he could not be. And he had the confirmation of Federigo's suspicions to fortify his own. Two proofs, however small, are a thousand times more powerful than one. And he was filled with wonder, too. He had looked upon this girl as the quietest and gentlest soul in the world, but now he could suspect that there was a great deal of force in her, also, and a silent and steady enthusiasm such as he himself had never dreamed of. He knew the meaning of that far-off, eager look, he thought.

"Listen to me, Federigo," he said to his spy, as they hurried toward the observation platform which had been prepared for the elite of the spectators. "Young Guillermo Estaban has been in Siddon Flat — that is the young fellow who recently joined my guard. Go to Estaban hastily. Ask him if he knew the name of the man who was reported to have been in love with the señorita a year ago — the man who disappeared into the mountains."

And he added to himself, as Federigo hurried off: "What a dolt I was not to learn every detail of that affair before I left the town! Before I took a step toward her!"

Such were the thoughts of Don Diego as he came to the high stand from which he was to watch the race; but, the moment that he reached that place, his reflections were scattered like dust before the breath of a strong wind, such was the excitement around him. Everywhere bets were being placed on the various horses. For that race the finest horseflesh in the mountains had been entered — imported stock from England and France or direct descendants of that racing blood, though most were perhaps a little high in flesh to show their utmost speed, and all were inclined to look something more like picture horses than the racing machines into which they could have been made. However, there was a good half dozen of them entered, because a five-thousand-peso stake was eminently worth running for in any country, and because, also, there was an excellent opportunity of making even more money by betting.

And every man who had a thoroughbred in that race was smiling up his sleeve at the idea that any other horse in that section of the world could possibly live with his own speedster for as much as a furlong of running. Not that there were only imported horses. There was the great Flinder, of course. And yet he was not the favorite, for though it was agreed that in a day's chase through the mountains he could have run any of those finely drawn horses to the ground, still a two-mile sprint was a different matter. Besides, he was carrying a heavy burden. Knowing men of money consistently bet against him at any odds. But as for the rank and file, they all placed their coin, without exception, upon the white stallion.

Flinder, Flinder was their only thought. And, as he stood yonder at the starting post, dancing on his toes, with the sun flashing and shimmering along his flanks, he seemed thoroughly capable of living up to their fine opinions of him.

As for the native-bred and half-blood horses, they had been scratched the instant it was known that Flinder was to be entered. One could not quite be sure. Perhaps on the rather soft and cuppy going on that racecourse, over a full two miles, endurance such as a cow pony possesses might have worn down the thoroughbreds. But there was no longer any such question now that Flinder was entered. He had the endurance of an express train; he would run as far as an eagle would fly, it was felt.

There was only a single doubt about the winner of that race in the minds of the rank and file. Would the new rider be able to make Flinder run? That doubt, too, was presently banished. For they could see Flinder, now, turning his head and looking at his rider with pricked ears, and turning his head still farther, and sniffing the hand which the giant held out to him.

And what a group for stone that horse and rider made! To see Oliver Tay on foot, one wondered where the horse would be found to carry him with any ease. But here was Flinder, who made even Oliver Tay look slender and medium in weight. And he stretched forth his neck and flaunted his tail and sent his neigh ringing over the heads of the crowd.

"Very beautiful! Very beautiful!" said one gay lady beside Don Diego. "But he will never win over those thoroughbreds. A wolf may be a grand animal, but it can't outfoot a greyhound, you know!"

"Nevertheless," said Don Diego, "I am betting on the white stallion. Will you tell your husband that?"

It happened that this same family was not altogether affluent. They could well use a few thousand of the silver pesos which Diego Venustiano tore from the earth. And so the gentleman came in haste. Would Don Diego really bet Flinder against the field? Flinder's chances preferred to those of all the others?

"Write the bet any way you care to," said Don Diego. "I'll take it, and in any amount."

For his heart was swelling in him with grief and indignation at the very thought of the troubles which might be lying ahead of him with Marian Barge, and he was anxious to find some sort of diversion, if only for a moment in placing bets on a horse race! If that was diversion for him, he found it in plenty in the following moments. Everywhere on the flat beneath the platform the crowd was offering money on Flinder, always on Flinder, and with no takers. But when it became known among the people of money that their host was actually betting on the white stallion against the entire field — there was an incredulous gasp and then a laugh of joy.

For they had not altered much from their ancestors, the conquistadors, in one respect; that is to say, they loved gold as much as did those high adventurers of an earlier century, who had crossed the ocean with their swords to find it. And now their descendants came hungrily to Don Diego. Had he really expressed a desire to bet the white horse against all and every one of the other horses on the field? Did he mean it as a jest, or would he be in earnest?

He stood up and laughed at them almost joyfully. "Gentlemen, gentlemen!" said Diego Venustiano. "You may write out the sums of your bets and place them in my hand. I shall cover them all. Signal for the race to be postponed for a moment. Now take your time and think over the matter and decide how good you feel your judgment to be, and how much you are willing to risk on it in hard cash."

They came in a swift drove. Only now and again one held back for an instant. "Nothing has ever been found that could keep up with Flinder in the open country — mountains or plains!" some objected.

But the more confident spirits appealed freely to reason; for those other tests were not tests at all, they said. No saddle had gripped the loins of the stallion, and the burden of no giant had weighted his stirrups. He had run free, unbridled, happy as an eagle on the wing. But now he was to be forced to submit to another's will — the will of a stranger, at that! And, furthermore, he was to be herded along with other horses. And, above all, he was to be forced to compete against the pride of the race track — trained sprinters! Over hill and dale, rough and smooth, no doubt he could kill off these specialists in speed. But in such a short race —

And, besides, let anyone look at the lines of him! Beautiful, to be sure, but not light and long enough in the leg to compete against these greyhounds! So said the wise, and so the timid took their judgment and went gaily to bet against Flinder and Don Diego — bet by many thousands at a time.

These bets were laid and finished when Venustiano saw the face of Federigo near by, and found that face so dark with gloom that it renewed the chill that had seized the heart of the rich man earlier in the day. He beckoned his servant to him. "Now, Federigo, you have made the inquiry?" he asked.

"I have made it," said Federigo. "It will not please you, señor."

"Speak, speak!"

"I was told that every person north of the Rio Grande knew that Marian Barge had been promised in marriage to Oliver Tay!"

Don Diego closed his eyes for a long moment.

When he opened them someone was calling, "May the signal be given for the start, Señor Venustiano?"

"Begin!" gasped Don Diego. And then he

leaned toward Federigo. "You have Martinez and Oñate also?"

"In the hollow of my hand!" said Federigo, with a little shudder, as though he were not altogether pleased by the sense of possession when it had to do with such fellows as that hardy pair.

"And they are ready?"

"For anything, señor!"

"That is well," said Venustiano. "I think that you will have to speak to them again, however. I think that you had better prepare them for the work which they will surely have to do."

"Señor, we still may be mistaken."

"Very well, but in the meantime we must be forearmed. Go to them at once. Find them, and ask them what would be in their minds if they knew that the man they were to face at midnight were none other than that same terrible Oliver Tay. Ask them, and if their courage fails at the thought, tell them that they may have more help."

"I shall, señor."

"But my mind is made up. Do you understand, Federigo? It is not that I dream any harm may come, but Caesar's wife must be above suspicion. Well, you would not understand that. However, this is what you must tell them: Oliver Tay shall die before the morning dawns. He shall die promptly at midnight."

The nostrils of Federigo expanded and contracted. "He is dead!" said the spy. "And their rewards?"

"Each shall be made rich. But twice as much shall go to the one who puts the first bullet through the heart of Oliver Tay. Go quickly!"

And at that moment there was a roar which was like a deep groan, coming from every throat in the audience.

CHAPTER XLIV

The Race

It was a wild glance that Venustiano cast around him, for it almost seemed as though the multitude had spied upon his thoughts and given them this groan for a token of their opinion of his plotting. But, an instant later, he brought his wits back from their agony to the earth and knew that this shout was merely the spontaneous cry which always arises when the racers are off from the start. And then another cry of agony came from all the crowd around the fences.

"Flinder! Flinder!"

For the darling of the crowd, the wild horse, the invincible Flinder, seemed to have been left at the post. Or could it be he had started so slowly, compared with the watch-spring uncoiling of the others, that he seemed to be left ridiculously behind them, though he was doing his best?

At any rate, the important fact was that half a dozen pairs of heels were flashing rhythmically down the soft track; and, in their wake, half obscured by the dense dust cloud which they raised, but still with the sun striking a silver shimmer from his flanks now and again, came the great stallion.

Bu
there
More i

"Wha

"Nothi
that crosse
gaining on

"Of course
gap, however,
it so rapidly. He
rein him in and r
shortest cut to the

Andrea Rulliano
little mirth. For, on
a very handsome and
of Flinder, and so were
and ladies around him;
Don Diego had to pay out
did it matter? He was so va
such a loss would be nothing
serve the good end of teaching
ion was best kept to mining an
Horseflesh was a flight beyond

Don Diego paid no heed to the
the shining faces in that dense litt
ther did he listen to the shouts of
despair that rose still from the peons
men around the track. What was im
him was one face, and that was the

Marian
platform. He
her breast, and h
parted with the
tainly he would
sake of a mere
could show so
way quickly an
was trembling
Don Diego,
that supporte
felt a dark
seemed to
anything th
heard. Cer
horse that
who was r
He star
of his lau
the silen
race —
rear, a
thorou
them
young
like
thro
to
co

ding close to the edge of the
hat her hands were clasped at
er face strained, and her lips
most intense excitement. Cer-
ever have dreamed that for the
horse race this woman of stone
much emotion. He worked his
d stood directly behind her. She
violently.
resting his hand against a pillar
d the sun screen above the stand,
ist whirl across his eyes. For this
im a more convincing proof than
t sharp-eyed Federigo had seen or
ainly it was not the running of the
made her tremble, but it was the man
ding in that race that mattered to her.
ed out across the field, above the heads
ghing, shouting companions, and across
t, stiff-standing multitude, and saw the
the great stallion running far, far to the
hopeless number of strides away, and the
ghbreds bunched in the lead. No, one of
was taking the lead now — a clean-cut
g mare, Esmeralda, a bright bay, flashing
a fine jewel in the sun as she bounded
ugh the soft, sandy going. For it was hardly
be called a track. It was merely a fenced-in
rse to be used this once; and the hoofs sunk
o, deep, at every stride.
wonder that Flinder was anchored, consid-
his weight and the mighty burden on his

back. And yet, was he really anchored? They no longer seemed to float farther ahead of him. And Don Diego, training his glass on horse and rider, saw Oliver Tay sitting easily in the saddle, his weight thrown well forward and the wind of the gallop blowing out his flashing hair. And the stride of the stallion seemed wonderfully light and free. Yes, watching Flinder at his work, and the glimmering of the sun on his muscles, one could not help feeling that that magnificent machine would conquer in the end.

He swept his glass to the thoroughbreds. They, also, ran wonderfully lightly; and yet it seemed to Venustiano that they lacked something of the huge stride of the stallion, something of the wonderful buoyancy of his gallop. He was no longer losing ground. A mile of the distance had been passed. The second turn was rounded, and surely now the white monster was winging his way faster than the rest. They swept nearer. They straightened toward the finish.

And now one could see the effect of distance and soft going. Beautiful Esmeralda was done. Her head was jerking up with each stride; and she was falling back, back. A brown gelding had the lead now; and a chestnut stallion was creeping up on his flank.

Perhaps the rider on Esmeralda realized that all was over, so far as his mount was concerned, and stopped urging her; but, at any rate, back she went and trailed behind the rearmost of the leaders. And then a white streak went past her, gaining almost two yards for every one she was covering. That was Flinder, coming mightily up from the rear.

And the men who watched around the fences suddenly came to life, shrieking his name, "Flinder! Flinder!" as though they felt that the power of their voices could, in some way, add speed to the racing horse.

Esmeralda was breathing dust; and still, with enormous strides, Flinder gained upon the leaders. There was another gone, a black horse on whom the going had told. Back he went, and now Flinder was past him, also, and still making toward the leaders.

Upon the ground there was pandemonium. Hats were flung wildly into the air, and hands brandished, and pistols discharged in a deafening tumult. But upon the stand there had fallen a sudden silence, so that Don Diego, leaning far forward, was able to hear Marian Barge whispering softly, over and over, "Oliver, Oliver, ride!"

It thrust a knife of pain into the very heart of Don Diego. He straightened and pressed the glass to his eyes again. There was no doubt now that the white stallion had a fighting chance. In three furlongs he would undoubtedly win, at this rate of running, but there was hardly that left to him — hardly half of it; and the chestnut stallion was showing wonderful strength. He was working free from the brown. Now he was in the clear running, right on the rail, stretched out straight as a string from head to tail, with a lightweight jockey in the saddle, swaying in rhythm with the stride of his mount.

Oliver Tay was working, too. Not with heel or whip, but leaning far forward to cut the wind with his wide shoulders; and through the glass, now, Don Diego could see the lips of the giant moving. He was calling on Flinder, and the stallion was answering with unbelievable power. Flinder reached the tangled knot of the three thoroughbreds who worked behind the leader. He went by them like a fast yacht past a slow freighter. He was not slackening for all the softness of the going, and it seemed as though the work had merely limbered and freshened his might. His ears pricked, and his nostrils spread until Don Diego could see the red lining of them; and still he seemed to gather speed, with his tail swept behind him and his mane blowing up into the intent face of Oliver Tay.

There was not a hundred yards left to the race, and still the chestnut was a good two lengths away, running honestly, very tired but never faltering. Then Oliver Tay loosened the tight reins which held the white horse, and in an instant it was over. It seemed to Don Diego as though the beat of invisible wings must have buoyed the stallion in his stride. He seemed to reach the saddle of the chestnut in one stride, and in another he was well-nigh a whole length in the lead and past the winning post.

The screech of the peons and the cattlemen roared in the ears of Venustiano; but more than that was the shrill cry of Marian Barge, half stifled in the uproar. "Oliver, Oliver, Oliver!"

And though Don Diego was richer by tens of thousands of dollars for the victory of the white horse, yet he felt that moment that he had become infinitely poorer. And Marian Barge, as though she had suddenly recollected herself, turned her head hastily, and found the burning eyes of Venustiano fixed upon her. She winced a little and smiled at him a very wan smile.

He decided that he would meet the issue firmly and more than half way. "I know that Oliver Tay is an old friend of yours," he said. "Of course you are glad to see him win!" That was surely opening enough, he thought, if she had anything to say to him; and he was not mistaken.

For she said faintly, "I think I shall have to speak to you — at once, Diego!"

It seemed the end of the world to Venustiano. But now he had to turn away among his guests and be the smiling host to them, never knowing what that conversation with the girl might unfold.

CHAPTER XLV
Don Diego's Plans

They could not have that talk at once, of course. And it was long hours before the entire party had at last been gathered together at the Casa Venustiano in the midst of the gardens that crowned the mountain. They were to spend the entire night there. A hundred guests — but there was room for them all! And at the banquet that night they were to learn that Marian Barge had been betrothed to Don Diego. And they could guess, then, that all of this festival had been in her honor who had given the prizes away.

Such were the plans of Diego Venustiano, but his face was very dark as he found, at last, his chance to speak with Marian alone. For it seemed to him that he had been living in a dream, and that his house itself was only part of a bubble which had been blown up, and which would vanish and leave him nothing but misery.

They were in the library. One vast window filled each end of the huge, vaulted room. There was a fireplace at one side into which even Oliver Tay could have stepped and stood upright, his lofty sombrero upon his head. And now, as the windows were thrown open, the soft, warm air of the evening blew gently in, purified with the fragrance of the garden. And with it came drifts and murmurs of voices, in humming conversation, and tinkling laughter of women.

They had wandered everywhere. They had drowned Venustiano with congratulations for his princely residence a thousand times repeated. And now an air of expectation was tingling through the house, while the great banqueting hall stirred with busy noise, and through the long windows a golden shadow of light fell out into the garden. All was happiness — except for Venustiano.

Marian stood beside the table with a hand on it. And in his misery he took note of the smallest details — the dazzling brightness of that hand against the dark wood, and how her hair was coiled at the base of her neck, and the wideness of her frightened eyes, and how the brilliant Spanish shawl seemed to be slipping from one shoulder.

"Now, my dear," said Venustiano, forcing himself into a tone paternally kind and a little gay, "what is troubling you?"

"So far," she said, "you have told no one — except Señor Rulliano and the señora, I suppose?"

"No one," he answered. "That is for tonight."

"I do not wish you to think," said she in a small, choked voice, "that I am wishing to dodge my promise to you. But I'm afraid of the future, and that's why I want to talk with you. I want to tell you that Oliver Tay — if you haven't known it already — is the man I was to marry!"

He was glad that he had had that news beforehand. It enabled him to merely nod, now, and wait for her to continue.

"And," she went on, "I thought, after a year of waiting for him and little word or none from him, that I no longer cared — a great deal. But when I saw him today I found that I was mistaken."

He felt the blow coming, and he stepped bravely forward to meet its shock. "You mean," said Don Diego, "that when you saw him come dashing onto the field, with his golden hair blowing over his shoulders, you thought that you still loved him?"

"Yes!"

"And he?" asked Venustiano.

"I don't know," said she. "But he sent me word that he wanted to see me. And —" She paused.

"Well?" he asked gently, seeing that she was very pale.

"I sent word for him to come at midnight. I intended to see him privately and not to let you know. But now I think that is not honest. And, besides, I am afraid!"

"Of what?" he asked.

"Afraid of myself. Because I am promised to you; and because I want to keep that promise. But if I see and talk with him I don't know what might happen."

He waited.

"And I think," she continued faintly, "that when he comes you had better arrange to send him away again. You could say that I am not very well."

He led her to a chair in front of the southern window. Through it, the eye wandered across the garden and through the trees which fringed the plateau — they had been transplanted from the valley beneath at a frightful cost of labor, every one — they had glimpses of the distant mountains through the night, with the loftier peaks dimly crowned with white.

"Now," said Diego Venustiano, "there are two things which I can do. The first is to say: 'Take this old lover of yours. Marry him. I shall see that you are well provided for.' And perhaps that would seem the generous thing to do. But, on the other hand, if I did that, I should wonder what would become of you and your husband. Money can't make happiness. I see that more and more clearly. And I doubt if money could tame him.

"My reason is that even you, Marian, have not been able to keep him true to himself and to you. He has wandered away. He has joined himself to the most famous band of outlaws in Mexico. And though he might come and talk of love to you, tonight, would it be because he really loved you, or rather simply because it would be a grand adventure to win you away from me and the Casa Venustiano? So, thinking of this, I feel that I have a right and a duty to be selfish and keep you to your promise to me, and tell you, my dear, that you must stay with me, and that you are quite right not to see this old lover. Will you blame me for that?"

She drew a soft breath. And then she said: "No, I haven't even thought of breaking my promise. Only —" She paused again, and then added with a sudden passion: "Only, make sure that I don't see him again. Keep him away from me. And, once we are married, I know that I shall be true to you. Will you do what I ask?"

Don Diego got up from his chair and leaned a little over her, from behind, so that she could not see the savage triumph which was in his face. "He shall never see you again!" he promised solemnly. "That is finished!"

He heard a catch in her throat. He knew that tears would be apt to come very soon; and he also knew that a woman never forgives a man for standing by after he has given her cause to weep. So he escorted her briskly to her room. And he only said at the door: "I am going to make you happy. You may depend on that. Why, Marian, I have done nothing but hard things all the days of my life, and I'm not afraid of this one. I have one new idea, however. Tonight, I am not going to announce our engagement merely. I'm going to announce our marriage, and tomorrow Father Ricardo shall marry us in the church. Do you agree?"

She could not speak to him. She merely made a mute little gesture of assent, and hurried on into her room.

But Don Diego went back, a happy man. He had laid his ground well, he felt. And if Oliver Tay died that night, with bullets through his heart, Marian could never blame the master of the house.

Federigo had the pair waiting for him. He went straight to see them. Seen at close hand, they did not appear less formidable. Martinez was an old hunter, with a bit of gray about his temples and a face as hard as iron. Oñate was younger, but in his dark eyes there was the patience and the ferocity of a great cat. They were mountain made, both of these fellows. The stamp of the wilderness was upon them. Surely they were the proper tools to kill with; for, if one of them fell in the work, the world would feel no loss. It would merely have one less incipient murderer among its ranks of men.

"Now, my friends," said Diego Venustiano, "Federigo has talked with you and let you know what is expected?"

"We know," said Martinez. And Oñate nodded.

"I could have taken a dozen men for the work," said Don Diego; "but I had rather use two good workers than a dozen bunglers. Besides, it makes the reward greater. What has Federigo paid you?"

"Five hundred pesos to each."

"I have with me a thousand more for each of you. And that is only a beginning. There will be more, hereafter. Tell me this — have you any doubt about your ability to handle the big man?"

Martinez murmured, "It is only the small wolf that can dodge the bullet, señor!"

As for young Oñate, he merely smiled, and his dark eyes glistened like the eyes of a hunting cat.

CHAPTER XLVI

An Extra Horse

When Oliver Tay rode up Venustiano Valley, you may be sure that he could not have moved at all, except with a crowd, had it not been for the darkness of the night. And, even so, he had had to maneuver a good deal before he could break away from his admirers. He had to leave first, and then make a swift detour and come stealing back into the barn where the white stallion was kept.

He saw the glimmering figure ahead of him, in a stall, and went straight for it, with his saddle over his arm. Not the gold-and-silver-mounted saddle which had been with the horse when it was won, but another and plainer one some vital pounds lighter; and before the morning there might be need of every pound saved that Oliver Tay could manage.

A shadow rose in the darkness before him with a wonderful suddenness, and a voice hissed in Spanish, "Who goes?" and the shimmer of a naked knife was at the breast of Oliver Tay.

"Yellow Wolf!" he exclaimed, starting back. "You are like a ghost, after the sun goes down. I forgot that you were here, and I have nearly had eight inches of steel in my heart as a result."

The Comanche laughed softly in the darkness. "All hunting is not done under the sun," said he. "I did not know you, brother, because I have not the eyes of a cat."

They went together to the stall.

"Beware!" murmured the Indian. "He is more a tiger than a horse, and if you go suddenly in to him —"

"We have known each other only half a day," said Oliver calmly "and, if we are not friends now, he will be of no use to me tonight!"

He stepped boldly into the stall, running his hand down the back of the great white horse until he came to the head of Flinder. And that monarch of the mountains snuffed the coat of his new master and then shook his head and stamped.

"He knows you!" murmured Yellow Wolf incredulously. "A good horse has more wits than most men. Do you ride now?"

"First, we must daub him over with this stain, brother. It is a pity to tarnish the silver of Flinder, but we must do it. Otherwise he will shine in this valley like a bright star, and the work that we have to do needs secrecy!"

"Good!" said the Indian, and without another word he fell to work industriously on one side of the stallion while his white friend worked on the other, and soon the shining pelt of the white horse was smudged over as with soot.

"This stain will be dry in five minutes, I think," said Oliver Tay. "Has Capiño been here?"

"He has been here."

"And what message did he leave for me?"

"That he and the others will be waiting for you in the poplar grove at the farther side of the lake."

"They will not fail me, then!" murmured Oliver joyfully. "And you are with me, Yellow Wolf. By heaven, all men are true to me! And now, if I am true to myself, I shall do a bit of work that will be remembered in one house in this valley." And he looked up through the door of the barn and toward the shining lights that gleamed from the house of Venustiano, on the mountain.

"He has his gold and his silver, and his servants and his flunkies, and his house and his mines and his cattle ranges; and against all of that I balance my handful of friends, Yellow Wolf, and we shall see who is the stronger. A friend is the finest wealth and the most useful. Tell me, *amigo,* have I ever offered you money?"

"You have never offered it," said Yellow Wolf.

"And is there anything money will buy from you which I cannot have for the asking?"

"Nothing," said the Comanche simply.

"I believe it," said the giant. "And with four hearts like yours to fight for me, Yellow Wolf, I think that I could conquer the world. That stain is dry, by this time. We'll saddle him."

The saddle was accordingly put on the back of the stallion. They led the monster out through the back entrance of the stable into the corral, surrounded as it was by a tall fence.

"I shall take down the top bar," offered Yellow Wolf.

But the giant answered: "If he will not jump a little fence like this, he is not the horse for me. Where is your own pony?"

"Here," said the Comanche.

He whistled, and at once a horse showed beyond the bars and whimpered with a half-choked neigh for its master.

"He comes to you like a dog to its owner!" said Oliver Tay, very well pleased at the sight of this.

"That is true," said Yellow Wolf. "For you have taught me to make a friend of my horse, rather than a slave. He will run farther and faster and truer now than spur and whip could ever make him before."

"We are ready, then. Come, Flinder. We are over this fence —"

The great horse lurched at a stride into what seemed to the Indian full speed for a racing horse; and, with a bound, he hurled himself high into the air. To Yellow Wolf, overawed, it seemed that half the stars of the heavens above were blotted out by the flying silhouette of this magnificent pair. And then there stood the stallion beyond the bars.

"He didn't flick a bar with his heels," said Oliver Tay, laughing in exultation. "He has wings hitched to these feet of his. We're away, Yellow Wolf!"

They swerved around the corner of the barn.

And in a moment they were picking their way down a narrow street of the village which Venustiano had built here.

"Faugh!" grunted the Comanche. "See them snorting and rolling in the dirt like pigs. Shall we not stop, brother, and take away a scalp or two that will never be missed by the townsmen in the morning?"

"Take scalps? Take scalps?" said Oliver Tay, too accustomed to his companion to be shocked by this suggestion. "Do you forget that this is the country of Venustiano?"

"No," sighed the Indian. "I remember! Lead me, brother. I have no thoughts, except those which you give to me."

And they whirled away from the edge of the town and made for the far-off shimmer of the waters of the lake, whose still surface took all the bright faces of the stars as clearly as though they were sunk here in the depths of another heaven. They reached the poplar grove beside Lake Venustiano; and, in the steep, dark shadow that lay between the edge of the trees and the lake itself, they could see three horses and three riders. Yellow Wolf hooted, like an owl that sends its soft, half-muffled cry along the ground as it hunts for prey in the twilight; and instantly the three men in the shadow came to life. They poured out on their horses and joined the pair.

"Carpio! Antonio! Capiño!" called Oliver Tay. "If a single one of you were missing I should have had to give up this work that I have in mind for tonight. But you are here; and I think before morning you will have made me the happiest man in the world!"

"So? So?" said Carpio Vega, shaking his wise head. "Then is there to be a woman in it?"

"First," said Oliver Tay, "I thank you for giving me this night, when you could have been taking in a little harvest among the drunken fools of the village."

"I have found a few odd moments," said Capiño with satisfaction. "I have not wasted the entire evening." And in his hand he raised a little necklace that sparkled red and faint in the starlight.

"Do not thank us, brother," said Vega. "What you wish, we wish. When we work for you, we serve ourselves. We owe you our blood. Do you think that we shall stop, then, and ask for thanks. No — speak clearly! We have done what you asked us to do. We have our horses here. They are all in good trim. We have not touched beer or wine, even, since dinner time. Our guns are looked to. We have enough food and provisions to last us for a month's ride — as we travel!"

"Bless you, Carpio! You have forgotten nothing. You have even remembered the extra horse, then?"

"That, first of all. Look at her! She is a sound mare, Oliver. I got her from a man who would not sell her for any price. But he would gamble for her. And I have not forgotten how to roll dice and make them answer me! So I took her away and left him crying. She is not a heavyweight, but you said that the extra horse would not have a great burden to carry. And as for speed and wind and gentleness, she is a perfect thing."

"She has the head and the eye, and the proper span between them," said Oliver Tay. "And now, friends, this is the direction in which we are riding." He raised his arm and pointed.

Vega and Morales were silent; but little Capiño broke out with a moan: "The Casa Venustiano! *Diablo, amigos,* I knew that he would go mad one of these fine nights! I knew that! And now we are to fly up the face of a mountain to rob the devil himself."

"Be quiet, Capiño," said Vega. "You need not go with us, if you are afraid."

This taunt brought a groan from the little man and then silenced him, though he writhed with a desire to protest.

"Very well," said Carpio Vega. "We are with you up the cliff, if you wish. Are you to blow open the treasury of Venustiano tonight?"

"No, Carpio. Tonight, at his banquet, Don Diego has announced to his guests that tomorrow he will marry Marian Barge. But the fool has lied. She will never see the morning rising over that house. The extra horse is for her, Carpio!"

CHASER XLVII

Spies

They traveled in single file, with Oliver Tay leading; and then, at a little distance behind him, came the three, closely grouped, Capiño and dark Antonio Morales and that calm hero, Carpio Vega. They led the extra horse with them. And far to the rear skulked Yellow Wolf on his little pony.

Half the time he was out of sight; and Capiño, who suspected everybody and everything in this wide world except the man of his worship — Oliver Tay — rode hastily up to that leader to communicate his latest ugly thought. "The Indian is sneaking back to the rear, and before long he will drop away and scoot off to send in a warning that will cause us all to die before another hour is out, Oliver!" said the sneak thief and knife fighter.

"Listen to me, Capiño," said the good-natured giant. "Whatever else you may do, don't waste your time trying to understand Yellow Wolf. I have lived close to him for a long time, but even I can't make him out. Only I know that I would trust him a little better than I would trust myself. Go back to Carpio. He will tell you that we don't have to fear Yellow Wolf."

"Listen!" broke in Capiño.

Across the night came the mournful booming call of the owl. And again it came.

"It is Yellow Wolf," cried Capiño, "calling us back into some sort of ambuscade. Oliver, you must not go!"

"Hush, you fool!" snapped Oliver angrily; and he brushed away the hand which Capiño stretched out toward him, "Do you think that I shall stay here when I hear such a signal? There may be danger for Yellow Wolf; and I have sworn to stand by him, as he by me."

Flinder bore Oliver back like a flying comet. Before Vega and Morales could well turn about the heads of their horses to investigate the call of the owl, which was their prearranged signal, Oliver Tay was shooting past them and plunging into the thicket from which they had just issued. He came abruptly upon a little clearing, and there reined in his horse barely in time to keep from trampling upon a singular group, which consisted of two men lying flat on their backs, with their arms thrown out crosswise, while above them crouched the Indian, a pistol pressed against the back of one and his knife point tickling the throat of the other.

"I would have killed one, brother," said Yellow Wolf gravely, "and brought up the other to you; but I thought that you might wish to hear them both talk. Is it well?"

"Very well!" said Oliver. "Yellow Wolf, you

are worth ten." He leaned over the two. They were both young Mexicans, utterly unknown to him.

"I saw their shadows sneaking behind us," said Yellow Wolf, "so I turned back and walked on their footprints until a chance came to make them stumble." He shrugged his shoulders. That story was at an end, so far as the Comanche was concerned, except that he could not help adding, "But if one of them is to die, this is a fine scalp, brother!" And he pointed to the flowing hair of one of his victims.

"Mercy, mercy!" gasped that frightened man. "Dear heaven! Hear me, señor, my deliverer, he has been cutting my throat; I am bleeding to death already."

"You are a fool," said his companion. "You are only slightly scratched. Sit up and wipe the blood away. This is Don Oliver Tay. He is no murderer."

Dios! Dios!" gasped the frightened fellow, sitting up. "I thought that I was dead. I half think that I am in heaven now! Señor, heaven be gracious to you!"

"Look," said Oliver Tay, bending a little above them. "I could turn my back on you and let Yellow Wolf take a pair of scalps. Or else I can stay here for five minutes and hear everything that you have to tell me."

The one was sullen and silent. But the frightened companion could not hold his tongue, and he began to chatter straightway. What he had to say was very simple. He was one of a number of spies who had been sent out that evening to comb the valley and, searching everywhere, to bring back whatever word they could of Oliver Tay or of Capiño, Carpio Vega, and Antonio Morales — all of whom were accurately described. And the instant that they had any tidings, they were to bring them straight to the Casa Venustiano and there make their report to the secretary, Federigo. He, Vicente, had never liked the business; but his companion, Agostino had lured him on into the adventure.

"I'll cut your throat for these lies," promised Agostino.

But Vicente babbled on. His tongue was at command until Oliver Tay gave the word, and Vega and Morales tied and thoroughly gagged the pair. By that time they knew whatever they wanted, and chiefly how Don Diego was guarding Casa Venustiano on that night. And how the men were posted and, with a finger-drawn chart in the dirt, all the lie of the land at the mountaintop!

CHAPTER XLVIII
The Rendezvous

In that tall and graceful campanile which Don Diego had built beside the new church in the valley there had been hastily installed a big bell, worthy of its place; and from that bell midnight was tolled with slow strokes; and the melancholy, brazen notes floated slowly through the air and welled up, one by one, to the Casa Venustiano on the heights above.

"It is ended," said Diego Venustiano to the girl, as they listened to the last of the count coming with long-dying murmurs through the open window of the library. "You see, he has changed his mind; and he will not attempt to see you. You may go to bed now, Marian, and have no fear. For you see that even an Achilles like your Oliver Tay knows that there is a certain point where discretion is the better part of valor; and I don't think that even he would willingly cross me — not in this valley where every man is my man."

"He has not come," agreed the girl faintly; "but still — ah, heaven help us!"

Don Diego started up from his chair and whirled at that cry. And he saw against the great arch of the doorway, as in a frame, the most sinister picture which it had ever been his fortune to behold — a tall Indian warrior, naked to the waist, the war feathers braided into his hair, and across the crook of his left arm was lying a sawed-off double-barreled rifle, with two huge mouths looking directly at him.

It had upon Venustiano the effect of a phantom. He could not believe his eyes. "It is some jest which one of our guests is playing on us!" he said through stiff lips to the girl. "There is nothing to fear. This is the Casa Venustiano. No one would dare — not even an Indian madman —"

That sentence remained unfinished, for the second door opened with a sigh at that moment, and against the black heart of the arch appeared the man for whom they had been waiting — Oliver Tay, looking loftier than human, and behind him three grim faces that had been seen before by Venustiano on that day.

"There is one dead man behind us, Venustiano," said Oliver Tay quietly. "If you call out louder than a whisper you will make the second. Close the door, Capiño. Carpio, watch that window; and, Morales, take the other. Yellow Wolf and I will handle the man."

He advanced close to them; and Venustiano said with equal quiet: "This is brave, Tay. This is a trick worthy of your fame. But tell me, are you mad enough to think that you can take the lady with you to —"

"Not a step," said Oliver Tay. "Not a step if she is unwilling to go. Marian, I haven't come here to drag you away. I have only come to persuade you, if I can. And, first of all, I wish to know why you have come here to Venustiano."

"There was no word from you, month after month. And my father was sick."

"Is that it?" asked Oliver gently. "I should have guessed that. And so you sold yourself, poor child? If there is nothing but this, are you ready to go with me, Marian?"

"Oh, Oliver, I have given Diego my promise! Tomorrow —"

"You have given him your promise; but I release you from it," said Oliver Tay.

"This is a new logic," said Venustiano. "Who are you, Oliver Tay, to dispense pardons for —"

"I was someone powerful for you, Venustiano, when twenty men were hungry to hang you over the edge of the cliff. Have you forgotten? I gave you your life freely on that day. But I never gave it to you so that you could steal from me. Do you understand, Marian? He was in the cup of my hand. I could have tossed him away, but I saved him. And now he has done this. That is why I can release you from your promise."

"Wait, Marian!" interrupted Don Diego hastily. "Let him tell me, first, how he could take you, even if you would go with him? How will you pass down?"

"As we came up, and more safely — with Don Diego along to guard us."

"I understand," said Venustiano. "You will take me with you with a gun against the small of my back. But even at that, after you are away, what can save you? A signal fire from the top of the mountain will block every pass that leads in the valley."

"Señor," said the outlaw, "we have ways of avoiding your outer guards as we have avoided the inner ones. You supplied me with a horse for this work, Don Diego. Have you forgotten Flinder?"

The face of the rich man darkened. He turned to the girl. "He is waiting for your decision," said he. "Will you weigh us both and then make your answer. I could say a good deal, my dear. I could speak of the work that I have done to make this house a home for you, and how I have treated all this great valley like a garden to make it pleasant for you, and how I have made the festival of the rodeo, so that there would be a proper place for the world to see the wife of Venustiano. But I shall not speak of that. I only beg you to see, my dear, that as the wife of Diego Venustiano you will be like a queen. And like a queen you can take care of your father. And in addition, your promise. What has he to offer you, compared with this?"

"I have only one thing to offer you," said Oliver Tay, raising his head so that the golden hair fell back from his shoulders and the light shone upon the tenseness of his face. "A long, long time ago I rode into Siddon Flat in the same stagecoach

356

with you. I was a callow young fool, Marian. Since that time I have ridden on a good many wild trails. I have done a great deal of wrong. The law wants my head, here south of the river. And the law is against me north of the river, also. But still there's a way for me to win back an honest, quiet life. Because, whatever has happened, good and bad, has helped to make a man of me. And there is always some way for a true man to make one woman in the world happy, if she cares for him. I don't offer excuses. For the last year I've run about like a madman, enjoying myself, forgetting everything except the joy of a free life.

"Now, perhaps, I should still be riding trails that have no end, except that Venustiano stole you; and suddenly that made me understand how much I loved you and that I could never be really happy without you. And therefore, Marian, I want you to understand, if you can, that I am ready to lead a new life, if you can come with me. I have no money except stolen money. I can't offer you that. I have no man except an outlawed one. I have no friends except thieves and robbers and murderers, made of gold and steel. I can only offer you my poor self, Marian, and my love for you. Is that enough?"

She took half a step forward, and then she turned and cast a glance over her shoulder at Don Diego — a glance filled with shame and pity and remorse and fear — then she ran to Oliver Tay, and she was lost in his arms.

"She has made her choice," said Don Diego. "You have nothing to fear from me. You are all free to go."

"I have seen your teeth, Venustiano," said Oliver Tay. "We'll trust you when we have to. And, in this place, you are a little too much of a king to be altogether honest."

So Diego Venustiano passed into the shadow of his greatest humiliation. He himself was forced to go with the marauders to the foot of the cliff, while his men looked on with amazement. He himself had to watch them mount — six people on six fleet horses, with Flinder among them, hardly less glorious, even with his darkened hide.

And the giant riding the great stallion called: "We're away, Diego. And now you're free to hunt us and catch us if you can. We ask for no more sporting chance than this good start."

What a hunt was that, which whirled up Venustiano Valley, with the hundreds of riders and the trained dogs and the terrific rewards offered in tens of thousands of pesos!

Twice they turned back and fought. And twice they checked flying bodies of pursuers, and then rode on. In and out among the mountains they dodged for three days. And then the strong arm of the great outlaw, Venales, reached out and gathered them in, and provided them with fresh horses, and provided for the pursuers false clews on blind trails.

Two days more.

They camped at last on the shoulder of a

mountain. Dawn was not far off. And under the broad moon they could see the silver face of the Rio Grande, beyond which lay a land where they would not be free, indeed, but where they would not, at least, be hounded so closely and so savagely. There they fell asleep, crushed with exhaustion, except Yellow Wolf, who seemed to be beyond the need of rest when he rode upon the war trail. He rose from his place beside the fire; and, raising the tip of a blanket, he looked down at the tired, white face of the girl.

"Oliver!" she whispered, and smiled in her sleep.

He turned from her and looked down into the face of the white man, stern, furrowed with resolution after the long ride, still with his will set against tomorrow and its dangers.

Then Yellow Wolf went back and sat down upon his heels. It was all far beyond him. For it seemed to him that there were a thousand things more precious in this world than a mere squaw. He patted his rifle. That was one treasure more beautiful. He touched the hilt of his knife. That was more priceless, also.

He raised his face and saw the crimson day beginning to flow up from the east; and he smiled to think that God had placed that beauty there for the red man to see, while the white men, always blind, slept.

He unrolled a little packet. And he took out and examined three well-cured human scalps. He smiled upon them tenderly. To each man his own happiness, thought Yellow Wolf. To each man his own strength. To each man his own weakness.

But, alas, what weakness was so great as the love of woman? For it seemed to him that already he saw the mighty shoulders of Oliver Tay bowed to the plow.